Lament for a
Lady Laird

MARGOT ARNOLD

Lament for a Lady Laird

A Penny Spring and Sir Toby Glendower Mystery

From the Library of:

KATE

Foul Play Press

The Countryman Press
Woodstock, Vermont

This edition first published in 1990 by Foul Play Press,
an imprint of the Countryman Press, Inc.,
Woodstock, Vermont 05091.

Copyright © 1982 by Margot Arnold

ISBN 0-88150-184-0

Printed in the United States of America

To My Godchild, Lucinda, and to Nigel—
May Their Days Be Long and Happy

WHO'S WHO

GLENDOWER, TOBIAS MERLIN, archaeologist, F.B.A., F.S.A., K.B.E.; b. Swansea, Wales, Dec. 27, 1926; s. Thomas Owen and Myfanwy (Williams) G.; ed. Winchester Coll.; Magdalen Coll., Oxford, B.A., M.A., Ph.D.; fellow Magdalen Coll., 1949-; prof. Near Eastern and European Prehistoric Archaeology Oxford U., 1964-; created Knight, 1977. Participated in more than 30 major archaeological expeditions. Author publications, including: What Not to Do in Archaeology, 1960; What to Do in Archaeology, 1970; also numerous excavation and field reports. Clubs: Old Wykehamists, Athenaeum, Wine-tasters, University.

SPRING, PENELOPE ATHENE, anthropologist; b. Cambridge, Mass., May 16, 1928; d. Marcus and Muriel (Snow) Thayer; B.A., M.A., Radcliffe Coll.; Ph.D., Columbia U.; m. Arthur Upton Spring, June 24, 1953 (dec.); 1 son, Alexander Marcus. Lectr. anthropology Oxford U., 1958-68; Mathieson Reader in anthropology Oxford U., 1969-; fellow St. Anne's Coll., Oxford, 1969-. Field work in the Marquesas, East and South Africa, Uzbekistan, India, and among the Pueblo, Apache, Crow and Fox Indians. Author: Sex in the South Pacific, 1957; The Position of Women in Pastoral Societies, 1962; And Must They Die? — A Study of the American Indian, 1965; Caste and Change, 1968; Moslem Women, 1970; Crafts and Culture, 1972; The American Indian in the Twentieth Century, 1974; Hunter vs. Farmer, 1976.

CHAPTER 1

The scene inside the office of the Pitt-Rivers Museum of Oxford was a cozily domestic one. Dr. Penelope Spring had abandoned her anthropological labors and was toasting crumpets, while Miss Ada Phipps, the long-suffering girl Friday for herself and the eminent archaeologist Sir Tobias Glendower, was equally busy brewing a pot of tea.

"Isn't it peaceful," Ada exclaimed, settling herself with a jiggle of her considerable bosom, which strained against a bright violet cardigan as if seeking escape. "The end of Trinity term and everyone gone but us—I do hope it's going to be a nice summer."

"Yes, it is a nice change from the usual furor," Penny answered as she gingerly tested a buttered crumpet. She accepted a cup of strong black tea from her companion and settled her dumpy five foot one figure into her own chair. She ran her free hand through her short, mouse-colored hair so that it stood up in spikes around her small head and added, "I can use a rest. What a year!"

Ada Phipps crunched into her thickly buttered crumpet. "What are your plans for the summer?" she asked with avid interest. It was so rare that she had her favorite employer all to herself and secure from constant interruptions that she was determined to make the most of it.

"All a bit vague at the moment," Penny said absently. "I've got to finish up this wretched book and get it off to John Everett in Boston. I've been at it for a year now, on and off, and he's getting a bit impatient. After that's finished, well, I just don't know. Sir Tobias is off replenishing his cellars for the next couple of weeks in Bordeaux. When he gets back, we may potter off to Greece, or I may go to Fiji and finish up a project there." Her voice trailed off as she considered her plans.

"I expect you'll be spending some time in America with your son," Ada prompted her.

"Well, no, not this year. Alex has gone off on one of those hospital ships for the summer, to South America, I believe. He's finished his internship, and with only one year to go to finish his residency, he decided he'd like a break. I don't expect to see him until Christmas." The thought seemed to depress her, and she consoled herself with another crumpet. "No," she repeated. "I really don't know what I'm going to do."

The door of the office opened, and Ada Phipps looked up in annoyance.

A uniformed guard with a long drooping gray mustache deposited a pile of letters on the desk. "It's late again," he announced with dismal relish.

"Ah, the afternoon mail," she exclaimed unnecessarily, and with quick fingers sorted through the pile. "Here's a couple of things for you. Oh! I've got a letter from my niece in Australia. The rest are for him and Dr. Jessup." The "him" in question was her other employer, Toby Glendower, with whom she cherished a long-standing feud, which both of them rather enjoyed.

Penny accepted her letters and looked at the uppermost one; a little frown creased her face. The writing teased at her mind, but she could not place it.

"I'm going to read mine now," Ada Phipps announced happily. "I don't often hear from this niece. She's the one I told you about who married the plumber and emigrated to Australia."

Penny, who had long since lost track of the ramifications of Ada's large and roaming family, said brightly, "Oh, yes, *that* one," and opened her own.

Ada's niece evidently was a woman of few words, for Ada soon finished reading and looked with impatient curiosity at Penny, whose correspondent had covered page after page with a distinctive, stylish script. She fidgeted in her chair, poured herself another cup of tea, and had replenished Penny's cup before the latter patted the letter into a neat pile and said, "Well, how extraordinary!"

"What is?" Ada said, her pale blue eyes agleam with curiosity.

"It's from a friend, a very old friend but one I haven't heard from in some time. And it's a rather pressing invitation to visit her this summer. Strange, when we were just on the subject."

"Where?" her secretary demanded.

Penny looked at the embossed heading on the letter. "Soruba House, Ardnan, near Kilmelfort, Argyll. That's Scotland, isn't it?"

"Why, yes." Ada Phipps leaped to her feet and extracted a gazetteer from the bookshelf behind her. She flipped to the index, opened it to a map, and after a brief consultation handed it across the desk to Penny. "There's Kilmelfort," she said in triumph. "South of Oban on the Sound of Jura. I didn't know you knew anyone in that part of the world. I have a nephew in Oban; he's with the police there."

"I didn't know I knew anyone there, either. This is quite a surprise. My friend is an American, but now, apparently, she's a lady laird of this huge estate." Seeing the unquenched gleam of interest in her companion's eyes, she decided to indulge her. "It's quite a story. Would you like to hear it?"

"Love to," said Ada with an ecstatic wriggle. "Isn't this *nice!*" A light summer rain tapped at the office window as she poured more tea.

"Well, my friend's name is Heather Macdonell. She was my roommate at Radcliffe for our first two years there. She's had a remarkable life—more worries and troubles than you would think one person could possibly handle—and she was always such a little slip of a girl. When we first knew each other, she was in pre-law, dead set on being a lawyer like her father, which wasn't the easiest thing for a woman back then. But then, at the end of her first year, her mother died, and that seemed to start a whole disastrous cycle for her. Her father fell ill shortly after with a lingering form of cancer, and she had to leave college to look after him. She had two younger sisters, but they were too young to be of any help.

Anyway, by the time the father finally died, they were wiped out financially—you know how expensive medical costs are in the States—and there was no question of her being able to finish college. In fact, she had to become an instant bread-winner. She was so sensible about it, too. I'd have been just devastated at that age, but she took a bookkeeping course at some secretarial college and went right to work. She went on studying at night—God knows how, what with looking after the two kids and keeping the house going—and finally became a CPA, an accountant. After that she just kept moving up in her profession, switching from accounting to the executive side and to bigger and better companies all the time. The last time I saw her, which was about five years ago in New York, she had a luxury apartment in a swank part of Manhattan and was, I would say, extremely comfortably fixed. She put one of her sisters through college, too. The other one had polio as a teenager—this was in the bad old days before the Salk vaccine—and was partially crippled."

"Do they all live together?"

"Oh, no. Both sisters married long ago and have grown-up families now. One of them—" Penny looked down at the letter again—"a niece, seems to be coming over to join her for the summer."

"But *she* never married," Ada Phipps said soulfully, deter-mined to wring as much pathos from the story as possible.

"No, she has always been much too busy." Penny grinned at her sentimental companion. "But it hasn't exactly ruined her life. She's one of the most together people I know and happy as a lark."

"And you've been faithful friends all these years through thick and thin. How marvelous!" Ada sighed.

"Well, not exactly." Penny was brisk. "We were never exactly bosom buddies in college. We just liked each other, and it has been one of those friendships that have continued in spurts ever since. I have lost track of her for years at a time and she of me, particularly when I was popping all over the world doing fieldwork, but somehow or other we always get back into contact again."

"How did she end up in Scotland?"

Again Penny frowned slightly. "I must say, that is one for

the books. Her explanation is a bit vague and assumes that my knowledge of the laws of inheritance is a lot more extensive than it is. I knew she was of Scottish descent, but I had no idea . . .'' Her voice trailed off, and she reread part of the letter. ''She is now 'the Macdonell,' and it is something to do with fee female, whatever that is. Somebody died, and even though she had never set foot over here, it seems that as her father's daughter she inherited all this. Weird! She was such a dedicated New Yorker, I somehow can't picture her lording it over some rustic estate.''

''I think it's thrilling,'' Ada said. ''Are you going to go and see her? That's a lovely part of the Western Highlands, my nephew says, and an estate, too!'' In Ada's world, estates were still peopled with butlers, well-manicured lawns, extensive stables, and leisurely house parties on which the sun always shone.

''I might,'' Penny said cautiously. ''She does seem very insistent about it.''

''You were just saying you didn't know what to do for the summer. Why don't you give her a call right now. I'll get the long-distance operator for you.''

''No, not now. Maybe later.'' Fond as she was of Ada Phipps, Penny was not about to be hustled, and there were some things in the letter that puzzled her slightly. If she did talk to Heather, it would be from the privacy of her cottage in Littlemore and not under Ada's insatiably curious gaze. ''I'd better go and finish off my bibliography for the book.''

''So romantic,'' Ada murmured dreamily. ''The Road to the Isles, Bonnie Prince Charlie, and all those Spanish galleons.''

''Spanish galleons?'' Penny echoed in amazement, not seeing the faintest connection.

''Yes, you know—the Spanish Armada. Lots of them were wrecked around that coast. I read an article in *Ladies' Magazine* just recently all about them. People still keep looking for them. Divers found one of them in Tobermory Bay in the Isle of Mull not too long ago. And Soruba House has a sort of Spanish sound to it. It's so exciting!''

''More probably Gaelic. Yes, well, I don't suppose Heather is into that sort of thing. She's got enough on her hands on land by the sound of it,'' Penny said as she left.

Back in her cottage that evening, she reread the letter to see whether her first impression had been justified, that all was not quite as it seemed on the surface. Heather had always been an enthusiastic soul and, perhaps because of the hard life she had led, impressed almost to the point of naiveté by material possessions. But even for her, the wording of the letter seemed a bit extreme. Everything was in superlatives: "the most wonderful situation," "the most gorgeous antiques," "the most fabulous boating, swimming, hiking," and on and on in the same vein. "I know your term has just ended at Oxford, so do come and as soon as you can," Heather had exhorted. "I can promise you the most exciting summer of your life." To Penny, who had had more exciting summers than she cared to count, there was something almost ominous in that last line.

Methinks the lady doth protest too much. There's something almost frantic about the tone of this, she thought. I wonder if she's all right. She's all alone up there. Perhaps it's getting to her after what she got used to in New York. Maybe I should give her a call and see what's up.

The phone rang, and she picked it up, so deep in concentration on her subject that she half expected to hear Heather's high-pitched voice on the line. But it was Toby's deep rumble.

"Nothing the matter, is there?" she asked anxiously.

"Certainly not," he replied huffily. He had just called to tell her his news and to collect hers.

"Oh, there's nothing much going on here. I'll have the book ready for John in a couple of days, and I've had an invitation to go up to the Western Highlands from an old college friend that I'm considering. That's about it."

"That should keep you out of trouble until I get back," Toby said cheerfully. "Don't forget to take your raincoat; it always rains up there in summer." After a few more minutes of inconsequential chitchat, he rang off.

Penny debated a few minutes longer and then, picking up the phone again, dialed the number on the letterhead. It rang for a long time, a weak peevish buzzing that seemed infinitely remote. She was just about to give up, when the receiver lifted at the other end and a high, breathless voice announced, "Soruba House."

"Heather? Is that you?"

"Yes, who is this?" The voice had a surprised and slightly impatient quality, as if Heather had been interrupted in the middle of something important.

"This is Penny, Penny Spring. I got your letter today."

"Oh, yes." There was no encouragement in the voice. Penny was about to get irked, when she remembered that Heather always sounded like this on the phone and had once admitted that she detested it as a means of communication.

"I wondered if you were serious about that invitation," she persevered. "I'll be finishing up some work here in the next couple of days and would be free after that to make a visit for a while."

The voice warmed perceptibly. "Of course I was serious. That would be super!" Super? Penny thought. Good grief, she's trying to go native. "It would be wonderful to have you. When can you arrive? Can you stay the whole summer?"

"Goodness, no," Penny said hastily. "I'm afraid I have plans for later on, but if you could stand me for a couple of weeks, I'd love to see you in your new-found glory. It was quite a surprise."

"To me, too!" Heather's voice was dry. "I'm still not over the shock of it. Yes, do come as soon as you can. I have so much to tell you and show you. Could you make it by this weekend?" There was an underlying urgency to her question.

"Let me see, today is Wednesday. Yes, I could probably leave by Saturday and be up there by Sunday. I'll drive. Are you all right?"

"Of course I'm all right." Heather's voice rose a little higher. "But it will be so nice to have company. I've been rattling around the mansion like a pea in a drum. You and Alison will be my first houseguests. She's arriving next week. She's my sister Margaret's oldest and in her first year of college—a brilliant girl."

"Well, that's nice," Penny murmured. "But are you all by yourself now?"

"There are lots of people on the estate," Heather said, evading the question. "And there's been so much to arrange. I've been so *busy* since I arrived."

"You'd better give me directions on how to get there."

Penny drew a notepad toward her. "I've never been to your part of the world before. Edinburgh's been my only port of call in Scotland, and that's on the opposite side. You'd better give directions from the border on up."

After some fairly complicated directions, Heather concluded by saying, "I'll come down to the gate on the Lochgilphead road to meet you; you'd never spot the entrance otherwise. There's really nothing to mark it, and it's two miles from the house."

Odd, Penny thought. No manorial pillars? She said, "Oh, heavens, that's a lot of trouble. Can't you hang out a flag or a shingle or something? I'll find it."

"No, no. I insist. I'm just longing to see you."

"Well, I've no idea when I'll be arriving, so to prevent you hanging around for hours, why don't I phone when I get to Oban. You can gauge my arrival time from there."

"Oh, all right. Then I can count on you for Sunday?" The urgency was back.

"Yes, probably in the early evening. See you then." Penny rang off and sat back with a perplexed frown. Yes, there was definitely something—but what?

Saturday she loaded her little green Triumph Spitfire and set off on the long drive north. She spent the night with friends in Carlisle and departed early on a misty Sunday morning. She made good time through the Lowlands, but as she hit the Trossachs and the beginning of the Highlands, the rain, which had threatened on and off, started to come down in earnest. She found that she had seriously underestimated the difficulty of negotiating the twisting Highland roads. It was already dinnertime when she reached Dalmally at the head of Loch Awe, whose steely gray waters stretched without end into the mist. Ahead of her stretched the dark and forbidding Pass of Brander, hedged in by mountains, and she decided to take a break, eat a hasty dinner at the hotel that stood on the loch's edge, and give Heather a call to report her lamentable lack of progress.

"I'm only at Dalmally," she reported. "And it's getting so late, I think perhaps I'd better stop over for the night in Oban and come in the morning, what with the rain and everything."

"No!" The negative was vehement. "Don't do that. There's

plenty of time. It stays light up here until eleven o'clock at night this time of year. And once you are through the pass, I'm sure you'll find the rain has stopped, and Oban is just beyond there. Then it's only an hour's drive from Oban to here—*plenty* of time. Please, do come tonight.''

''Well, I'll give it a try, but if I don't make it by dark, you'd better send up flares,'' Penny said, and made her way wearily back to the car.

As Heather had predicted, the rain did stop beyond the Pass of Brander. It seemed a very short time before she was entering the little highland port of Oban, with its harsh salt-laden air and its clouds of screaming gulls hovering over the trawlers bobbing in the choppy waters of the harbor. There was a short delay while she located an open gas station and filled the tank, and a further delay finding the right little road leading out of the town, which was shuttered in Sunday stillness. Finally, she was heading south again over a narrow road that edged like a cautious snake between the sea on one side and the low mountains on the other. The houses became fewer and farther apart, and she was in and through the little village of Kilmelfort almost before she had realized it.

''My God, this is isolated,'' she muttered, and slowed the car from its frantic speed. ''It can't be much further.''

She peered anxiously into the graying light at the unending vistas of heather and bracken, bog and sea. A couple of houses appeared on the left of the road, and she had almost slowed to a stop to ask directions, when she spotted a small red-jacketed figure farther down the road on the right-hand side, jumping up and down and waving frantically. She accelerated up to it; it was Heather, in the act of swinging wide a simple wrought-iron gate with a large ''S'' in scrollwork for its midportion.

''Super,'' Heather screamed above the roar of the engine. ''You made it!''

She bounced over to the car, a happy grin on her high-nosed, aristocratic face, and, scrambling in beside Penny, gave her a perfunctory peck on the cheek. ''Welcome to Soruba. Drive in, and I'll hop out and shut the gate. Got to keep the sheep and cattle in, you know.''

Penny drove in, parked, and looked around her as Heather

hopped out and wrestled the gate closed. All she could see was more unending vistas of bog, bracken, sea, and pines. "Fine," she said as her companion rejoined her. "But where is it?"

"All around us," Heather answered eagerly. "Drive on and you'll see. Welcome to the inheritance of the Macdonell."

CHAPTER 2

"Drive slowly," Heather directed. "There's still light enough to see, and I can give you a bit of a tour."

Penny obediently shifted into low gear and coaxed the car up the turf and gravel track. Their first encounter was with a small horde of black-faced Highland sheep that milled in front of the car in addled panic while Penny leaned on the horn; a black and white collie appeared and, with a contemptuous backward look at the inept human, masterfully drove the sheep away. A granite pillar appeared on their left.

"That's the Macdonell monument," Penny's hostess explained. "A sort of genealogy inscribed on it from the first Macdonell who grabbed this land down to World War I, when most of them were wiped out."

A little farther to the right was a small red wooden building, with a miniature wooden spire on its roof giving it a vaguely ecclesiastical air.

"That used to be a chapel for one of the Episcopal Macdonells. It's used as a tool shed now, but I may refurbish it."

They plunged into a thickly planted avenue of rhododendrons in full flower—pink, white, magenta, and mauve. The great clusters of flowers emitted a heady fragrance in the still twilight air.

"Aren't they marvelous," Heather exclaimed happily. "I'm so glad you came now while they are at their best."

They had mounted a little rise and were now in sight of the dark gray waters of the bay, when an overpoweringly unpleasant smell assailed them.

"Phew! What's that?" Penny asked. "Something dead?"

Heather wrinkled her nose. "No, but it's awful, isn't it? It's rotting kelp. High tides lift it into rock pools, and then it just sits and rots. I can't think what to do about it; there are so many pools. Oh, look down there. You can see the jetty and the boats."

"Boats?"

"Yes, there are two—a sailboat and a motorboat plus miscellaneous rowboats. That's a boathouse down there." The track had climbed up almost into the pines to the left of the road, and they passed another wooden building nestled among them. "That's an indoor gym and badminton court," said Heather. They rounded a sudden bend. "And here is the house."

It sat on a shelf of land, protected on three sides by low, sheltering hills dotted with pine trees. It faced the west, where the land dropped sharply to the gray-silver waters of the bay and looked out to misty islands, now wreathed in opalescent mist.

"The big island out there is Jura; the smaller, Scarba; and the one nearest to us, where you see the lights, is Sheena," Heather said in her best tour-guide manner.

Penny agreed that the view was spectacular, but as she drew up in the graveled sweep before the front door, she saw that the house itself did not live up to its setting and was unremarkable. Its nucleus was evidently an ancient gray stone farmhouse, to which additions had been made in the best ivy-clad Oxford-Gothic style of the 1860s. The front door was centered in the ancient part of the mansion and was surmounted by a sculptured stone, a mailed fist rising out of a shield, and an inscription deeply etched underneath it, which she could just make out: "CEUD MHILLE FAILTE DO SORUBA."

"A hundred thousand welcomes to Soruba," Heather translated. "And from me, too." She hopped out and started wrestling with one of Penny's suitcases.

Penny crawled out and stretched thankfully before reaching in for the other suitcase and her tote bag. "What now?" she asked.

"Go on in, the door isn't locked. Incredible after New

York, isn't it?'' Heather said. For some reason she hung back until Penny had opened one of the double doors and preceded her into a small square hallway. ''Just dump the bags here for the moment,'' Heather said, coming in behind her. ''We'll take them up later, but I expect you could use a drink first after all that.'' She opened a door to their right and switched on a rather dim electric light. ''Go on in and make yourself at home. I'll forage for some ice.''

Penny found herself in a room paneled from floor to ceiling in light oak; it was comfortably furnished with chintz-covered couches and easy chairs and a large black-oak, sixteenth-century cheese cupboard against one wall. She sank thankfully into one of the deep couches and stretched again to get the cramps out, looking around at a collection of water color landscapes, obviously executed by an amateur, but one of considerable ability.

Heather reappeared through a door at the other end of the room, bearing an ice bucket; she made for the cheese cupboard. ''I don't have a great selection, because I don't drink much myself,'' she confessed, peering into it. ''There's sherry, red wine, brandy, or Drambuie.''

''A fairly stiff brandy and soda would be nice, or brandy and water if you don't have the soda,'' Penny said.

''Yes, there's one of the old-fashioned doodads here that makes soda.'' Heather's voice came muffled from inside the cupboard. ''What do they call them—gasogehes?—just like Sherlock Holmes had and from about the same era.'' She gave a little shrill laugh. ''Highly appropriate from what I've heard of all your recent sleuthing activities.''

''Oh, you know about that?'' Penny said, thankfully accepting the tall glass and taking a long, satisfying swig.

''Yes, there was an article about you and your fellow sleuth in the *New York Times* magazine not too long ago—very exciting.'' Heather had helped herself to a small sherry and settled in an easy chair. ''You'll have to give me all the inside dope while you are here.''

''Toby and I fell into it by accident to start with. We were in a rather nasty mess involving murder in Turkey, and the only way to get out of it was to solve the murders ourselves.

Since then it has become, well, a rather weird recurring pattern," Penny confessed.

There was a short silence while they sipped their drinks. Heather was wearing a high cowl-necked green cashmere sweater and a kilt in muted shades of green, blue, and yellow. Her stylishly cut short hair, which was an improbable shade of greenish-bronze that Penny recognized as a recent New York high-fashion trend, clashed with her otherwise sedate image.

"Well, congratulations on all this. I must say you look the part to a T," Penny said dryly. "What a pretty kilt."

"It's the Macdonell hunting tartan. The dress tartan is ghastly—red and yellow with black stripes." Heather laughed self-consciously and touched her hair. "But I'm going to have to do something about this. It's fine for New York, but here! I haven't had time so far, since it means going in to Oban. I was thinking of having it bleached and silvered. Amy McClintock—she's the laird of Sheena, that island you saw— has white hair, and she looks super with it."

That word again, Penny thought resignedly. "I'd be fascinated to hear how all this came about," she said "I had no idea you were so nobly connected or that you had such 'Great Expectations'."

"No more did I," her hostess exclaimed. "It's a terribly complicated story, but I could give you the main events if you aren't too tired, or it could wait until later if you'd rather go right up to bed."

"I'm getting my second wind, and another of these would help." Penny smiled, holding up her empty glass.

Heather produced some cheese and crackers to go with the refill, and they munched companionably before Heather went on. "It began for me last October in New York. A letter out of the blue from an Edinburgh firm of solicitors asking me if I could prove descent from one Fergus Macdonell, who emigrated to America in 1746. If I could submit such proof to them as soon as possible, I would have news to my great advantage. Of course, I was terribly intrigued, and luckily I had kept all my father's papers with, among other things, the family genealogy. He often used to talk to me about our ancestor who had fought for Bonnie Prince Charlie and had fled from Scotland after the defeat at Culloden, so I wasn't completely in the dark. My sister Margaret, who is keen on this kind of thing, had joined the DAR some time ago and had done all the genealogy work for that, tracing back to *this* Fergus Macdonell's son who fought in the revolution. So I photocopied everything and sent it off. The next thing I knew, I was *the* Macdonell, because I was the eldest of the eldest surviving branch of the Macdonell clan and consequently heir to the Soruba estate, which is totally entailed to 'the Macdonell'; three hundred acres, this house, and all the farms. To say I was flabbergasted is the understatement of the year. I flew over in February to see what was what, and the first thing I asked the lawyers was how they ever found me. It was all extremely curious and more than a little embarrassing, actually. I don't suppose you noticed a sizable house on the left-hand side of the Lochgilphead road, just before you spotted me."

"Yes, I did. In fact, I was just about to stop at it and ask directions."

"Well, the man who owns it, Ian Macdonell, was under the firm impression he was next in line to inherit. Everybody else thought so, too—everybody, that is, except the old boy who just died. He was a history buff, and in ferreting through the family history, he evidently spotted this 'lost' American branch. He must have been a secretive old so-and-so, because he didn't say a word to anyone, but after he was drowned . . ."

"Drowned," Penny interrupted involuntarily.

"Yes, he was drowned out here in the Sound of Jura," Heather said with a slight frown. "These waters can be dangerous, and he was really getting past the age for sailing by himself. He was seventy-five. But as I was saying, after his drowning, his lawyers found an envelope that was to be opened after his death. I thought that only happened in old-fashioned novels. It was a tremendous shock to everyone, but I must say Ian has taken it with very good grace. The lawyers told him he hadn't any grounds to dispute it, and while he hasn't exactly greeted me with open arms, at least he's been civil."

"Losing an estate this size must have been one hell of a blow," Penny said bluntly. "Or isn't it profitable? I know a lot of them aren't in England these days, especially if the entail does not allow any land to be sold.''

"Well, the estate is self-supporting. All the farming land is rented out; the only thing that doesn't pay for itself is this house and its grounds. I'm not sure yet how much of a drain it's going to be,'' Heather confessed. "I think I can manage it if I'm careful. Luckily, the last Macdonell was single, like myself, and he had a lot of things done so that most of the house can be closed off and there's still a workable nucleus. I don't want you to see the place in the dark—it doesn't do it justice—but we'll do the grand tour tomorrow. It has fourteen bedrooms, and that's not counting the servants' rooms and other little extras like a ballroom and a huge formal dining room, besides the usual quota of drawing rooms and studies.''

"My God, it must cost a fortune to heat.''

Heather gave a triumphant laugh. "No, not really. I am very much indebted to my immediate predecessors here. Just after World War II, the Macdonell of the time tried to run this place as a private residential hotel for a while. He lived down in one of the farm cottages, where the Strachans, my tenant farmers, live now, but he sank a lot of money into the house. He put in a coal-burning central-heating system, some more bathrooms, and the electric-generating plant which gives us our power. The hotel folded after his death, but then the old boy who just died made further modifications so that the central heating need only be used in the occupied part of the house, and the rest can be sealed off. I just have three bedrooms and two baths open now—one for me, one for you, and one for Alison when she comes.''

"Then where does the other person in the house sleep?'' Penny asked, and was startled by Heather's violent reaction.

Heather sat bolt upright, her fists clenched and twin spots of color in her high cheekbones. "What other person?'' she said shrilly.

"Why, I thought I heard a door shutting and some footsteps just now,'' Penny said in surprise. "I naturally thought it was the maid or housekeeper or whatever you have here. You don't look after the whole of this place by yourself, do you?''

"You're mistaken, quite mistaken. There's nobody here

but us. Mrs. Mitton, the factor's wife, housekeeps with the help of a girl from the village and old Mrs. Gray from the lodge at times, but they all live out. There's nobody, I tell you!'' Heather's voice rose almost to a scream.

"Whoa there, calm down, Heather. No need to get bent out of shape," Penny said soothingly. "My ears are still buzzing from listening to the car roaring all day. I'm probably just hearing things." She stifled a yawn. "Maybe we should call it a day. I see the witching hour approaches, and by the time we get my bags up and I'm unpacked, it'll be past my usual bedtime. I'm not a great one for staying up late. Are you?"

With a visible effort, her hostess calmed down. "No, I've been keeping country hours since I came over again in May." She got up. "I've put you in the Spencer room. It has the nicest view."

They collected the bags and lugged them up a shallow-treaded staircase that fell just short of being impressive. At the first bend it opened out into a small landing with two massive double doors set into the left-hand wall.

"That's the way into the north wing," Heather said as she stopped to rest before climbing another flight to a much larger landing. "This is my room to the left, and those two other doors are to a bathroom and a separate john. Yours is here on the right." There was another short flight of steps directly facing them, again blocked by double doors. "That leads to the south wing. It runs over the ballroom, and that little flight of stairs"—she indicated a smaller staircase that ran up to the right—"goes up to four more bedrooms and a bathroom. It's blocked off at the top."

She led Penny in and switched on the light; Penny was relieved to see three hot-water radiators discreetly sheltered under the window seats of the three large windows of the huge room. It appeared almost cluttered by the mammoth pieces of furniture, which were dominated by a king-size four-poster bed complete with hangings. There was a colossal wardrobe that ran along the whole wall opposite the end of the bed and an equally large dressing table on the wall opposite the windows. There was a door leading off to the left of the bed.

"That's your bathroom and john," Heather said, opening a door to the left and inviting Penny to peek. "You'll share it with Alison, who'll have the room next door. And if you don't mind, she'll come through this way. Otherwise, the main entrance to her room is in the north wing, and that'll mean opening it up."

"Oh, no, not at all," Penny muttered absently, eyeing the high and enormous bed with alarm. "I hope I don't get lost sleeping in that thing. It looks as if it might swallow me whole."

Heather chuckled. "There's a footstool for shorties like us, and if you sleep in the middle, you run no danger of falling out and breaking your neck."

"I haven't turned you out of your usual room, have I?" Penny asked.

A faint shadow crossed Heather's face. "No, I started out in here, but then I switched to the one opposite. It looks out over the gardens and Soruba, the hill that gives its name to the house. It's—well—cozier." She crossed quickly to the long windows and stared out into the darkness. "No moon tonight, or you could see the view. It really is lovely. However, at least you can hear one of our local wonders." She threw open the bottom half of one of the windows, setting the long chintz curtains swaying in the warm, salt-laden breeze that blew in. "Come over here and listen."

Penny obediently stuck her head out. For a few seconds she heard nothing but the wind sighing in the pines on the hills behind the house, and then she became aware of a dull continuous rumble. "What is it?" she asked. "Sounds like a subway train."

"It's the Corrievreckan." Heather's voice held a touch of awe. "On rough nights it really roars. It's the second largest whirlpool after the Maelstrom in Europe, and it lies between the two big islands of Jura and Scarba. It is one of the things that makes the waters around here so dangerous." She shivered suddenly and, drawing back, closed down the window. "Remind me to tell you about it and the Macdonell curse tomorrow."

"Curses, yet. Good heavens," Penny murmured.

Heather became her usual brisk self. "Well, if you have

everything you need, I'll leave you. I usually have breakfast at eight, but if you don't want to get up until later, that's okay. Mrs. Mitton's a flexible soul.''

"No, I'm usually up before that," Penny assured her. "And after a good night's sleep, I'll be a lot peppier tomorrow, I promise."

"Good night, then," Heather said with some reluctance, and went out, closing the door behind her.

Penny suddenly felt very weary. She decided against trying to unpack and instead ferreted in her bags for her pajamas. Then she went into the bathroom for a perfunctory wash. Ever curious, she opened the adjoining door and fumbled around for the switch. The bedroom was a smaller version of her own, graced by only two windows and a much smaller four-poster bed. She switched off the light and returned to her own cavernous room. With some misgivings, she crawled up into the huge bed and settled herself in the middle of it before leaning across and switching off the bedside lamp. It was surprisingly soft and downy, and she immediately felt drowsy. The first waves of sleep were starting to lap over her, when her door came open with a soft click and swung wide.

"Is that you, Heather?" she mumbled, but there was no answer, and she felt too comfortable to get up. "Couldn't have latched it properly." She yawned and snuggled deeper under the covers.

Penny was almost asleep, when she heard the noise of a door creaking open and then the measured tread of heavy feet. Sitting up in bed with a start, she wondered frantically what weapon was at hand. She grasped her small, round traveling clock and edged cautiously out of bed, reaching the floor with a small thud and creeping cautiously to the open door. She peered out on to the darkened landing; the footsteps were still audible but seemed to be dying away. There was a crack of light under her hostess's door. She crossed the landing and knocked softly.

"Heather, are you there?"

The door opened to reveal her friend's small figure clad in a dressing gown; a startled expression was on her long face.

"We've got an intruder by the sounds of it," Penny whispered. "Got anything we can bean him with if he gets into this part? It sounds as if he's in the south wing."

Heather stood as if frozen. "So you heard it, too? I haven't been imagining things?"

"Imagining things? Of course not! There's someone here," Penny snapped. She put on the landing light.

Heather shook her head stubbornly. "You don't understand," she said. "There's no intruder. There can't be. Look." She pointed at the double doors to the south wing, which had flat steel bolts top and bottom that were firmly in place. "It's locked as well."

"Well, he probably got in a door and is wandering around the south wing. Shouldn't you call the police or the factor or someone?"

"You don't understand," Heather repeated. "It's impossible. That's the only door into the south wing, and all the windows are shuttered."

Penny felt a little prickling at the nape of her neck. "What are you trying to say, Heather?"

Her friend's face suddenly crumpled. She reached out and grasped Penny with thin, wiry hands. "I don't understand it, but I think the place is haunted." She gasped. "I've been terrified, half out of my mind with worry. Oh, Penny, what am I going to do?" She began to shake uncontrollably.

"If that's a ghost, it's a mighty solid-footed one," Penny said grimly. "But one thing for sure, I'm not about to investigate it tonight. I'm much too tired, and you're much too upset. Safety in numbers, come on. There's room in that bed for six of our size. We'll lock the door and sleep together. And to heck with Bigfoot! But tomorrow, I promise you, we'll get to the bottom of all this."

CHAPTER 3

When Penny awoke, it was to sunshine streaming in through the long windows and a pale-blue cloudless sky. There was no sign of Heather, and the miniature barricade Penny had erected in front of the door, which she had locked, was gone. It was eight o'clock, and so she zipped through a quick bath, put on slacks and a sweater, and, feeling fully restored and ready for anything, sallied forth to find her hostess and breakfast.

Heather was neither in her room nor in the lounge, but Penny heard her calling, and so she followed the sound to see Heather's head popping around the door down the hall. The head shook a warning and then said brightly, "In here. Mrs. Mitton has just brought in the coffee."

Penny followed her into a small, white-paneled room, bright with sunlight, where a tall thin woman with a faded face that probably had once been beautiful was placing a silver coffee pot on the round dining room table.

"I eat in here all the time," Heather explained. "The other dining room is too vast, even if it is nearer to the kitchen." She performed the necessary introduction, which Mrs. Mitton acknowledged with a dignified nod.

Then Mrs. Mitton asked in the lilting voice of the native Gaelic speaker, "And would Dr. Spring be wanting porridge, or would she be wanting the cold cereal?"

Dr. Spring tactfully opted for the porridge, which was steaming gently on a hot plate on a pretty little eighteenth-century Hepplewhite buffet off to ths side. This was followed by fresh-made oat bannocks and honey.

When Mrs. Mitton left the room to get fresh coffee, Heather said, "Don't mention last night in front of her. I thought after breakfast we'd go for a walk to see the gardens. I'll explain everything then."

"I wasn't about to," Penny said with some asperity. "But before we go sight-seeing, I'd like to take a look at the south wing, if nothing else."

"I was going to wait until they had finished cleaning up there. Then we wouldn't have to worry about being over-heard," Heather said nervously. As Penny gazed curiously at her, she added, "By the way, thanks for all the support last night. That's the first decent night's sleep I've had in a month."

Mrs. Mitton reappeared, and so Penny launched into a hasty report of her trip.

"And at what time would the Macdonell be wanting luncheon served?" Mrs. Mitton asked primly.

"One o'clock suit you, Penny?" Heather asked, keeping a wary eye on her housekeeper. Penny, her mouth full of bannock, nodded.

"And no doubt ye'll be wanting coffee and shortcake for your elevenses?" the housekeeper continued. "Here or in the lounge?"

"That'll be nice," Heather said. "But just leave it in the kitchen, and we'll fetch it ourselves when we come in. We'll be looking over the grounds."

"Very well." Mrs. Mitton's tone verged on the disapproving as she departed silently.

"It's very nice to be looked after," Heather said with a faint sigh. "But after a lifetime of doing it for myself, I do find it a bit constricting."

"I'm sure you'll get used to it," Penny said with a grin. "But I know what you mean. I'm finished. How about a quick peek at the south wing before we go out? I've got to go up for my jacket, anyway."

They made their way upstairs, and somewhat surprisingly Heather fumbled under the stair carpet of the top step and produced an old-fashioned key.

"This makes it easier for the cleaning women, rather than

having to get the keys from me or Mrs. Mitton all the time,''
she explained.

They slid the bolts back, and Penny tried the doors, which
were indeed locked tight. They opened on to a few more steps
and then a broad corridor, dimly lighted by an oriel window
over another small staircase at the far end. There were two
doors, one to the left and one to the right; Heather threw both
of them open.

"As you can see, the shutters are all in place," she said,
turning on the lights. Both rooms were large, and their ordi-
nary bedroom furnishings had the forlorn air of things that
had not been used for a very long time. They were, however,
to Penny's probing eye, remarkably dust-free.

"Do they clean all these regularly?" she asked.

Heather shook her head. "No, it's the air here, so unpol-
luted that there is virtually no dust. So far as I know, these
haven't been cleaned since I got here. I think Mrs. Mitton
told me they just got done twice a year in the spring and fall
cleanings."

Penny examined the windows. "There's a hasp broken
here," she exclaimed, and, sliding the bottom half of the
window up, pushed the shutter, which opened with a sharp
click on to the same spectacular view of the bay she had
enjoyed from her own windows. It was about thirty feet to the
ground, but thick ivy grew up the walls and stretched above
her head to the story above. "Well, it wouldn't be easy, but
an active man could do it. Is there anything missing?"

Heather shook her head. "Nothing. There is nothing valuable in this part of the house. Why on earth would anyone
want to climb in?"

"Ah, there you have me," Penny confessed, leading the
way up the staircase to another little landing, which yielded
on to two smaller bedrooms and a box room that were
unshuttered. Peering out a window, Penny found the height
so vertiginous that she hastily drew her head in. "Unless he's
a human fly, I doubt that he came in this way," she muttered.

"Do let's go out now," Heather said impatiently. "I have
so much to tell you."

As they reached the broad corridor, Penny said, "Talcum

powder, lots of it, that's what we need. We'll sprinkle it around under that window and across the corridor before the doors. That should give us a line on Bigfoot. He'll never spot it, and we should get good prints. We'll do it before we go to bed tonight."

"Talcum powder," Heather was beginning, when she let out a frightened yelp, as a gray head appeared at their feet, grinning savagely up at them. "Oh, Mrs. Gray. How you startled me."

The little bent old woman looked up at Heather, her bright dark eyes snapping under bushy gray eyebrows. "Forby, I was just cleaning the stairs and was wondering who was so early abroad in the south wing. Will ye be opening it up the noo?" She had the lilt of the Highlands in her voice.

Heather recovered herself. "No, we were just locking up again. I was showing my guest, Dr. Spring here, the house. We'll be up to the lodge in the next day or so. Maybe you'll guide us to the Wishing Well."

"Och, aye, I can do that well enough," the old lady said, looking at Penny reflectively. "That is, if the leddy is up to a guid lang walk. Would ye be wanting to see the Giant's Grave also? He doesna get many visitors these days, puir soul."

"Sounds great," Penny said hastily. "And I'm used to walking."

"Ye'll be needing the rubber boots, then," the old woman said in a tone of dismissal, and turned back to her work.

They passed a large girl with a glum face vacuuming the formal drawing-room and emerged into the bright morning sunlight. Crossing the broad sweep of gravel in front of the house, they descended a steep flight of stone steps to a sunken lawn fringed by large elms. Tall privet hedges loomed to their left, in the middle of which sat an ornate wrought-iron gate.

"Inside there is an Italian garden planted by an eighteenth-century Macdonell after he'd made the Grand Tour," Heather explained absently, but kept walking to where the lawn sloped down to a small burn, which they crossed by a small wooden bridge. As they climbed the moss-covered path that meandered across the shoulder of the hill, Heather said in a far away voice, "This is Soruba. I believe it means 'Place of Dreams.' "

Their footsteps made no sound on the brilliant emerald moss, and they could hear the tinkle of the burn. The heavy cloying scent of the rhododendrons massed along the path, mixed with the cleaner tang of the Scotch pines whispering above in the gentle westerly wind.

"I hate to break in on this bucolic peace," Penny said, "but we've simply got to talk about what happened last night and what has been going on here."

"Just a little farther," Heather pleaded. "We're almost at the Laird's Seat." They had rounded the flank of the hill and were now in full view of the bay. A stone seat had been cut into the hillside, and she sank onto it with a grateful sigh. Then she pointed mutely down to the jetty, where a small sailboat and a larger powerboat bobbed gently.

"Yes, very nice," Penny said impatiently, settling beside her. "But what about this other business?"

"The odd thing is that it didn't start at once," Heather said in a perplexed voice. "As I told you last night, I came over to settle in the house in May. Here we are in the third week of July, so it was just about, oh, six weeks ago, about mid-June, when I started to hear things."

"In the south wing?"

"No, not entirely. At first, when I was sitting in the lounge at night, it was just the sound of a door shutting with a bang. Naturally I assumed it was Mrs. Mitton come back for something she'd forgotten, but when I asked her about it, she would look at me with her blank gray eyes and flatly deny it. After that, I thought it was my imagination playing with the noises you hear in any old house, but then I started to hear footsteps and some nights—" she bit her lip "— the pipes, the bagpipes playing softly, and always the same tune—a lament."

"Where?"

"It seemed to come from the ballroom, but I was too frightened to look."

"I don't blame you," Penny said grimly. "All by yourself like that. Has something been going on every night?"

Heather shook her head. "No, at first it was only now and then, but in the last week or so, it has been more frequent, and the footsteps have become heavier—and nearer." Her voice trembled. "I thought I was losing my mind."

"Well, I assure you that isn't so, because I know I have all my marbles and that last night someone opened my door and was marching around in the south wing. Did the door ever open when you were in that room?"

"It was the reason I moved," Heather replied. "It happened almost every night."

"Probably there's a board with a latch that connects with the south wing and is triggered when someone steps on it. I tested it this morning, and it does open very easily. Now, think back to the time all this started. Was there anything you can think of that you either said or did that may have stirred someone up?"

Heather's brow was wrinkled with perplexity. "No, nothing I can think of at all, unless. . . . But that's kind of silly."

"Nothing is silly when you have a weird set of happenings like this. Out with it."

"Well, Amy McClintock—she's the lady laird of Sheena I was telling you about—gave a dinner party in my honor at the castle." She pointed to a crenellated tower that was just visible at the northern end of the nearby island. "All the local 'acceptables' were there. There aren't many, as you can well imagine. Anyway, someone asked me what my plans were. Was I going to use Soruba as a summer place like the old laird did, or was I going to rent it, or what?" She fell silent.

"And?"

"Well, you know how carried away I get sometimes. A bit overenthusiastic? I said something to the effect that I had so fallen in love with Soruba that I didn't intend to leave it ever, not until my dying day. I wasn't expecting them to break into wild applause, but it seemed to fall singularly flat. Nobody said anything for a minute, and I felt pretty silly."

"And who all was there?" Penny asked, feeling a prickle of unease running up her spine.

"Amy McClintock and her husband, Gareth. She is really

the McDougall, but she likes to go by her married name. I was a bit surprised when I met them both, because he must be a good fifteen years younger than she is, and I found out from Mrs. Mitton that he used to be her gillie, so in a sense it's a bit of a misalliance. Not that that matters to me, of course," she continued as she noted Penny's wry smile. "And she has been terribly nice to me, and he seems very fond of her and harmless. Then there was Ian Macdonell and his wife, Margaret."

"The disappointed heir?" Penny interjected.

"Yes, but as I said, they neither of them seem to hold it against me. Then there was Cranston Phillips, a very interesting man. He lives in that smaller house by the Macdonells and is an artist. He shares it with another man, Bennett Rose, who's a photographer and skin diver. He specializes in underwater photography, I gather."

"Gays?" Penny asked.

"I don't think so. Rose might possibly be—he's a bit effeminate—but Cranston's a real he-man type, a great sailor, hunter, fisherman, and, I would say, has an eye for the ladies. He's very gallant. Then, 'below' the salt," she went on with unconscious arrogance, "were the Strachans and the Camerons, who are both my tenant farmers. Dennis Strachan and his wife, Meg, farm the home farm. They are Lowlanders who moved up here, oh, about twenty years ago. They live in the largest of those three cottages you see grouped together down there." Again she pointed to a row of red-brick houses not far from the jetty. "And Hamish Cameron operates the bigger farm. Their house is over on the Ardnan side, behind us, and his wife, Deirdre, is the Mittons' daughter—a real beauty. The men could not keep their eyes off her, Gareth McClintock included, which I did not think suited Amy too well. Her husband, Hamish Cameron, is a rather unpleasant man, a wheeler-dealer and a skinflint. He goes in for antique dealing on the side and has a shop he runs in Lochgilphead. He spends a lot of time combing the Highlands for antiques."

"And it was about a week after this party that you first heard the noises?"

"Yes, just about. But as I say, I can't really see any connection."

"Your announced intention of staying here permanently may well have been bad news to three of them. Ian Macdonell for obvious reasons, and the Strachans and the Camerons because with you on the spot all the time, they won't be as free as they have been."

"No, that doesn't make any sense," Heather interrupted heatedly. "What the Strachans and Camerons do on their farms really has nothing to do with me. They have a completely free hand. I'm a lot more dependent on them than they are on me, because if either of them quit their tenancies, I'd really be on the spot. As for Ian, he enjoys all the same rights he had in the old laird's time. He has free run of the hunting and shooting on the estate, and frankly, I don't think he'd have the money to run the big house. He's an ex-army officer, and I think he has very little outside of his pension. Actually, his inheritance has only been postponed. He or his son will inherit the place after I die, anyway."

Penny looked at her in surprise. "You mean it wouldn't go to your sister Margaret and her heirs as next in line?"

Heather shook her head. "No, that's not the way it works. If I had children, it would go to them, but I don't, and so it would revert to the next eldest male line, which is Ian's. This will all be his one day."

"It wouldn't be the first time an heir-in-waiting tried to hurry up the process," Penny muttered stubbornly. "Even if all he is trying to do is to scare you out so he can rule in absentia. And it also strikes me that Hamish Cameron might have his eye on some of those antiques you are talking about and would like you off the scene so he could get hold of them."

"But that doesn't make sense, either," Heather replied. "For one thing, there is a complete inventory of what is in the house, and for another, he has had months when the house was empty when he could have taken what he wanted. I almost wish I could believe you and that there was someone human doing all this, but I'm afraid it's a whole lot deeper and darker than that."

"All right, what's your explanation?" Penny asked. "What do you think it is?"

Heather looked at her with troubled blue eyes. "I think what we are hearing is the late Colonel Macdonell, and I think what is coming to pass is the curse of the Macdonells," she whispered. "I can see I'd better tell you about that. You may not want to stay on, and if you don't, I can't say I'd blame you."

CHAPTER 4

"I'm getting chilled sitting here." Penny stood up abruptly. "Before we discuss curses and suchlike why don't we go on to the jetty and look at the boats and then swing by the farm cottages. I'd like to get a look at them, in any case. You can tell me as we go."

"Oh, all right." Heather seemed taken aback by Penny's matter-of-fact manner. They continued on the same downward-running path until it split into two branches, one running to the left around the hill and the other to the right toward the beach. "We've just been over what is known locally as the Laird's Walk," Heather explained as they took the right branch. "The laird in question was Colonel Hector Macdonell, who died in World War I. I'll show you a portrait of him when we get back to the house, but to make any sense of his story, first I'll have to tell you about the curse."

They recrossed the burn by another little bridge and were in sight of the kelp-strewn beach, which they skirted, aiming toward a wider turf-gravel track that ran directly down to the jetty. Again, Heather appeared to go off on a tangent. "As you'll see when we go down to the memorial, the Macdonells have been mainly military men, farming their ancestral acres between wars, but there have been a few exceptions. The man who collected most of the worthwhile stuff in the house and planted the Italian garden was one of them. He got into trade in some way and made a big success in the ship chandling business. He died in the 1840s, and his son was the one who built all those additions to the house. He not only went on with his father's business but launched out into shipowning, too. This was in the early days of steamships, and he made a small fortune by buying old sailing ships, shoving in a steam engine, and beating his competitors in the west here hands down. But as you may well imagine, a lot of these ships were death traps. Incidentally, it was he who built this jetty and had a channel dredged—long since silted in, of course—so that some of his ships could come directly here. I suspect that perhaps he didn't want any officials to see some of his cargoes. The story goes that sometime in 1864 he sent one of these steam sailers on a quick run to Colonsay, one of the outer islands. The direct route is between Jura and Scarba, past the Corrievreckan, which is safe enough if the tide and weather are just right. However, just before they got to the Corrievreckan, the engines failed, and the ship began to drift into it. When the captain hoisted sail to escape from the vortex, he found that the sails the Macdonell had provided were rotten and just ripped away. He had his eldest son aboard, a lad of fourteen, and just before the ship was sucked under and they all perished, he was seen with the lad in his arms, screaming curses on the Macdonell to the effect that the Macdonell had killed him and his eldest, so no eldest Macdonell heir would ever live to enjoy the fruits of Soruba again.''

"How do you know all this if everyone perished?" Penny said, interrupting. They were strolling on the stone-built jetty now, the gentle waves providing a sibilant background to their voices.

"I should have said all but one," Heather amended. "One of the sailors clung to a large piece of wreckage and managed to escape. He was washed ashore on Jura and told the story at the official inquiry." She shaded her eyes and looked out over the sparkling waters. "Oh, look, that's Cranston's boat. Isn't she a beauty?" Penny saw a large white powerboat cruising past the southern end of Sheena. Two figures were visible: one large and burly, and the other slighter, clad in a skin diver's outfit. Heather waved energetically, and the figures returned her greeting. "He often fishes out there at anchor, while Bennett dives," Heather explained, and turned back up the jetty. "Where was I?"

"At the official inquiry," Penny said. "How did you get to know all this?"

"Mrs. Gray told me. She knows a lot about local history," Heather said. As Penny snorted gently, she added with a touch of tartness, "But it's not just an old wives' tale, it's a matter of official record. There's a bound copy of the inquiry in the study. You can read it for yourself."

"What on earth does it have to do with this Colonel Macdonell or your own situation?" Penny asked.

"Because the curse has come true ever since," Heather said shortly. They had reached the red-brick cottages, which were larger than Penny had thought from a distance. They were built in a row, the middle one appreciably smaller than the two that flanked it. From the one nearest to them came the faint skirl of bagpipes. "That'll be Jamey Mitton practicing," Heather said. "He's the local piper, plays at all weddings, funerals, and so on. He's very good."

"Is he, now," Penny said thoughtfully. "Who lives in the other cottages?"

"The little one in the middle is occupied by Mr. and Mrs. McDougall. They are both very old now, but he used to be the factor here for going on fifty years. They are Mrs. Mitton's parents. She was born here on the estate and has lived here all her life. After she married Mitton and Dierdre was born, they moved into the larger cottage, and her parents moved next door. The Strachans' place is at the end."

"Do they have any children?" Penny asked.

"No," Heather said with a laugh. "When you see her, I think you'll know why. She's a better man than he. The Strachans have some Highland cattle that run free. If you meet any of them, there's nothing to be alarmed about," Heather continued in an absent voice. "Just yell and wave your arms, and they'll get out of your way."

"Thanks a lot." Penny grinned faintly. "But go on with your narrative."

"Well, the curse seemed to start almost at once; within a year, the heir of the Macdonell shipowner was drowned right here in the bay. Since that Macdonell had fourteen children, six of them boys, it didn't present too much of a problem. His second son, Colonel Hector Macdonell's father, eventually inherited the estate. He had two sons, and the elder died of a ruptured appendix when he was a freshman at Edinburgh

University, so Hector, the younger one, inherited. Like so many of the Macdonells, he was a military type, and when World War I broke out, he formed a volunteer regiment of infantry, mainly recruited from his own kinsmen and the people around here. It was positively feudal. He had two grown sons and one daughter. The sons were in the regiment with him. Here things get a big vague, but it seems he made some terrible blunder at the battle of Ypres, which resulted in the slaughter of most of the Macdonells, including the two sons. He wasn't killed in the battle, but he was shot shortly thereafter. Some say he was shot by one of the survivors; others claim that he was so overwhelmed by what he had done that he blew his own brains out."

Heather's voice began to tremble. "It is his ghost that is said still to walk around here. There are many reports of it. Even Jamey Mitton . . ." Her voice trailed off as they emerged from the track opposite the wooden building that housed the badminton court. Penny opened her mouth to speak but after a look at her friend's troubled face closed it as they turned into the drive.

"Anyway, the estate then passed to Hector's daughter, who married, had a son, and promptly died. The son was raised by his father's family and never really lived here. He was the one who, after World War II, fixed the place up as a hotel. But he'd been badly wounded at El Alamein and never completely recovered. He was here only about five or six years when he died."

"Of natural causes?" Penny peered keenly at the tall, shuttered windows of the ballroom and the thick ivy that clustered around the south wing as they strolled past. Her quick eyes noted a dead strand of ivy about twenty feet from the ground.

"Yes, as a result of his wounds, apparently. He had never married, so the succession then passed to this Edinburgh lawyer, who came from a remote branch, like mine, that isn't even on the memorial." They had reached the front door, but Heather hovered in the sunlight, evidently reluctant to go in.

"Why don't we look at the Italian garden?" Penny suggested quickly, and they strolled on. "You mean there was not a single surviving line from all those kids of the shipowner?'' she asked.

Heather shook her head. "No. As I said, the carnage among the Macdonell kin in that World War I battle was unbelievable. No one survived in that line. This Ian Macdonell, who believed himself the lawyer's heir, came from a cadet branch of the same man who sired my ancestor, Fergus. His forebear was too young to get caught up in the 1745 rebellion, but he emigrated to Northern Ireland, and his family has been over there up to this time."

"Ireland, eh?" Penny said thoughtfully. "Did he move here because of his expectations, then?" They had reached the Italian garden and entered through the pretty gate, only to find that the formal-sculpted flower beds edged with low box hedges were empty of all but a few straggling rose bushes.

"I'm going to have to do something about this," Heather said with a sigh before answering. "I think it was partly because of all the ghastly trouble they've been having over in Ulster. He was regular army, and he's about my age or a bit older, so I suppose he figured it wouldn't be too comfortable a place to retire."

"How many children does he have?" Penny asked as they came to a small ornamental gazebo at the end of the garden and turned back toward the gate.

"Just the one son. He's away at Sandhurst becoming an army officer. Of late the Macdonells don't seem to have been a very prolific family." Heather gave a wry grin. "But you must admit, it is rather strange how the sea captain's curse has worked out."

"With considerable help from two world wars and the very imperfect state of modern medicine," Penny said dryly. "And if we are going along those lines, I must point out that the curse seems to be wearing a bit thin. Even the Macdonell who died after World War II enjoyed his inheritance for several years, and he was still in the shipowners' line. And the old boy who just died was scarcely nipped off in his prime if he was seventy-five, and he must have enjoyed his inheritance for close to thirty-five from what you've told me. Even granting the curse—which, frankly, I don't—I don't see that you have a lot to worry about."

Her tone did nothing to lighten the shadow on Heather's face as they climbed the stairs from the sunken garden. "There's still the colonel," Heather said stubbornly. "Come on, I'll show you the portrait."

"Yes, and I would like to see the ballroom and more of those antiques you told me about," Penny added as they went through the formal drawing room into a wider hallway with big double doors.

Heather ushered Penny through a door directly ahead of them into a white-paneled room whose walls were lined with bookshelves. In the spaces between them were a motley collection of weapons and framed photographs, many of them of military groups. A full-length painting hung over the marble fireplace; it was of a large, florid-faced man with a bushy walrus moustache, clad in a cockaded tam-o'-shanter, a brown hunting jacket, and a kilt whose violent colors of red, yellow, and black assaulted the eye.

"That's the colonel wearing the dress tartan of the Macdonells. As you can see, the background is the Italian garden."

Penny examined the portrait. "Looks harmless enough. In fact, he looks downright stupid. I must say I couldn't get too upset over him, dead or alive."

Heather made a disapproving noise. "You don't understand," she said again.

"What I understand is that you're in a fine state of nerves. It's no wonder, shut up in this great place and in a whole new ambience, which is as alien to you and what you've been used to as the other side of the moon," Penny said firmly. "So let's have it out. You tell me your theory of what has been going on, and then I'll tell you mine."

Heather walked over to the window and stared out at the view. "Before I ever started to hear anything," she said in a low, troubled voice, "I had heard about the colonel's ghost, first from old Mrs. Gray and then from Jamey Mitton. Jamey was the batman to the World War II Macdonell. He's from Inverness originally, a real Highlander, but he came here with the Macdonell to look after him. That's how he met and married Mrs. Mitton. But when he came, he really knew nothing about this part of the world or the family history.

He's a very down-to-earth type, not a man given to fancies at all. Well, he told me that when his master was lying sick with his last illness, he came for a walk up here to clear his head, along the Laird's Path. He saw a man dressed like that''—she nodded at the portrait—''and followed him along the path, thinking it was one of the hotel guests out for a walk. The figure turned into the Italian garden, but Jamey did not see or hear him open the gate, so, thinking this a bit queer, he hurried up to it, and there was no one there in the garden at all. The Macdonell died two days later. Mrs. Gray told me that he always appears when something is going to happen to the family. She says she saw him just before the last Macdonell was drowned and tried to warn him.'' Her voice trembled, and she bit her lip.

"Mrs. Gray is a regular ray of sunshine. So you think you are being warned of some approaching doom?"

"That's about the size of it."

"Okay, that's your theory. Now let me tell you mine. Nothing happened here until after that dinner party when you announced your intention of staying at Soruba House forever more. I think someone at that party was very upset by that. You were an unknown quantity up to that point, a successful American businesswoman from New York who wasn't all that likely to want to settle in an isolated spot like this. But your declaration changed all that and evidently did not suit someone, so he—they—decided to do something about it. For some reason, he doesn't want you here, so he is mounting a war of nerves to scare you away. And he has plenty of material to work with, what with the curse and all those ghosts. Think about what has happened so far—pipes playing, doors opening by themselves, footsteps in a locked wing, all the standard ingredients of a two-penny dreadful. But as I think I demonstrated this morning, somebody active enough could have climbed up into the south wing by the ivy, and unless my eyes are deceiving me, that is just what someone has been doing, because there is a thick branch of dead ivy out there where no dead branch ought to be. As to the pipes, let's take a look at the ballroom."

She hurried out and waited impatiently while Heather searched under the carpet for the key and opened the doors.

She clicked a switch, and two large crystal chandeliers sprang to dim life on the high-beamed ceiling. The ballroom was completely empty but for an ancient grand piano and a large harp that stood forlornly on a raised dais. Penny tried the piano, which gave out an untuned dissonance, and twanged the harp but could not produce anything like the note of a bagpipe. She tried all the windows, but they were firmly locked.

"Well, a piper standing in the bushes outside, playing at a normal range close by the wall, could well be mistaken for someone inside playing softly." Heather looked unconvinced, and so she went on hastily. "Let's see all those antiques."

"That set in your bedroom is eighteenth-century Italian marquetry, and there are two smaller sets, one in my room and one in Alison's. There are various other bits scattered through the house: a desk in the study, a cupboard in the drawing room. Then there's the dining room."

She had been leading the way into the north wing, and now she flung open another door. They entered a huge, gloomy room, decorated with dark green damask walls on which hung a collection of family portraits, heavily framed in black and gold. It was dominated by an enormous cherry-wood dining table, around which were sixteen Chippendale chairs. At the lower end of the room loomed an equally enormous sideboard flanked by two identical serving tables on which sat enormous wine coolers.

"The dining table and chairs alone have been valued at twenty-five thousand pounds. A cherry-wood Chippendale is very rare," Heather said with a touch of awe.

"Do have you any idea of the total value of the antiques?" Penny asked.

"I know exactly, since it was on the inventory of the old laird's estate. It is one hundred and fifty thousand pounds, and that does not include the paintings around the house, which for some reason have never been appraised."

"Well, that's a nice hunk of change, I must say. That might well bring an avaricious gleam to anyone's eye."

"Perhaps. How about some coffee? It's after eleven," Heather said, abruptly changing the subject.

"Good idea." When they were settled with steaming cups

and a plate of homemade shortbread on the table between them in the lounge, Penny continued. 'Look. Obviously, one way or another we have to get to the bottom of this thing. I'll make a bargain with you. If we hear footsteps and all the rest of it tonight and there are no marks on the talcum I'm going to spread around, I'll take your theory seriously. We'll get the best exorcist in the business and make a dignified retreat for the moment. But if I'm right and we find evidence of an intruder, we'll do some serious investigating my way. Okay?''

"Okay." Heather smiled faintly at her. "But either way, it's pretty awful, isn't it?"

There was a light tapping on the door, and Mrs. Mitton appeared. "The MacDougall—er, Mrs. McClintock—is on the phone for you. She wonders if you and Dr. Spring would be free to dine with her and some friends tonight on the island."

Heather sprang up. "Oh, that's nice. Will that be all right with you?" She looked enquiringly at Penny.

"Fine." Penny agreed. "I can hardly wait to meet your neighbors." As Heather left, Penny looked after her with a worried frown. "Particularly since I think one of them may well be trying to get rid of you—permanently."

CHAPTER 5

"My, you do look smart." Penny admired her friend's evening clothes, which included a long black velvet skirt, a short Bonnie Prince Charlie black velvet jacket, a white blouse with a frothy lace jabot, and a sash of the Macdonell dress tartan peeping out under the jacket.

Heather gave a little embarrassed laugh. "Thank you. Actually, to be absolutely correct, I should wear a long skirt of the dress tartan, but I so disliked it that I had this outfit made instead."

"It looks marvelous." Penny glanced ruefully at her own emerald-green dinner dress, which she had worn too many times. "I feel positively shabby. But what worries me is, now that we're all dressed up like this, how the hell do we get out there without reducing our clothes to tatters?"

"No problem. I'll run us down to the jetty in my Mini. I have it tucked in a garage by the kitchen, and Mitton will drive us over in the powerboat and leave us off. The Strachans aren't going to be there, so Gareth McClintock or someone at the party will give us a lift back. I usually drive myself, but not when I'm dolled up like this."

As they bumped across the waters of the bay, which were a lot choppier than they had been earlier, toward the beckoning lights of Sheena Castle, Penny realized that she was keyed up with anticipation. She had spent a very profitable afternoon. After lunch, Heather had confessed that she had made a habit of taking an afternoon nap to make up for her broken nights. Thankful to have some time to herself to think things out, Penny had retired to her room, armed with several books from

49

the library. She had stretched out on a chaise longue drawn up to the window and done some quiet research.

She had read the account of the official inquiry into the shipwreck, which corresponded with Heather's story, but she had found one suggestive bit of information that her hostess had omitted. The name of the drowned sea captain had been McDougall. Knowing how Celts of all kinds loved to cling to feuds and long-standing hatreds, she wondered how significant it was that at least two of the people nearest to her beleaguered friend were of the McDougall clan: her hostess of the evening and the dignified Mrs. Mitton. She looked thoughtfully at the long saturnine face of their pilot. Mitton was very tall, but his broad shoulders somehow diminished his height, and he wore a long, drooping moustache that accentuated his general air of silent melancholy. Heather had heard the pipes, and he was a piper. Were there any others around? she wondered.

She had also read a manuscript written by the World War II Macdonell, including an analysis of the battle of Ypres and a rather pathetic attempt to whitewash the memory of his maternal grandfather, Colonel Hector Macdonell. Even given the bias of the writer, it was plain to see that the ghastly catastrophe had been the colonel's doing and that he must have been every bit as stupid as his portrait indicated. She simply could not take anyone that stupid seriously, and so she had sprinkled with added diligence all the talcum powder she could find in every vulnerable part of the south wing.

"We're almost there," Heather announced. "There's Gareth McClintock at the jetty."

The roar of the powerboat sank to a gentle chugging as Mitton came alongside and was drawn close to a flight of stone steps by a boathook wielded by a brawny young man in Highland evening dress. Mitton hung on to a large iron ring and drew the boat up to the steps, and the young man, still hanging on to the boathook, held out his free hand and expertly transferred them to the steps.

"Bye, Jamey. See ye the noo," he said, and nonchalantly released the boat, which departed as Mitton raised a hand in silent farewell. He straightened up and grinned at them, showing beautiful even white teeth in an olive-skinned face, with twinkling brown eyes under dark brows. A Burt Reynolds but with Clark Gable's jug ears, Penny thought instantly—a very attractive male animal. Gillie or not, I don't wonder that the McDougall married this one. She was further charmed by the lilting but very broad accent with which he acknowledged Heather's introductions.

As they walked up the wide gravel path toward the castle's main entrance, Penny noted that despite its ancient design, the building was comparatively modern, approximately of the same period as Soruba's Victorian additions. Her impression was confirmed as they entered the hall, which was filled with trophies of the chase and Landseer animal portraits, and proceeded into the muted light of a very Victorian-looking drawing room. There was a small group of people in front of the large stone fireplace, where a token fire was burning. A white-haired woman, clad like Heather but with a tartan skirt, detached herself from the group and came over to them, hands outstretched. She pecked her counterpart on the cheek.

"Heather, so good of you to come at such short notice. I couldn't wait to see your famous guest. I'm delighted." She turned to Penny, and her slightly bulbous blue eyes took a careful survey. "I am the McDougall. I am so happy to have you here, Dr. Spring. Welcome to Sheena Castle and our wee group of friends."

Penny instantly disliked her hostess, who had captured her arm, squeezed it fondly, and steered her toward the fireplace.

The McDougall raised her voice as if the assembly were a little hard of hearing. "Now, I'd like you all to meet this very exciting person, an old friend of Heather's, Dr. Penelope Spring, from the University of Oxford no less. She is an archaeologist and such a very clever person." Her "r"'s rolled and trilled up and down the scale.

"Anthropologist," Penny said, correcting her firmly, shaking hands and trying to sort out who was who.

"Archaeologist, anthropologist—I'm afraid it is all the same to us simple souls," her hostess proclaimed with a shrill laugh. "It's all far too clever for me at any rate. We lead such quiet lives around here."

You might, but I'm willing to bet somebody here doesn't, Penny thought grimly, accepting a glass of sherry and standing somewhat apart from the guests. Some of them were easy enough to identify: the beautiful Deirdre, who was certainly spectacular, with her long flaxen hair and amazingly large, dark-lashed violet eyes; the big and burly Cranston Phillips, who looked more like a successful farmer than an artist and who would have been good-looking save for his eyes, which were small and of a rather washed-out shade of brown. The Ian Macdonells were both slightly overweight and had a long-married look to them. He had the ruddy, weather-beaten look of a dedicated outdoorsman, whereas she was very pale. Penny was momentarily confused about Hamish Cameron, whom she first supposed to be the smallish man with thinning hair who was hovering protectively at Deirdre's elbow. But that turned out to be Bennett Rose; Hamish Cameron, who was talking to his host, was as handsome as his wife was beautiful, with a long, chiseled face, jet-black hair and eyes, and the beautiful hands of a musician. Although they were all affable, there was a curious sense of exclusion, which applied not only to herself but also, she saw, to Heather. We're outsiders, she thought, and I have the feeling that is all we would ever be. It did nothing to cheer her on her friend's behalf.

A maid appeared, clad in old-fashioned black, with a white cap and apron. "Dinner is served, ma'am," she announced.

"Too bad Alastair couldn't make it," Amy McClintock said, looking at her husband. "Alastair is Gareth's brother, such a busy young man; he's a policeman, you know. Still . . ." Again the vacant laugh rang out. "It would have unbalanced the table tonight."

They went into a dining room as cavernous as that of Soruba, but here the vast dining table was of light oak surrounded by matching chairs of mid-Victorian vintage. We'll have to bellow at one another, Penny thought gloomily, and was thankful that she had on a long-sleeved dress, for the room was decidedly chilly. She was seated at her hostess's right, and Heather sat at the other end of the table to the right of her host. The dinner was long, lukewarm, and mediocre, but the wine was extremely good, which surprised Penny. She remarked on its excellence and was rewarded by another of her hostess's laughs.

"Ah, that's Cranston's doing. He's so clever about things like that. We all depend on him."

Penny's initial impression of her hostess was confirmed as she seesawed between vapidity and a faint arrogance that Penny found extremely trying.

"So nice of you to dash up at a moment's notice to keep poor Heather company. Though I believe some relative of hers will shortly be on the scene. I do hope, though, that you aren't going to be selfish and keep her all to yourself. We so enjoy Heather and her quaint ways."

Penny stifled her irritation. "Yes, Heather's niece will be arriving for the summer in a few days."

"And will you be staying all summer, too?"

"My plans are indefinite. I might," Penny said in a voice loud enough for the rest of the table to hear.

"I always thought anthro— whatever, spent their time scurrying off to faraway places and studying things," her hostess remarked, eliciting a guffaw from Ian Macdonell.

"Just what I am doing at the moment," Penny said dryly. "This is certainly a faraway place and new territory for me. I am sure there is much to be studied right here."

"Oh, really?" Amy McClintock said, evidently taken aback. "Goodness me. I never thought of that."

There was an ensuing awkward pause, which Cranston Phillips broke with a remark about sailing conditions in the bay.

"Your friend, Mr. Rose, is an underwater photographer, I believe," Penny said, and an imp of mischief prompted her to continue. "A friend of mine recently was showing me an article about that Armada galleon treasure found off the Isle of Mull, beautiful underwater photos. Did he do those, by any chance?"

"Er, no, I don't think so," Cranston Phillips said uneasily.

"That same article mentioned that there were others around here. Has he tried his hand at locating them?" she asked with deliberate innocence.

"Treasure, Spanish galleons, here?" her hostess put in with excitement. "Oh, wouldn't that be thrilling. Don't tell me that's what Bennett's after off the south end of the island. I know I've told you a thousand times, Cranston, the fishing for you is better farther out. And don't forget," she added coyly. "If you did find anything, it would be treasure trove, and some of it would belong to me."

"Nothing as exciting as that. Bennett likes the rock formations and the sea growth around there, that's all. But"—he gave a deep-throated laugh—"believe me, if we did find anything, Amy, we'd not only tell you, we'd trumpet it to the entire world."

They retreated to the drawing room for coffee and brandy, and there was a painful interlude during which Amy tried to persuade her evidently unwilling spouse to "play for Dr. Spring." Gareth McClintock eventually brought out a set of bagpipes and with ill grace blasted out a few Scottish dance airs, confirming Penny's opinion that the pipes should be played only out of doors. When the music died away in an uncanny caterwaul, she waited for the ringing in her ears to die away and reflected that here was piper number two.

The pipes had evidently been a bit too much for Margaret Macdonell, for she collected her husband and, pleading a headache, took an early leave. Cranston Phillips and Bennett Rose were not far behind; their excuse was an early business appointment in Oban. Penny would gladly have followed them, but Amy had Heather in deep conversation, and so she was forced to make rather stilted chitchat with the Camerons, who did not have much to say for themselves. When Gareth rejoined them, he did nothing but glower, his piping apparently having thrown him into a towering rage. It was with considerable relief that she finally managed to catch Heather's eye and give her a discreet sign to leave.

Since the other boats had gone, Gareth had to ferry them all back, and his wife accompanied them down to the jetty, still talking to Heather. As they embarked in the powerboat, which was a larger version of Heather's, she delivered a final admonition. "Well, if you make up your mind about it, let me know. I have a very good firm in Glasgow that supplies them."

Once the boat was under way, Penny muttered into Heather's ear, "What was that all about?"

The roar of the engine hid their voices from the others, who were standing on either side of Gareth, looking at the starlit waters. Heather grinned at her in the gloom. "Oh, Amy is very upset that I don't have my staff in uniform and is determined to bring me into line. Somehow, though, I can't see Mrs. Gray hopping around in a cap and apron, and as for Mrs. Mitton, well, she's so dignified, it would be like trying to get Queen Victoria into drag. Anyway, like it or not, they will have to get used to informal American entertaining. When Alison comes, I'll give a barbecue for the whole group and see what happens. How did you enjoy the evening?"

"It was very interesting," Penny said guardedly.

"Meaning you were bored." Heather's tone of voice was cheerful. "They don't exactly sparkle at witty repartee, but they all mean well, you know. What did you think of Amy?"

"To be honest, I found her rather trying. A very limited woman."

Heather sighed. "It's funny, she seems to have that effect on most people, but she's been awfully kind to me—taken me under her wing from the start and is always popping over to see me. She's not had much of a life, you know. Her mother died when she was seventeen, and she looked after her father until he died, oh, about ten years ago. That's when she came into the castle and quite a bit of money. She was well into her thirties by then. She's hardly ever been away from it, so it's no wonder she seems limited to you. And while the marriage has been okay in some respects, I think in others it has brought problems. People around here are so narrow, and many of them won't even come to the castle or have anything to do with her. I think she's lonely."

Penny forebore to point out that Heather's life had been even more difficult but that she had risen above it, and so she fell silent as the engine spluttered to a stop and they slid alongside the Soruba jetty. Gareth seemed to have regained his good humor on the trip; he flashed another winning smile as he helped her out. She had turned back to the boat, intending to thank him again for the evening, when she witnessed an interesting tableau. Hamish Cameron was busy securing the mooring, with his back turned, and Deirdre had extended her hand to Gareth to help her out of the boat. There was an expression of such heartrending yearning on both of the young faces that Penny's heart did a flip-flop of its own as she hastily turned away. So that's the way of it, she reflected as she followed Heather up the steps and into the car.

The evening, unstimulating as it had been, seemed to have done wonders for Heather's spirits. "How about some cheese and crackers and a nightcap?" she suggested as they entered the darkened house. "We can play some records or talk. It's still quite early. I must find out if Cranston can get me some of that wine. It was very good, I thought."

Penny agreed. When they were settled cozily in the lounge, she brought up a matter that had been at the back of her mind all evening. "Heather, how many bridges have you burned behind you in the States?"

Her friend looked at her for a long moment before replying. "Most of them, but some could be rebuilt. Why? Do you think this is all a mistake?"

"No, not exactly, but I'd like to think you had an out if the going got really rough."

"The biggest bridge I burned was the apartment," Heather said with a rueful laugh. "It seemed such a good idea to sell it at the time, what with real estate prices in Manhattan going through the roof. I paid only sixty-five thousand for it, and I sold it for a hundred and fifty. I've had such good advice on investments in my various jobs that it's unnecessary for me to go on working if I don't want to."

"You've done very well, magnificently, in fact," Penny said. "It's just that when the newness of all this wears off—even supposing there's no further harassment—I can't see you being satisfied with this kind of life."

"I've always loved the country," Heather said somewhat defensively. "And there are lots of things I can do here that I could never afford in the States that will keep me busy as a bee: sailing, swimming, riding, growing things, looking after the people on the estate."

"All alone?" Penny was blunt.

"Hopefully not." Heather gave her a quick grin. "Oh, don't worry. I'm not about to up and marry a gillie, even supposing I could find one, but I do have a plan in mind. I'm hoping to entice Alison to transfer to Edinburgh University. She's always been just wild about European things, and she's a history major. She also likes all the country things I do. I'm hoping she'll so fall in love with the place that she'll agree. We've always gotten on well together.''

"Well, aren't you the crafty one," Penny murmured. "Then we'd better get cracking and lay our night wanderer low before she gets here. Let's take a gander at the talcum powder and see if we've had any visitors.''

They walked upstairs and undid the south wing doors. The talcum spread in unblemished glory in all directions.

"No takers as yet. You bunking with me tonight?'' Penny said as they closed up.

"No, I'm feeling fine," Heather insisted. "Also, I thought we might find these useful if you are right." She produced two knobbly shillelaghs and laughed. "I think if the footsteps come for us, we might use these to effect.''

"Good thinking," Penny said, and went off to her bed.

She lay awake for some time listening, but there was no sound to mar the stillness of the night, and her door remained firmly shut. She drifted gently off to sleep and did not wake until the sunshine reached the four-poster bed. The first thing she did was head for the south wing. The talcum was still traceless and unmarred.

"I already looked," her hostess said behind her. "Unless it was one of his off nights, I think we've laid our ghost to rest.''

CHAPTER 6

"It's been four days now and not a weird sound to bless ourselves with," Heather exclaimed happily. "Whatever it was, your presence here seems to have done the trick. And tonight Alison arrives, and we can really start to whoop it up."

Although Penny said nothing to diminish her friend's new-found joy, she was not convinced that the matter was closed. She had learned from Heather that the only person who had been apprised of her expected arrival had been Amy McClintock. It had occurred to her that whoever was behind the scare campaign had been unaware of her presence in the house that first night and that she had heard something she had not been meant to hear. It was also apparent that the fact that nothing else had happened, that her trap had remained unsprung, might be related to the fact that the redoubtable Mrs. Gray had been in earshot when she had first suggested the plan and could well have passed the information on. The more she saw of Mrs. Gray, the more she was convinced that underneath the very unprepossessing exterior lurked a formidable intelligence, one that intimidated even the aloof Mrs. Mitton. No one, she noticed, ever crossed the old woman, and the maid from Ardnan was frankly terrified of her. She was determined to find out more about Mrs. Gray.

"Why don't we have Mrs. Gray take us to the Wishing Well you were talking about?" she asked. "It's a nice day, and we don't have to get into Oban to meet the train until nine tonight."

"Super. We'll take the Mini and run into Kilmartin first to

pick up a packet of that tea she's so fond of. She gets offended if you offer her money for little extras like this, but she's very partial to that tea. Then we can drive up to the main gate—it's quite a stiff climb if you walk it—and maybe even take the car a little way on the track to the well. It'll save our legs if you want to see the Giant's Grave she was talking about.''

"Do you know anything of her background?" Penny asked as they drove to the nearest store in Kilmartin.

"A little. She was married to a farmer who used to have the Cameron farm. He was years older than she—twenty-five, I believe, so he's been dead a long time. They had one child, a son, fairly late in life. She must have been in her mid-thirties. She's seventy-five now, which is hard to believe, since she's so strong and agile.''

"Where's the son now?"

"I don't know. I believe for a while the old laird had him as a junior factor, but there was some sort of trouble, and he was fired. He went away, and she never talks about him. The laird let her have the wee lodge at the main gate, and with her old-age pension and the money she gets from helping in the house, she makes out all right. She's a remarkable old soul.''

"Yes, she strikes me that way, too," Penny agreed as she followed Heather into the little country store and waited while her friend purchased a pound of Indian tea.

"Mrs. Gray will have none of this tea bag nonsense.'' Heather laughed. "She gave me a long lecture one day on the virtue of tea leaves. She tells fortunes by them, among other things.''

They drove back from Kilmartin along the edge of Loch Craignish and through the hamlet of Ardnan that nestled on its edge before starting the steep climb up to the main gate of Soruba, which stood on the crest of the hills overlooking the house. While Heather knocked on the door of the tiny red-brick lodge just inside the gate, Penny looked down at the peaceful outlines of the big house and beyond it to the shimmering waters of the bay. Cranston Phillips's boat was anchored off the south end of Sheena, she noted, and there was a small sailboat approaching it from the direction of

Kilmelfort. She wished that she had her glasses to see who was in it. Another sailboat with a bright blue sail was just setting off from the Sheena jetty.

"She'll be right with us," Heather said. " 'Hae ye got your rubber boots?' " she quoted with a grin. "I assured her we had."

Penny climbed into the back seat of the Mini as Mrs. Gray, with an ancient tam-o'-shanter sitting jauntily on her gray head, got in beside Heather.

"Aye, it's guid to save your legs if ye can," she announced. "It's a guid lang piece to the Giant's Grave, and ye'll be wanting to turn on the track beyond the gate, yon that heads up Soruba." She pointed a gnarled finger, and they started to bump up a grass-grown track between the heather and gorse, until the jolting became so spine-wrenching that Mrs. Gray opined, "Ye'd do well to stop. No sense in wrecking such a sweet wee car." Climbing out, she started off up the track at a rate of speed that soon had Penny puffing.

"We're on the southern side of Soruba now," Heather said, trying to catch her breath. "If you headed right up over the crest and down the other side, you'd end up on the Laird's Walk."

Mrs. Gray had swerved off on to a smaller track to their right; about ten yards along it she came to a sudden halt and beckoned.

They caught up with her, and she gestured downward. A large granite outcrop stuck out of the hill, its base moss-covered. Below it was a small round stone basin into which water dripped through the moss with a faint tinkling sound.

"The well," Mrs. Gray announced. "It may be small, but it's powerful. A coin in there, and ye may wish your heart's desire."

Penny examined the basin with interest. It looked like a small baptismal font or even the bottom half of an ancient grinding quern. Whatever its original purpose, it was extremely old.

The old woman was looking at them with keen dark eyes. "Are ye not going to make a wish?" she challenged.

"Certainly," Heather said hastily, and dropped a coin in with a small splash, keeping her eyes tightly shut. Penny saw that there was quite a collection of coins at the bottom of the basin, some of them green with age. For such a remote spot, the well had certainly had its quota of visitors.

"Aye, there's many a person makes his way here," Mrs. Gray said, seemingly in reply to her unspoken question. "And some of them would surprise ye. But it's a wonderful power it has. I mind well the time I brought puir Amy McDougall here after her father went. 'Throw a coin,' I told her. 'And it's a fine braw man ye'll be getting.' And so she did. Though one person's heart's wish is often another's heartbreak," she added after a little pause. "Ye'll not be wishing, Dr. Spring? I see a tall man in your future."

Penny fumbled in the pocket of her windbreaker, extracted an American quarter, and tossed it in obediently. "That's an offering to the spring," she said. "I have nothing to wish for. There are enough tall men in my life already."

"Then it's a sensible soul ye are. Men! They're more trouble than they're worth," Mrs. Gray said with sudden vehemence.

"Mrs. Gray is 'fey,' " Heather said.

"Aye, that I am. Seventh child of a seventh child, so I have the second sight. It's often a sore burden." The old woman sighed and started back down the path. "We'll be off to the Giant's Grave."

"Are you a Macdonell by birth?" asked Penny.

"Losh, no. I'm a Campbell, and this is Campbell country, ye ken. One time we had it all. Clachan I'm from, though for fifty-six years I have roamed these hills." There was a bleakness in her voice as she looked over the heather-covered terrain. "Aye, fifty-six years ago I was brought here as a bride. It was a sad place then and sad times, with the great house shuttered and no living voice to cheer its walls."

"You must have seen a lot of changes in all that time," Penny said, encouraging her.

"Some things never change." Mrs. Gray looked at her with fathomless dark eyes. "But aye, changes there have been, some for the better, some for the worse. During the war, now, that was a busy, happy time." Noticing Penny's startled expression, she continued. "The house came to life then. They brought a girls' school up from Edinburgh the first year of the war, away from the bombing. Packed to the rafters for five years, and such noise and laughter!'' The wrinkled face lit up momentarily. "Young Moira McDougall joined them, and such things she learned. She's never got over it," she said with a sniff. "Airs she has put on ever since, and ideas above her station."

Penny struggled to place this new name and after a few seconds decided that it had to refer to the redoubtable Mrs. Mitton. To make sure, she asked, "Not Amy McDougall?"

Mrs. Gray shook her head vigorously. "Nae. It was a Catholic school, ye ken, and the auld laird of Sheena had very strong views against the Papists. Furious he was that they should be allowed here, and he shut himself and the family up in the island all the time they were here."

Penny began to see the wisdom of the rubber boots as the ground flattened out and they squelched through green-mossed bog and crossed little rills of brown peaty water, rushing toward the sea, which lay to the south.

"Yon's the grave." Mrs. Gray pointed a crooked finger at a long low mound showing up against the flat terrain in the middle distance. "We'd best hurry; there's a rain storm coming." She increased her pace.

Penny looked up in surprise at the cloudless sky, and Heather shrugged as they struggled to keep up with their guide. She reached the mound before they did and climbed it, looking toward the beach, which formed a silver crescent of sand several hundred yards beyond. Penny examined the large blocks of stone that ringed it.

"What's the story of the grave, Mrs. Gray?" Heather called up to the still figure above them.

Mrs. Gray started out of her reverie and climbed down toward them. "Some say that in the olden days a giant came out of the ocean and laid all the farms around here to waste, until the people banded together and crept upon him, rocks in their hands, as he slept. They battered him to pieces and then covered him with rocks where he lay. Others say that it belongs to a time when the men of the north came with a longboat, and they fought the people here in a great battle in which many were killed on both sides. Then peace was made between them, and they buried their dead together, here in this long grave, and went away again.''

"The Vikings?" Heather looked at Penny.

"Certainly sounds like it," Penny answered. "But this has the look of a long barrow to me. Toby could tell in a flash. Maybe you could lure him up here to take a look at it."

"We'd best be on our way if we dinna want a soaking," Mrs. Gray said decisively, and nodded behind them.

They looked around to see great rain clouds rolling over the high top of Jura. "Good heavens," Heather exclaimed. "That was sudden." They retraced their steps in a hurry.

"My niece will be arriving tonight, and I'd like to show her this," Heather panted at their guide. "Is there another way to it? We don't want to bother you all the time."

"It's nae bother, but see yon path?" The old woman pointed. "If ye follow the Laird's Walk and take the left branch around Soruba, it'll bring ye on to that. From there ye'll see your way. Would you like to take it now?"

"There's the car."

"Och, aye. I was forgetting that."

They walked quickly over the route they had come, but even so, the first raindrops were spitting at them before they reached the red Mini.

"You're a very valuable person to have around, Mrs. Gray," Penny said wryly. "Not only are you knowledgeable about the land, but the skies as well."

The old woman looked at her with a sly grin. "Aye, and that's not all I know, either."

As they dropped her off at her tiny lodge, she turned back to the car for a second and stuck her head in Penny's open window. "Ye're a sensible soul," she said softly. "So I tell ye now, there's trouble ahead, bad trouble. Guard the Macdonell well. She's a grand wee lass, and we have need of her."

"Our local Cassandra is certainly working hard to impress you." Heather laughed as they drove down the steep incline to the house. "And with a sop to the laird thrown in, too, I noted. Though I have never considered myself a 'grand wee lass.' She really is a bit much at times."

"I would never underestimate the interesting Mrs. Gray," Penny said noncommittally. She would do nothing to upset her friend's new-found contentment but was well aware that the old lady had been transmitting a series of veiled messages all during their excursion. If anything else happens, she thought, a long conversation with her will be my first order of business, but I hope to hell it won't be necessary. And the Giant's Grave will be a fine excuse if I have to get Toby in on this.

Mrs. Mitton was waiting for them at the door. "The McDougall was here," she announced. "She was sorry not to have found you. She could not wait, she was so upset."

Heather looked at her in surprise. "Oh, really? I had no idea she was coming. I'll give her a call."

"She is not on the island. She told me she had urgent business in Oban and would not be back before evening. I said that you would not be here this evening."

"I wonder what that was about," Heather said when they were alone again. "Amy always calls before she comes. She's very punctilious about that. Do you suppose she got the dates mixed up? I invited her over tomorrow afternoon to meet Alison and make plans for the barbecue. Well, that's too bad. Perhaps we'll run into her in Oban and see what's what."

"How does she get there?" Penny was becoming sensitive to the difficulties of escape from this isolated corner of the world.

"Oh, they have a landing over near Cranston's place, and there's a garage by it where they keep the car and Gareth's motorbike. That reminds me, I'd better call Cranston. He's asked us all for drinks tomorrow evening."

They went into Oban early in the evening for a brief sight-seeing tour of the little fishing port and dinner at a waterfront hotel. There was no sign of Amy McClintock.

On their way to the railway station, Heather said cheerfully, "It'll be so good to have Alison around. You are in for a surprise. She's not a bit like any of the rest of us. Her father is of Scandinavian extraction—he's an Ingstrom—and she takes after him, big and blond. When the family wants to tease her, they call her Brunhilde. She's great fun."

The train was an, hour late, and when Alison Ingstrom finally debarked, dusk was already falling.

"Too bad you didn't get in on time," Heather said as they

drove back over the Lochgilphead road. "You won't be able to see a thing of our lordly demesne. First thing tomorrow morning, Penny and you can come down to this gate and pick up the mail and get the first part of the guided tour. I simply must do something about organizing things for this shindig I'm planning."

"Sounds fine," Alison said amiably.

When they reached home, Penny tactfully excused herself to let aunt and niece catch up on family news. "I think I'll go for a stroll before turning in," she announced. "The rain has cleared, and it's a fine night."

"Don't get lost," Heather called gaily after her. "Better take a flashlight. There's one on the hall table. I usually go for a walk too—but not tonight."

Penny found the flashlight, crossed the gravel, and descended the steps, intending to take a few turns around the Italian garden. Deciding to venture a bit farther, she opened the gate and suddenly sensed a movement on the bridge over the stream. She advanced cautiously.

"Hallo," she called. "Is somebody there?" She trained the flashlight in that direction, but its powerful light revealed nothing. She shifted the beam slowly along the Laird's Walk and again sensed movement. Then she saw it—the flash of a red, yellow, and black kilt that quickly disappeared behind the thicket of rhododendrons. She stood transfixed for a second, her heart pounding, and then set off at a resolute trot for the bridge.

Crossing the bridge, she hurried along the walk, with the flashlight illuminating the mossy path ahead. She spied nothing else, although she kept going until she reached the Laird's Seat. Aiming the beam into the still emptiness, she noticed that lights still burned in two of the cottages below.

"Well, whoever it was had a fair turn of speed," she said aloud to herself as she made her way back, her ears still straining for any sound. She had reached the base of the steps leading up from the lawn, when from behind her, somewhere on the dark flanks of Soruba, came the faraway sound of a bagpipe. She listened, her mouth set in a grim line. It was playing a lament.

Slowly mounting the steps, she was almost at the door

when she spotted something on the ground. She shone the light downward and barely choked back a scream at the sight of a disembodied head gazing up at her with opalescent eyes. It was the severed head of a deer, dead for some time by the look of it, for there was no evidence of blood. She stared at it, her anger building. Another warning for Heather, she thought. Well, whoever you are, it just isn't going to work. She picked the head up by the ears with a grimace and deposited it behind the nearest bush.

"I'll deal with that in the morning," she announced to the night. "And after a long talk with Alison, I'm going to do something about the joker who put it there."

CHAPTER 7

The next morning, she and Alison drove to the back gate on the Lochgilphead road to pick up the mail.

"Is there somebody else besides me sleeping in the north wing?" the girl asked casually.

"Not so far as I know," Penny said guardedly. "Why?"

"Oh, it's just that I woke up some time in the night—you know how it is the first night in a strange bed—and I thought I heard footsteps—heavy ones—going down the corridor."

In the north wing? Penny thought. Well, that's new territory, anyway. She came to a prompt decision. "Alison, you strike me as a sensible girl. I don't want your aunt to know I have told you this, because she is determined that you enjoy yourself while you're here and would not want you upset. But I'll fill you in on what I think has been going on." The telling took some time. "I think the general idea is to scare her away," Penny concluded. "It is possible she may be in some sort of danger, too. I intend to get to the bottom of it. Are you with me?"

"Wow, I'll say! So Mother was right, after all. She's been worried for some time about the odd tone of Heather's letters. Certainly I'm with you. This is exciting."

"I hope it doesn't get too exciting," Penny said grimly. "You'll be meeting the most likely suspects at this artist's place tonight. I'll be interested to see what you think of them all. Now, let's get on with the sight-seeing. The memorial first."

"Well, if the going gets physical, somebody is in for a surprise." Alison grinned. "Not only is my size a factor, but

I happen to be a red belt in karate. Mighty handy that has
been at times!''

They inspected the bronze genealogy plaque on the granite
shaft. ''Violent lot, the Macdonells,'' Alison observed, peering at the details. ''Not a lot died in their beds according to
this. Makes me thankful for my peaceable Scandinavian side.''

''Which in times of yore produced the Vikings,'' Penny
pointed out with a wry grin. ''We'll have to make an early
visit to the Giant's Grave, I see, which may well be the burial
place of some of them. We'd better get on to the chapel now.
Heather was very keen for you to see it, because she's
wondering if it is worth fixing up again. I have the key.''

They drove up to the quaint wooden building, and Penny
unlocked the flimsy padlock, pushing open the Gothic-style
double door. Light filtered through a stained-glass window in
multicolored patches on to the wooden floor, disclosing a
jumble of unrelated objects. Three pews were pushed against
one wall, with a bundle of moth-eaten prayer hassocks on top
of them. There was a collection of garden tools, including a
ferocious-looking scythe, an ancient wood-burning stove, discarded bits of furniture, and a large collection of empty
bottles.

Alison explored the room; in one corner she found something that interested her, and she hunkered down with a little
exclamation. ''Ha! Come and have a look at this. It doesn't
seem to fit with the rest of the junk.''

Penny peered over her shoulder at an almost-new plaid
traveling rug tidily folded on a discarded couch. Alison plucked
something off it. It was a very long fair hair.

''Not mine,'' she announced. ''It's too light. How'm I
doing, chief? It looks as if someone has been using this
shack.''

''It does indeed,'' Penny said thoughtfully.

''Somebody else have the key?''

''I don't know, but that padlock could be opened by a
six-year-old with a hairpin. Let's get back and ask Heather.''
She carefully closed and locked the door after putting a
couple of matchsticks in the crack. ''A trick I learned from
my colleague, Toby Glendower,'' she informed the fascinated

Alison. "A good way of telling on the quiet if a door has been opened."

They started back toward the house but were surprised by a figure appearing out of the rhododendrons and holding up an imperative hand. He was a medium-sized man with very fine fair hair and a boyish-looking, unlined face. Normally one might have called him almost pretty, but there was nothing pretty about the way he glowered at them.

"This is private property," he shouted. "No tourists allowed. I hope you haven't left any gates open behind you, or you'll be liable for damages."

Penny poked her head out of the car. "We are house guests of the Macdonell," she snapped. "I'm Dr. Spring, and this is Miss Macdonell's niece. And who might you be?"

The glower disappeared in a flash and was replaced by a weak grin. "Oh, I'm so sorry. I had forgotten. One has to be so careful," he stuttered. "I'm Dennis Strachan. I farm this land."

"So I've heard. Well, if you'll get out of the way, we'll be on ours."

"I'm sorry for the mistake," he repeated. "But now that you are here, would it be too much trouble to swing down by the farmhouse and pick up some things for Miss Macdonell? I have a brace of ducks and some eggs she asked for. Besides," he added with what was intended to be a winning smile but came out as a grimace, "I'd like you to meet my wife. We were disappointed we couldn't make it to the island the other night to meet you."

"Well, all right," Penny said grudgingly. "But we'll have to meet you there. There's no room for a passenger."

"If you drive slowly, I'll hang on to the luggage rack," he said, and did just that.

At the gate of the cottage, he jumped down and led them to the rear door of the house, which stood open.

A deep voice floated out of it. "That you, Dennis? Where the hell have you been? I've been worried sick."

"Here are some visitors for you, Meg," he called, with a warning note in his voice. "They'll take the things up to the big house and save you a trip."

A big, rawboned woman appeared at the door, wiping her

hands; a startled expression was on her face. She topped her husband by two inches and had the shoulders and arms of a stevedore. She had dark hair and eyes, and the black hairs of an incipient moustache on her upper lip showed clearly against her very milky skin. Astonishment turned to suspicion as she took in Alison's blond beauty. Her husband said hastily, "This is Miss Macdonell's niece, Alison, and her guest, Dr. Spring."

"Oh, pleased to meet you," Meg Strachan said with no great enthusiasm. "Come on in. I'll have the things ready for you in a jiffy." The farm kitchen was large and very clean but singularly devoid of personality. "Wipe your boots," Meg said automatically to her husband.

"Perhaps you would care for some coffee?" he said to Penny as he obediently wiped his feet on the doormat.

"No, thank you. We ought to be getting back, but I'm sure we'll be meeting again very soon."

"We'd be honored if you came here for dinner some night, wouldn't we, Meg?" he said, persisting.

"Yes, I expect you could use a good meal if you've had to put up with Moira Mitton's cooking."

"Er, yes, some time that would be very nice." Penny was purposefully vague and escaped as soon as the ducks and eggs were produced.

They made a short detour to dispose of the deer's head, and Penny suggested to Alison that she say nothing about what had happened that morning.

"I see what you mean about Mrs. Strachan," she said to Heather at lunch. "A very unlikely couple."

"She just dotes on him, too; she's fearfully jealous. Every time I have to talk to him, she stands in the background and glares."

"You wonder how he puts up with it."

"She's a marvelous cook and manager, and I believe also had the money to get them started in farming. She may not be a pinup, but I think he knows which side his bread is buttered on."

"I gather she doesn't get on with Mrs. Mitton."

"Neither of them gets on with the Mittons. He's jealous of Jamey's hunting and piping skills, and I think she suspects

Mrs. Mitton of having designs on Dennis. All too ridiculous, really.''

"Strachan's a piper, too?'' Penny enquired, chalking up number three.

"Yes indeed, but not on a par with Jamey. No one around here is; a man of many parts. Which reminds me of the surprise I had him prepare for you.'' She smiled at Alison. "We can look at it after lunch.'

She led the way out to the drive and pointed down at the lawn, where the freshly painted lines of a tennis court had appeared. Jamey Mitton was bent over one of the net posts. He looked up as he heard them.

"It's all ready now,'' he called.

"Thank you very much, Jamey,'' Heather called back. "Alison, how about a couple of sets before Amy gets here? You don't play, do you, Penny?''

Penny shook her head firmly. "I think I'll run into Kilmelfort for a few things. Anything I can get you?''

"No, I can't make a shopping list for the barbecue until I've huddled over it with Amy,'' her friend replied.

Penny returned with several more cans of talcum powder and surreptitiously slipped into the house and up to the north wing. She spread the powder in the same fashion as she had in the south wing. Nothing seemed amiss in any of the rooms, but she discovered a back staircase that presumably ran up from the kitchens, although she could not find a key to unlock the stout door that barred its bottom end.

To cover all bases, she went into the main kitchen, where she found Mrs. Mitton gazing out the window above the large sink.

Mrs. Mitton started as Penny came in. "What can I do for you, Dr. Spring?''

"Nothing. I was just doing some more exploring. Tell me, is there a back entrance to the north wing in here? And if so, where's the key kept?''

"It goes up from the old dairy next door. And the keys are kept with the others in yon case on the wall. Would you be wanting it?''

Penny went over to the case and ascertained that the key

was on its hook. "No, I simply wanted to know. Is this case locked at night?"

"Why, no." Mrs. Mitton looked at her in blank astonishment. "Why should it be?" Unable to think of a sensible answer, Penny shrugged her shoulders and retreated hastily.

The tennis players came in, flushed from their exertions and eager for a shower.

"I can't think where Amy could have gone," Heather said, looking at her watch. "It's four already, and we're supposed to be at Cranston's by six." She came into Penny's room and peered through the glasses at the Sheena jetty. "Well, neither of the boats is there, but I don't see any sign of her on the water. Strange."

The three of them showered and changed, and there was still no sign of her. Heather telephoned their house and after a brief conversation came back more puzzled than ever.

"Neither she nor Gareth is there. I talked with the maid. She didn't know anything except that they were going to Cranston's later on. What could be up? Well, I hope she isn't mad at me for yesterday. I suppose we'll find out soon enough."

When they arrived at Cranston Phillips's small house, they found the Camerons and the Ian Macdonells already ensconced with drinks in their hands, but there was no sign of the McClintocks or, for that matter, their host. Bennett Rose was doing the honors and appeared far more energetic and affable than he had been at the island dinner party.

Their host finally arrived, somewhat windblown and breathless, bearing a bag that clinked. "We were running low on gin and vodka, and in our present company, that would never do," he said heartily. "Bennett been treating you all right? Better watch out, Miss Ingstrom, he's got quite a way with him when he wants."

The drinks flowed freely, and the noise level and general merriment increased. Penny was amused that the silent Ian Macdonell had obviously taken an instant shine to Alison, whom he positively monopolized, stroking his grizzled moustache like some old-time villain and guffawing heartily at intervals. Alison, with a twinkle in her eye, played up to him. Penny kept her ears open and managed to learn several interesting things. Bennett Rose, despite his Scottish burr, was a Canadian and made much of the fact that his father had been stationed with the RCAF in the area in World War II. And Cranston Phillips, far from being the long-entrenched resident of the area that he appeared, had been the Macdonells' neighbor for only two years. This she learned from Mrs. Macdonell, who was now bright of eye and had a pink flush on her sallow cheeks.

"It's been so different since he came," she confided tipsily. "I don't know what any of us would do without him. He's so helpful, and he really brings the place to life. We were such a quiet lot before he came, positively dull."

The only jarring note was struck by Hamish Cameron, who had been drinking heavily. He came over to Heather with an excited gleam in his dark eyes. "We're friends, aren't we?" he challenged in the harsh voice that contrasted with his handsome features.

"Why, of course." She was startled.

He leaned toward her confidingly and asked, "Then you promise you'll give me first refusal on anything?"

"Like what?"

"Anything you sell off from the house, anything at all. I'll give you a good price for it."

The awkward pause that followed was broken by Cranston, who came up, clapped the tall man on the shoulder, and said, "Now, Hamish, no business talk here. This is a party, so relax. That's an order." He gave Heather, who was looking embarrassed, a conspiratorial wink.

Bennett put a record of some Scottish dance music on the elaborate stereo system that lined one wall and, tearing Alison away from the faithful Ian Macdonell, proceeded to give her an impromptu lesson in the Highland fling. Cranston, after a glance at Hamish, who had slumped sleepily into a chair, tried to draw Deirdre into the dance, but that provoked another unexpected response.

Her beautiful violet eyes were slightly glazed from the drinks as Deirdre shook her head and looked around at the group. "No, not tonight, Cranston. But I have an announcement to make which may be of interest to you all. I'm going to have a baby."

There was a chorus of exclamations. "Why, how very exciting. Just marvelous," Mrs. Macdonell hiccuped.

"Isn't it?" said Deirdre, and burst into tears.

"I think we ought to be going home," Heather murmured to Penny. "It's after eight, and Mrs. Mitton will be furious at having to keep dinner. You'll have to drive, I'm afraid. I've had it." They disengaged themselves with some difficulty, and Heather issued general invitations for the coming barbecue.

"No sign of the McClintocks," she said morosely on the way back to Soruba. "And what's worse, no one seemed to miss them. Poor Amy."

"Cousin Ian seems a real old swinger," Alison said with a grin. "He was letting down what is left of his hair with a vengeance, telling me all about those terrible Irish Catholics who are at the bottom of the world's ills. He's an ardent Orangeman."

As they walked into the house, the phone was ringing. Heather rushed to answer it. "I hope this is Amy," she exclaimed as she lifted the receiver, but it was the broad accent of Gareth at the other end, a slightly slurred accent, as if he too had been drinking.

"Is Amy with you?" he demanded belligerently.

"Why, no, Gareth. I was expecting her, but she never showed up. Isn't she on the island?"

There was a mumbling on the other end, which gradually clarified into a final, ominous sentence: "She seems to have vanished into thin air."

CHAPTER 8

"What did he say?" Penny asked anxiously. It was after breakfast the next morning, and Heather had just been on the telephone to Sheena Castle.

"There's still no sign of her, so I told him he should call the police. He told me to mind my own business. He also sounds as if he has a horrible hangover. Not that I'm feeling any too frisky myself."

"I've just been up taking a look through the glasses. I can see the powerboat at the jetty but no sign of the sailboat. Would she have gone off in that anywhere?"

Heather shrugged. "I just don't know. It certainly sounds as if they've had some kind of fight. Maybe I should take a sail around the bay to see if I can spot it docked anywhere. I don't want to interfere, but then again, I am worried. Do you want to come for a sail, Alison?"

Her niece let out a faint groan. "The very thought of bobbing up and down out there makes me queasy all over again. I'm not used to all that strong stuff they were drinking last night. I'm usually a chablis sipper. What I'd like is a good long walk to clear my head."

"Why don't I take Alison over to the Wishing Well and the Giant's Grave?" Penny said quickly. "Then we could pop down to Ardnan and make some discreet enquiries about her there, while you are out scouring the bay. To your knowledge, has she ever done anything like this before?"

Heather shook her head. "No, never, but then, I've only been here three months. I was tempted to call Margaret Macdonell and ask her, but it would be terribly embarrassing if this was some sort of semiannual event and it got back to Amy that I'd been snooping. Still, I can't just sit around twiddling my thumbs and worrying, so if you don't mind showing Alison around, Penny, why don't we meet back here at lunchtime?''

Penny and Alison went off in search of rubber boots, Alison's camera, Penny's binoculars, and windbreakers. Although it was not actually raining, the sky was full of roiling clouds, driven swiftly before a westerly gale. After a brief consultation, they decided to try the alternative route around Soruba that Mrs. Gray had indicated. They set out at a leisurely pace along the Laird's Walk.

"Did you pick up anything interesting at the party last night?'' Alison asked as they strolled. "I was kept so busy that I forgot to observe anything or pump anyone.''

Penny gave a little annoyed cluck. "Drat! That's something I had meant to ask Heather, but this other business put it out of my mind. Yes, I had a snoop around the house while you were all Highland flinging it, and I would say that if Cranston is a professional artist, he certainly isn't a very active one. Most of his framed paintings I looked at were dated some time back, and I didn't see any sign of work in progress. He must have some other source of income, because they appear to live quite comfortably.''

"Maybe the other guy, Bennett, is rich or something. They were certainly lavish with the booze. You were the only one there who wasn't crocked. Old Ian was soaking it up like a dry sponge. He certainly had money on his mind. Complained the whole time about inflation and taxes. Blamed it all on the 'terrible Irish Catholics,' of course. He really is a nut on that subject.''

They reached the Laird's Seat and took the left fork where the path branched. It veered sharply around toward the east, and on this side the hill of Soruba was ribbed and rocky and quite unlike the smooth green face it turned toward its namesake. They had just rounded one of the rock ridges, when they almost collided with someone hurrying in the opposite direction. It was Dennis Strachan, and he looked angry and flustered.

"Oh, it's you,'' he exclaimed, coming to a abrupt halt.

"Some damn fool left a gate open and let the cows out of one of my fields last night. They make like arrows for the sea garlic near the shore, and it ruins the taste of their milk for a week. I've found all but one. If you are going for a walk, will you keep your eye out for her. And if you spot her, let me know. I'm going to beat down the other direction now. Oh, and my Highland bull is somewhere around here, too. If you see him, give him a wide berth; he's not too friendly."

When the path forked again, Penny hesitated for a moment, peering ahead. "That's the Giant's Grave in the distance, but I think if we still keep on this left fork, it will bring us pretty close to the Wishing Well, so let's go there first. For one thing, it's easier walking." After several minutes, she spotted the giant granite outcrop that sheltered the spring. "Going to throw your coin in the fountain?" she asked Alison with a grin. "If Mrs. Gray were here, she'd probably promise you a 'braw young man' for it."

"That'd be nice." Alison grinned back and searched in the pockets of her jacket. "Do you think the well would object to an American quarter? It's all I have on me."

Penny laughed and peered into the crystal depths of the basin. "Sure. It's part of the mighty American dollar, acceptable the world over. As a matter of fact, I threw one in myself. You can see it there under that other coin."

"Then here goes," Alison cried, and tossed it in. "I wish for a braw young man, whatever that is. Do you suppose it's a compendium of bare and raw?"

Chuckling, they turned back and headed toward the Giant's Gravel. A watery sun was trying to break through the flying clouds, creating a giddying effect of swiftly changing light and shadow as they plowed through the heather.

Alison let out a little whoop and plunged forward. "Oh, look. I've found a white one." She held up a sprig of heather full of white bells. "Isn't that supposed to be lucky?"

"Yes. Probably means you'll get a nice braw young man. One has to be mighty careful about wishes, you know."

They reached the mound. While Penny prowled around the base, looking at the stones, on some of which she could make out curvilinear designs, Alison climbed up on top of the mound and clicked away with her camera. Looking out toward the bay, she suddenly let out an exclamation.

"Penny, come on up here. There's something out there in the water that I can't make out."

Penny climbed to the top of the mound and gazed through her glasses. At first she thought she was watching a large fish with a long tail wallowing on top of the water, but as she adjusted the glasses, she realized with a sinking heart that there was a capsized sailboat, its bright blue sail fluttering underwater like a tail. "Oh, dear God," she exclaimed. "We'd better get down there. It looks like Amy McClintock's boat, but I can't see any sign of her."

They hurried down to the beach. On closer inspection, the partly submerged hull of the small boat showed an ugly hole in the fiberglass side. Alison quickly stripped off her sweater and jeans and, clad only in a bra and bikini panties, started to stride out into the waves.

"What are you doing?" Penny called anxiously.

"I'm going to have a look. I think I can tow it in. The tide's coming in," Alison called over her shoulder. She plunged into the waves, striking out with a powerful stroke. Penny, who wasn't a strong swimmer, watched anxiously as she reached the wreck and swam around it. She disappeared in a dive and then resurfaced, spluttering, some yards away. "No sign of anyone," she called in a puzzled voice. "And it's a bit odd. The *other* side of the hull has a hole in it, too. Only the sail is keeping it from sinking like a plummet. I'll try to push it ahead of me."

"Just be careful," Penny called back. "I'm no great hand at lifesaving. If it's too much for you, we can go for help."

Alison appeared not to hear her. She doggedly urged the boat toward the shore, with the waves bearing it forward. Penny waded a little way in, and between them they managed to heave it onto the sand, with water streaming from the large gashes in its sides.

"If we can't get it higher than this, the next tide'll take it out again," Alison said. She panted, shaking water out of her long hair like a dog.

"We can get help by then. There's plenty of time," Penny said in a grim tone. "I think what we'd better do now is look around the bay. The damn boat isn't that important; its occupant *is*. You go to the right, and I'll take the left."

They separated and made for the kelp-strewn rocks that edged the sand. Penny searched the rock pools beyond for several minutes without result and then, climbing up a slippery rock, trained her glasses on the bay. Her nerves were steeled for the sight of a bobbing object, but there was nothing.

A quavering call came from the right: "Penny, come quickly."

She scrambled down to see Alison signaling frantically. The tall girl rushed to her, her rosy cheeks pale and her eyes panic-stricken. "I've found her," she stuttered, "but I think she's dead."

They breasted a rise; below them in a tidal pool, a white-haired figure lay spread-eagled and face down. Penny felt a little rush of gall to her throat.

"All right, you wait here. I'll go and see," she muttered, and splashed down into the pool, her mind churning frantically. One touch on the icy flaccid wrist showed her that Amy McClintock was beyond mortal aid and had been so for some time. She stood staring at the body, wondering whether she should examine it, whether she should move it, where they might get help the quickest.

"She's dead, isn't she?" Alison's voice trembled from the rocks above.

"I'm afraid so." Looking up into the girl's stricken face, Penny made a quick decision. "Look, one of us has to go for help, and you're a lot fleeter of foot than I am. By my reckoning, we are much closer to Ardnan than to Soruba. I think there's a constable in the village, but if not, there's certainly a call box, and you can ring the nearest police post from it. Tell them we've found the McDougall from Sheena Castle. If you cut across that low hill over there, I think you'll be looking right down at the village. I'd better stay here to make sure nothing else happens to the body. There will have to be an inquest. Get your things on, and off you go now. Okay?"

"Okay," Alison said, her voice quavering.

Left to herself, Penny heaved a deep sigh and turned her

attention back to the body. It was clad in dark blue slacks, a navy and white windbreaker, and a pair of rope-bottomed sandals. One sandal had come off, revealing a wrinkled grayish foot. When had it happened? she wondered. Certainly she wasn't dressed for a party, and so it had to have been before Cranston's do of the previous night. On her way over to see us yesterday afternoon? But how did she end up here?

She tried to picture the coastline, wishing fervently that she had Toby's photographic memory. What she could recall made it seem very unlikely that if the boat had capsized between Sheena and Soruba, the wreck could possibly have ended up where it had.

Bracing herself, she gently eased the body onto its back, prepared for the glare of dead eyes. But Amy McClintock's eyes were mercifully closed. Her white hair was plastered sleekly around the bony face, which in death looked old. The face showed some post-mortem battering from the rocks.

Penny was no forensic expert, as Toby Glendower had become, but there were a few features about the body that struck her as odd. She had done some informed browsing in forensic annals, and now she cudgeled her brains to remember the typical symptoms of drowning. One was a condition of the skin known as "goose skin." Although she looked carefully at all the exposed parts of the body, she could see no sign of it. Another odd factor was that the face was congested and cyanotic, but this was not necessarily a symptom of drowning, either.

Amy had been wearing a turtleneck navy sweater under her jacket, and Penny gently eased it down from the neck, seeking signs of goose skin. There were none, but she found something else. There were little blue bruise marks on the side of the neck and a particularly heavy one near the Adam's apple. Penny stared at it thoughtfully and then tried fitting her own small hands around the neck, but their span was not great enough. She turned her attention to the other exposed parts of the body and found a continuous abrasion running all around one wrist, as if the wrist had been chafed by a rope. She examined the other hand. There was nothing, nor did the ankles reveal anything similar. Very perplexed, she climbed back up on the rocks and wandered over for another look at the damaged boat, trying to imagine the circumstances under which it could have been battered in on both sides of the hull. Perched on a rock and gazing seaward, she gave herself up to contemplation. *Maybe I'm being overly fanciful. If nothing else had been going on here, it probably wouldn't even have occurred to me, but, damn it, strange things have been happening, and so when Alison brings help, I'm certainly going to say something.*

Help, when it did come, was in more substantial form than she had imagined. Alison was accompanied not only by a worried-looking constable but by two brawny men with a stretcher and an elderly man carrying the little black bag of his trade.

"This is Dr. Young," Alison said, panting. "He was holding a clinic in the village. And this is Constable Menzies."

"Will you be doing the autopsy?" Penny asked Dr. Young.

The doctor looked startled. "I have no idea, but possibly so."

"In any case, before you examine the body, may I have a private word with you? There are some things I would like you to take a good look at."

The two men and the constable hauled the damaged boat safely beyond the high-water mark. The policeman looked at the holes in the hull and scratched his head in perplexity. "That's a rum go. You ever see anything like that, Tom, in all your sailing days?" Tom admitted that he never had.

The doctor went off toward the rock pool, and Penny joined the group around the boat. "Is it all right if we go back to Soruba now?" she asked the constable after a quick glance at Alison's troubled face. "We'll be available there at any time if you need our statements. This has been quite a shock for us. And Miss Macdonell will be worrying because we were supposed to be back for lunch and we're already quite late."

The constable was evidently not used to such situations and was still chewing over the problem of the boat. "No, that's all right, madam," he said absently. "We'll take care of all this. You go along now, and I'll be up later to get your stories."

They set off in silence for what seemed an interminable

walk back to the house. "Heather's going to be terribly upset," Alison said in a choked voice. "What a ghastly thing."

"Well, it's best not to dwell on it," Penny said firmly. "The first thing is to get you home and warmed up. Let me do the telling. You go change as soon as we get in, and then after a strong drink and lunch, we'll both be able to face up to it a lot better."

But when they got back to the house, there was no sign of Heather.

"The Macdonell waited lunch for you for a long time," Mrs. Mitton said with icy disapproval. "Then she went ahead and had hers and, I believe, has now gone for a walk. She was somewhat upset. Will you be ready for your lunch now?"

"There was an emergency, and we were unavoidably delayed." Penny did not explain further. "Yes, we'll have it right away."

Despite her protestations that she didn't think she could eat a thing, Alison had downed a hearty meal and was looking almost normal when they heard the front door open with a bang and hurried footsteps. Heather ran down the corridor, her stylish hair in hopeless disarray. She clutched at Penny.

"Oh, thank God you're here," she sobbed. "I've found a skeleton in the woods, and not only that, somebody just tried to shoot me."

CHAPTER 9

"Ada, is there any way I can get in touch with Sir Tobias?" Penny's voice was urgent over the phone.

Her question was answered by a little gasp at the Oxford end. "Why, he just this minute walked in as the phone rang."

"Then please put him on," Penny insisted, not caring to think what his early return from the Bordeaux vineyards meant.

"That you, Penny? How's the holiday?"

At the sound of his deep rumble, she was filled with overwhelming relief. "Yes, I'm here, and I need you as quickly as you can make it. Heather's life may be in danger, and I think there has been a murder."

"What do you mean, you think there has been a murder?" The rumble took on an exasperated edge.

"Well, there's been a drowning death—a friend of Heather's. I don't think it was a drowning, but we won't know for sure until the autopsy. It's almost beside the point. Some very odd things have been going on around here, culminating yesterday in an apparent attempt on Heather's life after she had found a skeleton in the woods. This is one hell of an isolated spot, and I'm surrounded by unknown factors. The only person whom I can trust besides Heather is her niece, and she's just a young kid. I badly need both you and your expertise; you're the bones expert, after all. Can you come? You could fly to Glasgow, get a train to Oban, and I'll meet you there in the Triumph."

An almost palpable shudder came over the wire. "Thanks,

but I think I'll drive up in the Bentley," he said. "Rattling around the Highlands in that torture chamber of yours is not my idea of bliss. Shall I fix it up to stay with old Corky, or do you want me nearer at hand?"

"Old Corky?"

"Yes. Surely I have told you about old Corky. The head of my house when I was at Winchester? Lord Corcoran? When he recently retired from government service, he bought Craignish Castle on Loch Craignish, about six or seven miles from you. Nice chap, fine taste in wines. Haven't seen him in about five years."

"No, I'd very much like you right here," Penny said firmly. "We're a household of women, and since I'm pretty sure a man is at the back of all this, I'd just as soon have a man in the house, namely, you."

"Oh." At the prospect of a household of women, Toby became instantly lugubrious. "Won't that look a bit odd, me suddenly appearing?"

"No, I have a ready-made excuse for the neighborhood. I think I've found a huge long barrow, known locally as the Giant's Grave. You may know about it already, or you can look it up and see if it is listed. That can be your reason. You've come to investigate it."

"Have I, now?" He did not sound overly enthused. "Well, all right, if you think it is necessary."

"I do. When can you start?"

"Right away, I suppose," he said with a faint sigh of resignation. "I just got in, and I haven't even unpacked the car yet. I'd stopped by the office to pick up the mail and was heading home. I can start now, but I probably will stay somewhere on the road overnight, so I'll arrive some time around noon tomorrow if you give me the directions."

"Great. By the way, what brought you back from France so early?"

There was a short pause at the other end. "I'd bought all the clarets I needed, the weather was simply frightful, and, well, I had an uneasy feeling something was wrong," he ended lamely.

Penny smiled fondly at the phone. "Bless your Celtic intuition. Your timing was just perfect. It's all settled, then?

Put Ada back on the phone, will you? There's something I have to ask her. See you tomorrow.''

Ada Phipps's voice was squeaky with curiosity. ''What's happened? Are you in trouble?''

''No, no,'' Penny said soothingly. ''I'm fine. I just wanted to ask you the name of your nephew in Oban. There's been a bit of trouble here, and I may want to contact him.''

''It's the same as mine: Jack Phipps,'' Ada said. ''He's a sergeant. I don't have his address with me, but you can contact him at the Oban police station. You're sure you are all right?''

''Quite sure,'' Penny said. ''Don't worry about me, Ada. Everything is fine now.'' She hung up, feeling a hundred percent better.

It had been twenty-four hours since the discovery of Amy McClintock's body and Heather's dramatic collapse. Penny and Alison had given her a sleeping pill and tucked her into bed, where she had rapidly sunk into a long, exhausted sleep. Since she had been quite incoherent as to the whereabouts of her grisly find and of the attack, there was no point investigating until she had calmed down. Not that they would have had the time, in any case, for Constable Menzies had arrived shortly thereafter to take their statements at laborious length. Alison had been holding up very well to that point, but as he questioned her about finding the body, she suddenly burst into tears and went rushing out of the room.

''A crying shame. A fine young lady like that having such a horrible thing happen to her,'' the constable declared, glaring at Penny as if it were her fault. ''No wonder she's upset like. I'll not bother her again today. Wait till she's herself again, I will, before I question her further. Do you have anything to add to yours?''

''Nothing really relevant,'' Penny said slowly. At this juncture she was not about to burden the constable, who was clearly a man of slow and painful thought, with the added complications of Heather's story. ''As I said, we aren't too firm on the times of all this, except within general limits. We weren't clock watching. Our single encounter was with Dennis Strachan, who was out looking for some of his cows. He may be able to give you a more exact idea.''

Constable Menzies snorted derisively. "That Lowlander. A fine farmer he is. Can't even keep track of his own cows."

"He said someone let them out," Penny said mildly, surprised by his contemptuous tone.

"More likely he was drunk and didn't remember to pen them in," the constable replied, gathering up his uniform cap and preparing to leave. "Running the home farm into the ground he is—a crying shame! Them quiet drinkers is always the worst."

Surprised into silence by this new bit of gossip, Penny accompanied him to the door. The policeman was evidently in a confiding mood, for as he stepped out on to the drive, he turned and added, "There's something very queer about that boat, very queer indeed. I don't like the looks of things, Dr. Spring, I don't. I think we've got big trouble on our hands." His gloomy prediction did much to confirm Penny's own fears.

But it was her conversation with Heather, later that evening, that persuaded her to send for Toby. "I guess you were right about the state of my nerves," her friend confessed with a sheepish grin. "I've never done anything like that before in my whole life."

"And I've never before seen so much Valium as you have in your medicine cabinet," Penny said worriedly. "You have enough in there to tranquilize the whole area. Are you hooked on that stuff?"

"No, it's not what you think. As you know, the jobs I had in the States were stressful, and we all took Valium on occasion. I had a prescription, and over here they are far more liberal about refills, so I just stocked up. I had been on them before you arrived, but I haven't touched one since then. And now I'm fine again."

"Fine enough to tell me what happened?"

"Sure. Come to think of it, it's not much. I no doubt overreacted. It's probably nothing."

"Tell me anyway."

"I was upset at not finding a trace of Amy and no sign of the boat. Then, when I came back for lunch and there was no sign of you two, either, I got all uptight and decided to go for a walk in the woods to calm myself. It was somewhere

behind Mrs. Gray's cottage, but these woods are funny. They
have boggy patches almost like sinkholes, and you have to
watch yourself. I've gotten so that I can recognize them, and
I was edging my way around the edge of one of them when I
saw something white sticking out of the pine needles. I took a
closer look, and there was this skull glaring at me. It was the
last straw. I panicked and started back toward Mrs. Gray's,
intending to get her help, when suddenly there was a high-
pitched whine past my ear. At first I thought it was a hornet,
and I'm scared of those, so I looked around. Then there was
another, closer whine and a 'splat,' and wood splinters flew
out of a pine tree just above my head; I knew it was a shot.
So then I was really terrified and took to my heels, just
running as fast as I could to get away. I came out of the
woods about halfway down the drive from the main gate. The
rest you know.''

"And you didn't see anyone?''

"Nary a soul. But the more I think of it, the more probable
that it was someone just out hunting birds or deer—maybe
even Mitton—and when they heard me crashing around—I
wasn't dressed for the woods, you see—they mistook me for
game.''

"Maybe. But with your permission, I'd like to get Toby in
on this. I'd like him around for a number of reasons, but if
you have found a skeleton, he's the one to identify what it
is.'' Penny looked at her friend. "May I invite him up?''

"Well, it's all right with me, but wouldn't that be a
frightful imposition, dragging him all the way up here? It is
not as if anything actually happened to me.''

"I wouldn't say that. How steady are you at the moment?''
Penny demanded.

"Oh, I'm fine.'' Heather looked at her, her face tighten-
ing. "There's something else, isn't there? Something about
Amy?''

Penny nodded. "I'm afraid so. Alison and I found her.
She's dead.''

Heather's hand flew to her mouth. "Oh, my God! Drowned?''

"We found her on the beach by the Giant's Grave. The
sailboat, too. It had been badly damaged. By the way she was

dressed, I'd say she was on her way to see us yesterday afternoon when it happened.''

"Oh, poor Amy. Another victim of the bay. Who will be the third, I wonder,'' Heather whispered.

"Third?''

"Another local superstition that always seems to come true. When a drowning occurs, there will be two others within two years. First the old laird, now Amy. Who next?'' Her voice rose slightly.

"That's morbid.'' Penny looked intently at her friend, trying to gauge her mood. "And in this case probably untrue. I don't think Amy was drowned at all.''

"What? What are you trying to say?''

"I think Amy McClintock was strangled, murdered.''

"You must be mad. Who would want to murder an inoffensive soul like Amy?''

"That's what I intend to find out,'' Penny assured her. "And that's why I need Toby Glendower here. Together we have yet to fail.'' This proud boast fell somewhat flat, since her friend seemed not to be listening. Her brow was furrowed, and she was gnawing at her under lip.

"On the beach by the Giant's Grave,'' Heather echoed. "How on earth did the boat end up there? If she was on her way here when something happened, there's no way the boat could have drifted in that direction. The pattern of the tidal currents is all the other way.''

"Maybe she had sailed down that way for some reason,'' Penny said. "To visit someone, perhaps?''

"No one lives down there. There's only the grave and the well, and it's a nasty place to land, with lots of rocks. It's why people always go to the well on foot.''

"The well,'' Penny began, and then let out a little exclamation. "Of course! Why didn't I think of that before? Heather, when we went to the well, you threw a coin in first, didn't you? And then I did. Mrs. Gray didn't throw any, did she?''

Heather shook her head. "No. Why?''

"Because when Alison and I went this morning, there was a coin lying on top of the silver quarter I had tossed in.''

"I don't know what you're getting at.''

"Don't you see? Somebody else had been to the well to make a wish. Perhaps it was Amy."

"But why should it be? You heard Mrs. Gray. Amy had her 'braw young man.' Why should she go to the Wishing Well?"

A series of vignettes were flickering past Penny's eyes: two young faces yearning for each other, long fair hair on a plaid traveling rug, two drunken husbands. "Maybe she was wishing to keep him," she said softly, and left it at that.

Secure in the knowledge that Toby was on his way, Penny felt the need for some action. She wrote copious notes on what had happened so far; inspected her talcum-powder traps, which were unmarred and seemed secure; and then decided that a quiet chat with Mrs. Gray might be in order. She drove to the crest of the hill and tapped at the lodge door. After a long interval, Mrs. Gray opened the door a crack and, with a very unwelcoming expression on her face, peered through it.

"What do ye want?" she demanded harshly.

"I wondered if you had heard the news and if we might have a little chat." Penny was a bit nonplussed.

"Och, aye, I saw the constable. Puir Amy McClintock, she hadna much of a life," Mrs. Gray said, but made no move to open the door wider. "I'm in no mood for chitchatting. My rheumatics is acting up, and the news was a shock, ye ken." Her eyes evaded Penny's.

"The Macdonell has also had a nasty shock," Penny said quietly. "Yesterday afternoon she was walking in the woods behind your cottage, and someone shot at her. Would you know anything about that?"

The old woman shook her gray locks vigorously, a panic-stricken look in her eyes. "Nae, I know nothing about that neither. Now leave me be!" She slammed the door, and there was nothing left but to retreat.

Lacking something better to do, Penny drove down to the disused chapel and checked on the door. The matchsticks were no longer in place. She unlocked it and went over to the discarded couch; the traveling rug was no longer there. She stood for a long time, looking thoughtfully at the array of empty bottles. She had little doubt that the long fair hair had come from the head of the beautiful Deirdre. It was only natural that a girl like that should be the focus of attention in this isolated community. But who else? Against the love-stricken looks of Gareth McClintock, another image began to form in her mind—a childless, good-looking man married to an ugly, overpossessive wife, a man failing at his work and with a drinking problem. One thing for sure, she thought as she carefully relocked the door. I certainly have a lot to tell Toby.

CHAPTER 10

Penny surmised that much of Heather's lack of enthusiasm about Toby's arrival was due to the fact that she was afraid of announcing yet another houseguest to her forbidding house-keeper, whose spirits seemed to be worsening. Penny volun-teered to break the news herself. She quickly discovered that she had underestimated the effect of Toby's title, for at the sound of it, Mrs. Mitton's faded face positively lit up, and she was assured, almost with warmth, that it would be an honor to have such a distinguished gentleman at Soruba. Should the bay room in the south wing be prepared for him? Penny agreed that that would be just fine. When Mrs. Mitton enquired about his presence for lunch, she said that she could not answer for it, since he might be dining with his friend Lord Corcoran at Craignish Castle. At this heady news, Mrs. Mitton almost floated out of the door in a euphoric cloud of snobbery to set the household to work.

This minor triumph accomplished, Penny found that she was too restless to settle down, and so she took the car and drove down to the back gate to await Toby's arrival. It was a gray day with a light rain falling and the coast road stretching empty and desolate before her, but she noted a lot of activity out on the water. Cranston's big boat was heading out to sea, apparently toward the Corrievreckan. Another sailboat was making its way toward the Sheena and was overtaken by a powerboat coming from the direction of Kilmelfort, at which juncture the sailboat bore off toward Scarba, while the pow-erboat docked at the Sheena jetty, whereupon several figures, two of them in uniform, emerged. She was so absorbed in all this that she failed to notice a car drawing up beside her, until a familiar voice boomed in her ear, causing her to jump.

"A bad business, this," Hamish Cameron observed, nodding toward the island. "That'll be the police launch. I wouldn't care to be in Gareth's shoes this morning." There was an undercurrent of satisfaction in his voice.

"Oh?" she said cautiously. "Has there been any further word on the accident?"

"Not that I've heard. I thought you might have." His dark eyes searched hers. "But no doubt they'll be asking him why he did not give the alarm sooner. A maid at the castle says that Amy went off after lunch that day we had the party at Cranston's and was never seen again, and yet he wouldn't do a thing about it. Upset they all are. Well, one thing for sure, they won't have to put up with him and his ways much longer." Now the satisfaction was evident.

"Oh? Why not?"

"Because the new laird will no doubt send him packing."

This had not occurred to her. "Who is the new laird?"

"Someone in Canada, I believe. A regular invasion from over the water we're having." He snorted. "Not that this one is likely to stay. A doctor, I am told, from Toronto."

"Surely, as her husband, Gareth will have some rights of inheritance?"

"Och, aye, he'll not be leaving empty-handed, that's for sure." This thought seemed to depress him. "Plenty of money Amy had, plenty, but he won't get the castle. Would you be waiting for someone?" The change of tone was abrupt.

"Yes, I am. An archaeologist friend of mine, Sir Tobias Glendower. He's going to look at the Giant's Grave for the Macdonell," she said glibly, but she was unprepared for his reaction.

He stared at her as if he were seeing her for the first time, his eyes widening and his hands suddenly clenching on the steering wheel of his car. "So that's who you are," he said. "I knew your name was familiar from somewhere. He's the man who found that treasure with you in Israel a couple of years ago, isn't he? Well, if it's treasure he's after around here, he'll not find any." With that, he gunned the engine and raced away, leaving Penny dazed by his vehemence.

Penny was still mulling over the meaning of this conversation, when the powerful purr of another engine brought her attention back to the present. She looked up to see the familiar black outline of Toby's Bentley bearing down on her. She hopped out with a glad cry, waved her arms at it, and opened the gate. Toby poked his knoblike head with its handsome thatch of silver hair out the driver's window.

"I told you it always rains up here," he announced dismally by way of greeting. "Why aren't you wearing a raincoat?"

"Because I came in the car, you goof," Penny said as she closed the gate behind him. "Follow me up to the old chapel. I want to have a talk with you there about what's been happening before we go on to the house and you have to be sociable."

Penny motioned Toby to one of the pews as she sat down on the dilapidated sofa. He cleared away some hassocks, settled himself in a corner, stretched out his long, spindly legs, and with a contented sigh stuffed and then lit his briar pipe.

"Now then," he said, fixing her with his stern, round blue eyes. "What is this all about?"

"So much has been happening that I scarcely know where to begin," Penny said, "but here goes." She related the odd happenings at Soruba—the footsteps, the bagpipes, and the deer's head—and interlaced the narration with side trips to the Macdonell curse and the restless spirit of Hector Macdonell. Toby's expression was stern but unimpressed.

"That's really only the beginning of it," she went on. "I'm convinced myself that Heather's announcement of her plans to stay here permanently triggered all this. She made it at a dinner party at the castle of this woman who has just been killed—murdered, I think—where the guests, almost without exception, have sides to them which warrant looking into. To start with, there is the beautiful Deirdre, daughter of Heather's factor and housekeeper, who is married to a rather unpleasant man called Hamish Cameron. She is so staggeringly lovely that she is enough to make any man's pulses pound a little harder. We found evidence in this very hut that she had been looking kindly on at least one of the locals. Now, it could be Gareth McClintock, the dead woman's husband, or it could be Dennis Strachan, who works the home farm and who has a nagging wife and a drinking problem.''

She stopped and indicated the array of empty bottles on the floor. "But that, as you can see, really does not explain all this business up at Soruba House, and so the rest of the people at that dinner have to be considered, too.

"There's Ian Macdonell, the disappointed heir, hurting for money and a fanatic Protestant Ulsterman. There's Cranston Phillips, an artist who doesn't paint and who spends a lot of time on his big powerboat with his friend, Bennett Rose, an underwater diver and photographer. The thought had crossed my mind that they may be up to smuggling of some sort. He apparently keeps the neighborhood supplied with quite excellent booze, and that may account for their comparative affluence. And then there is Hamish Cameron, a tight-fisted Scot if ever I saw one, who is in the antique business and has his eye on the very valuable antiques up at Soruba."

She paused and sighed deeply. "There are so many possibilities, but I think the crux of the matter lies in the fact that someone wants Heather off the scene, and the big question we have to answer is why. The death of Amy McClintock may be totally unrelated, but I'm beginning to wonder if someone did not want to get rid of her as well, and again, the big question is why."

Toby exhaled a cloud of fragrant blue smoke, his round blue eyes thoughtful behind his round glasses. "An onslaught on lady lairds. Interesting. Very."

"I thought you'd think so," Penny said happily. "And with both of us on the scene, I think it may discourage whoever is behind this from trying anything else."

"We can't stay here indefinitely," he pointed out. "So tell me about this shooting incident and the skeleton."

She obliged. "And there's an interesting aftermath," she added. "This old Mrs. Gray I told you about—from being quite helpful in a left-handed sort of way, she suddenly shuts up like a clam. It struck me she was frightened of something or somebody. When we return to the scene of the shooting later on, I plan to have another go at her. I have a feeling there is not much happening around here that she doesn't know.''

"Where's the evidence you found here?'' he demanded, wriggling a little on the hard pew.

"Oh, it's gone. I forgot to mention that.''

"Then someone else has a key to this place?''

"For all I know, the whole neighborhood may, but there's one thing certain. Either there is a very ready informant up at the house, or someone has been keeping very close tabs on me,'' Penny said. "The traveling rug, complete with our femme fatale Deirdre's hairs, disappeared from here like a flash.''

He uncoiled from the pew and stretched. "Well, maybe we'd better go to the house and start in. And my story is that I'm up here to look at this mound? It is not listed, by the way.''

"It actually looks as if it could be interesting. And you don't have to do anything about it if you don't want to. Maybe your first order of business is to get in with our three pipers. They are all I've found so far.''

"I'm surprised at you, falling for that,'' he said, and reached into his pocket. Suddenly the small building was full of the lilting cadences of a French folk song played by a musette. He pulled out a small object and held it up. "You remember Benedict Lefau? He sent me this. It's all the rage in the States just now, and Lefau Enterprises have gone in for it in a big way: miniaturized tape recorders. You wouldn't need a piper at all, just one of these little gadgets and a recording of bagpipe music. I went through the Bordeaux region, recording any tune that struck my fancy, and someone intent on scare tactics of this sort would only have to record a bagpipe lament on a cassette and play it on one of these.''

"How stupid of me. Why didn't I think of that? Then it could be anybody. Oh dear, back to square one. It's so good to have you here, Toby.''

"It's nice to be here. I was finding things a little dull,'' he confessed. They beamed fondly at each other.

"Be very nice to Heather,'' she instructed him. "After the hard life she has had, this was a dream come true that's turned into a nightmare. And Alison is a really nice kid, so you can forget being a misogynist for a while."

He had evidently taken her words to heart, for he was quite affable when the anxious-faced Heather greeted them at the door, and he completely won the heart of Mrs. Mitton, who hovered in the background, by greeting her in her native Gaelic, which was only one of his many languages.

At lunch he was so charming and his audience, including Mrs. Mitton, who was positively glued to his elbow, so captivated that Penny grew nervous. She knew that when he put himself out to that extent, he later usually became melancholy and morosely silent. As it turned out, she need not have worried, because events were to sweep him along at too fast a tempo.

Heather had been so restored by his appearance that she volunteered to lead them at once to her gruesome discovery in the woods. The rain had cleared, and the sun had broken through. As they walked through the rain-sweet pines, the tangy scent and the warmth lulled them into a sense of peace and well-being.

Coming into a small clearing, Heather said nervously, "This is it, over there." She gestured at something white, glimmering among the pine needles. Toby knelt briefly and then came over to where they stood in huddled apprehension. He was trying to keep his face suitably solemn, but his eyes were twinkling.

"Well, Miss Macdonell, I don't think you have to worry about that anymore. The skull is that of a long-dead sheep, some unfortunate ewe that got stuck in the sinkhole."

"Oh, really? How could I have been so silly? But it looked uncannily human to me."

"An easy mistake if you are not used to skeletons," he said smoothly. "Now, if you would show us the site of the shooting?"

But this proved not to be so easy, since Heather was uncertain in which direction she had started to run. They searched in a widening circle around the glade, but after half an hour of frustration, Heather was almost tearfully apologetic and Penny was growing increasingly hot and bored.

"I vote we give this up," she announced. "If someone

was taking unsuccessful potshots at Heather, he'd probably have picked up the spent cartridges. Our chances of finding the bullets in all this are zero, so why bother? But while we are out here, why don't we introduce Toby to the Giant's Grave and the Wishing Well?''

"We'll need boots," Heather objected.

"Then let's go back to the house and pick some up. There's plenty of time."

They hiked back to the house but were surprised to see Mrs. Mitton peering anxiously out of the front door. She hurried toward them, her usual dignity thrown to the winds.

"Oh, it's the terrible news I have. The McDougall—it was murdered the poor soul was. Strangled, they say, and dead before she ever went into the water. And that's not the worst of it! They've taken Gareth McClintock away with them. 'Official questioning' they call it, but Mair at the castle says that they'll be arresting him for the murder before the day is out!" Penny and Toby exchanged grim glances as she rattled on. "From Constable Menzies I had the news. He's now in the kitchen with Isobel giving him a cup of tea. It's the questions he'll be wanting to ask you again, Miss Alison, Dr. Spring." She broke off with an apologetic glance at Toby. "Such a terrible thing to happen, sir, on your very first day here. What will you be thinking of us."

They rushed back to the house, and Constable Menzies duly appeared, his face as long as a fiddle.

"I see Moira Mitton has babbled the news to you. Well, no matter. Forby, the doctor is most grateful to you, Dr. Spring. Had you not noticed whatever it was you did, he would not have found the method of the puir lady's death in so short a time. But there's no doubt about the strangulation. The hyoid bone cracked, and the Adam's apple collapsed. Strong big hands it took." He looked wonderingly at his own meaty hands. "And not a drop of salt water in her lungs, so she was dead before ever she hit the water."

"Did he say when it happened?" Penny asked. Although her worst fears had been realized, she was not so startled as the rest of the group.

"Only approximately. Between two and six on the day in question. But there are many, many questions yet to be answered." He nodded with gloomy satisfaction. "Aye, you mind I said there was something very peculiar about that boat, and right I was. Yon was stove in deliberate and meant to sink like a plummet, and the puir lady with it, tied on by the wrist, the doctor says." Penny gave a little exclamation as that minor mystery was clarified. "But the murdering scum that did it forgot about the sail—kept the boat afloat, it did, long enough, by the grace of God, until you and the young lady came along. So all his evil doings were for naught. No profit will he gain from it all."

"You say 'he.' Does that mean the police already have someone specific in mind?" Penny asked, anticipating his answer.

"Ah, that I am not at liberty to say," Constable Menzies said primly.

"We understand that Gareth McClintock has been taken in for questioning," she said bluntly.

"Mr. McClintock is helping the police with their official inquiries," he said, agreeing cautiously. "And more than that I canna say."

"Well, I can." A new voice broke in from the doorway to the lounge. A very tall young man in policeman's uniform stood on the threshold. "I can tell you now, all of you, that Gareth had nothing to do with his wife's murder." He glared angrily at Heather.

Alison immediately put herself protectively between him and her aunt. "Who might you be?" she demanded. "And there is absolutely no need to shout. We're not deaf."

"I'm shouting because I'm angry," he growled at her, not a whit abashed. "I'm Alastair McClintock, and I know my brother is innocent."

"Well, there's no reason to get so worked up about it," she flared back. "No one is saying he's guilty."

"That is just what they are saying," he roared. "Gareth has just been arrested for Amy's murder, and"—he turned in sudden appeal to Penny—"I need help."

CHAPTER 11

The story, as Alastair unveiled it after Constable Menzies had taken a reluctant departure, was an unpleasant insight into the petty jealousies and pent-up hostilities toward a man who had dared to "look above his station." All the servants at the castle had had long and varied tales to tell the police of how the poor mistress had suffered long and grievously from his bad moods and savage temper, of his many unexplained absences and the rows that followed his reappearance "often the worse for wear from the drink," and of his refusal to notify the authorities when she had "gone a-missing," though they had begged him.

"But this is all tittle-tattle and hearsay," Penny objected. "Where is the evidence?"

Alastair admitted that it was still all circumstantial, but the police felt that there were sufficient grounds to justify an arrest. The most damning testimony thus far had come from Amy McClintock's solicitor in Oban, who had reported that she had appeared in his office the day before the murder very upset and with instructions to draw up a new will for immediate execution, wherein her husband was to be left the minimum required by law. The will was yet unsigned; under the old will, Gareth stood to inherit all the McDougall money and possessions, except what was excluded by the entail.

"When she returned from Oban that night," he explained, "the servants say that there was a terrible row and that he stormed out, took the powerboat, and disappeared. They did not see him again until six o'clock the next evening, when he reappeared drunk. He shut himself up with another bottle and, apart from a few local phone calls, did nothing to locate Amy, despite their demands for action.''

"And what does he say to explain all this?" Penny interjected.

"That's just it; he won't say anything, not a single bloody word." Alastair looked at them grimly. "He just sits and glowers. A very stubborn man Gareth can be when he has a mind to it; not a word in his own defense, not a word of where he was or what he was doing."

"And yet you think him innocent?" Toby asked in his deep voice.

"I know he is," Alastair cried. "And if you knew Gareth as I do, you'd be sure, too. He's the gentlest soul I've ever met. Oh, he has a bad temper at times, but it's all shout and bluster, and then it's over. They are saying he killed her for the money—that in the quarrel she told him she'd changed the will, and that he killed her before she could sign it. But he'd never do that. Gareth didn't care about the money or any of the things there. He's a very simple man; all this state and fanfare that Amy kept at the castle meant absolutely nothing to him." He broke off and bit his lip, as if he had said too much.

"Then why, if he is innocent, won't he defend himself?" Penny asked briskly.

"I have no idea, no idea at all," said Alastair, his long jaw set and his fine-lipped mouth clamped in a tight line.

And that I doubt. Gareth is not the only stubborn McClintock, Penny thought, looking at the determined face. She marveled at how one family could produce such physically dissimilar offspring. Alastair was as different from Gareth as it was possible to be. He was extremely tall and thin, with sandy hair and a good-humored face set off by a twinkling pair of green eyes. Only in his great breadth of shoulder did he resemble his brother, but he had none of Gareth's intense animal magnetism or brooding charm. Of the two, she decided, Alastair was probably the smarter and had the stronger character. It would be useless to press him at this juncture as to his own theory of his brother's whereabouts. Instead, she asked, "What is the police theory about the murder?"

He stared at her a long moment before replying, and when

he did so, it was as if there were a constriction in his throat that he kept trying to clear. "He knew she was coming here to see Miss Macdonell that afternoon." He gazed briefly at Heather. "They think he waited somewhere in the powerboat and then waylaid and strangled her. They claim he tied her loosely to the sailboat and rammed holes in it so that it would sink and take her with it, making it premeditated murder."

"And how do they account for where the boat and the body were found?"

"They are still working on that." He looked faintly puzzled.

Heather gave Penny a quick glance and opened her mouth to say something but was silenced by a warning shake of the head from Penny. "When you came in, you asked us for our help. Why do you think we could afford you any?"

"Because I know your reputation in matters of murder. Amy showed Gareth an article about you, and then when I heard from Hamish Cameron that he was coming"—he nodded at Toby—"I couldn't help but feel that there was something more to your presence here than just chance."

"I am a very old friend of the Macdonell." Penny was being deliberately unhelpful. "And Sir Tobias is up here to investigate a possible archaeological discovery." His face fell. "The case against your brother is far from watertight, as you must know. Why do you think we, rather than your fellow police officers, could help you?"

"Because around here he is not likely to get a fair hearing. People's minds are already made up," Alastair cried. "You are outsiders and can look at things objectively, and you have a reputation for getting to the bottom of things. I know he's innocent, but I need help in proving it. I have to find the real murderer. Naturally, they are not letting me in on the actual investigation. In fact, in view of the extraordinary circumstances, my chief has put me on indefinite leave of absence until the case is closed. Chances are, the Oban police have already been called in, and they may even bring in Scotland Yard."

"You say you know he is innocent," she said softly. "Do you literally mean that, or do you just think that?"

"I know," he said.

"Then why don't you tell us?"

"I can't."

"Because Gareth won't let you?"

There was no response.

"Well, if you want us to help you, there are a great many questions you are going to have to answer," she said firmly. "First of all, has Gareth ever expressed any animosity toward Miss Macdonell? Did he resent either her presence here or her friendship with his wife?"

He looked at her in astonishment. "Why, no! He was thankful she was around to get Amy off his back—I mean, to have a friend in the vicinity. Amy didn't have many friends."

"So he would have no reason to want Heather out of Soruba?"

"Why, none. On the contrary, he is happy that Soruba is coming to life again, and he likes Miss Macdonell; she doesn't talk down to him like so many others around here do."

"And what of his relationships with the other people on Soruba estate?"

"Relationships?" His tone was wary.

"Yes, with the Mittons, for example." By his hesitation, she sensed that this was delicate ground.

"Jamey Mitton is his closest friend, indeed, more like a father. He taught Gareth all he knows about hunting, fishing, game keeping, even the pipes. Gareth has never liked Mrs. Mitton."

"And what about Mrs. Gray?"

"That old witch," Alastair said contemptuously. "Ever since he and Allen Gray had their fight, they've never so much as spoken."

"Mrs. Gray's son?"

"Yes, it was quite a few years back, but things like that go on a long time around here."

"And Isobel?" Penny asked, determined to cover all avenues.

"Isobel Menzies, the constable's daughter, who works here? I don't think they've exchanged half a dozen words in their lives."

Isobel's connection with the local law was news to Penny, but she didn't comment, nor did she ask about the Camerons.

If her suspicions were correct, she did not expect an honest answer. "How about the Strachans?"

Alastair shrugged. "The only time he had any contact with them was on the rare occasions when Amy invited them to the castle. He did not particularly care for either one."

"Forgive me for asking this, because it is really none of my business," Penny said softly. "But I couldn't help but notice, as we've been talking, how differently from your brother you speak. Is there a reason?"

He looked at her with a slight frown. "Yes, and I don't mind telling you, because it gives you a measure of the man, who *is* a man. Our father died when Gareth was fourteen; he's the eldest of four, and I'm the youngest. He had to leave school and go to work to keep the family together, and he wouldn't allow any of the rest of us to leave school to help out. We all went through to Scottish A levels, and my sister and I went to college. She's a teacher now. Every coin he could scrape together went to us. When I've saved enough, I'm going back to take my bar exams, and maybe then I can repay him for all he has done for us." He looked at her defiantly. "Gareth hasn't had it easy, whatever you may think."

She turned to Toby, who had been listening quietly.

"No connection has been established between one set of events and the other," he said noncommittally. "But I would say that the more informed people we have working on this, the quicker we'll get to the bottom of it."

"My feeling, too," she said with relief. "In that case, Heather, I think the floor is yours. I'd like you to tell Alastair— just as you told me—what has been going on at Soruba, and I'll take it from when I arrived."

Alastair looked mystified. "Well, I thank you for your help, but do you mean that something else has been happening?"

"Quite a lot," Penny said grimly. "Go ahead, Heather."

"That's why you asked me all those questions about the household," he said when Heather had finished. "You think someone connected with the house has been aiding and abetting whoever is responsible?"

"It's a possibility. Though informing, perhaps inadvertently, may be the better word for it. The big question is why."

"Could they be looking for something?" he ventured.

"What? They had months when the house was empty, when they could have looked to their hearts' content. No, I think the events have been triggered by Heather and her presence here."

There was a minor interruption as Mrs. Gray poked her head around the door. "Mrs. Mitton asks if ye'll be wanting your tea soon?" she enquired of Heather, and positively glowered at Alastair McClintock.

Heather looked hesitantly at her guests. "Do you still want to go to the Giant's Grave, or shall we leave it until tomorrow?"

"I think we should go today," Penny said. "There's something I want to show Alastair, and I feel we should get some shots of it in situ with your camera, Toby."

"Then, no thanks, Mrs. Gray," Heather said. "We'll skip tea for today, but we'll have an early dinner, say at six-thirty?"

"Och, aye," the old woman mumbled. As she turned, her gray hair fell away from the side of her face to reveal an ugly bruise.

Penny gazed thoughtfully after her. Either Mrs. Gray had had a bad fall, or someone had hit her hard. She wondered whether that would account for the old lady's suddenly bad disposition.

They piled into Toby's Bentley and set off along the now-familiar path to the well, but the size of the car soon proved a handicap, and they decided to go the rest of the way on foot. The young couple, their heads close together in earnest conversation, strode ahead of the others, and Heather looked at Penny with a grin.

"Looks like an immediate click to me," she said in the vernacular of their own youth.

"Well, I hope she keeps him busy," Penny said. "We have a lot to talk over that I would just as soon he didn't hear. What do you make of Gareth's silence, Toby?"

"He may be protecting someone, or he may be playing it very smart. By saying nothing, he puts the onus of proof on the police. Although the circumstantial evidence may seem damning, a good defense counsel could make mincemeat of it, unless they can come up with some solid factual evidence.

And if he is protecting someone, he may also be protecting himself, because the someone can provide an alibi. Revealing it at this point may give the police an extra handle in strengthening his motive for the murder.''

"I see we are thinking along precisely the same lines," Penny said. "But if he and Deirdre Cameron are having an affair and that child she is carrying happens to be his, that constitutes one hell of a motive for getting Amy out of the way, leaving aside all the money he stood to lose if she lived any longer. Alastair is convinced of his innocence, so I think Gareth undoubtedly has told him what his alibi is. But supposing it is just something that he and Deirdre cooked up between them if the going got rough. It isn't the first time that sort of thing has happened."'

"But that would be so cunning," Heather broke in. "Honestly, I can't see Gareth in that light at all. He has always appeared to me as a sort of innocent. Amy never let her hair down entirely about the marriage, but I did gather that it was she who did all the running and more or less proposed to him because he was so shy."

"Well, he looks like a macho type to me," Penny said. "But how about Deirdre? Innocent or macho, any man is putty in the hands of a clever woman."

"Well, you've talked to her," Heather said. "How does she strike you? I've never had the feeling she's a great brain or anything like that, just a very lovely girl who is attractive to men but isn't particularly happy. Hamish Cameron may be very handsome, but he is also bossy and a regular skinflint."

"We'll have to dig more into all of their backgrounds, that's for sure," Penny reflected. "A wild thought came to me just now about Bennett Rose. He's a Canadian, and the new heir to Sheena is from Canada. What if there is some sort of devious plot to frame Gareth and have this new man collect everything and split it with Rose?"

Toby snorted gently. "As you say, a pretty wild idea. No, if we've committed ourselves to helping this young chap—whom I must say I like—I think we'll have to proceed on the assumption of any good defense counsel that our client is innocent. As of tomorrow, we'd better split forces. I'll do some record delving in Oban and have a chat with old Corky to see if he has any ideas or information on the local scene. You take on Heather's staff. For a start, who has been beating up on Mrs. Gray?''

"Oh, so you noticed that, too," Penny exclaimed as Heather looked at them both in amazement.

"Isn't there something I could do?" Heather interjected.

"Yes, there is, if you feel up to it," Penny replied. "It would be very useful for you and Alison to pay social calls on the Camerons, the Strachans, Cranston, and the Macdonells and get them all talking about what has happened. It is something Toby and I cannot very well do ourselves as outsiders, and it may turn up a few useful tidbits."

"All right," Heather said, a shade doubtfully.

They were interrupted by a shout and looked up to see Alison summoning them from across the heather. "Hurry up," she called. "There's something here you simply have to see. It's astounding."

They hurried toward the granite outcrop a little way ahead and came puffing up to the Wishing Well. Penny gazed into its crystal-clear depths.

"Well, I'll be damned," she cried, and turned to Toby. "There's not a single coin in there. Someone has pinched the lot."

CHAPTER 12

The next day, the forces were dispersed. Toby drove off to Oban, Alison and Heather went visiting, and Penny zeroed in on the household staff. Still basking in Toby's reflected glory, she had remarked to Mrs. Mitton that Sir Tobias had so much enjoyed her homemade Scotch broth of the night before.

"Such a gentleman," Miss Mitton said with a sigh. "And such a saintly character. He reminds me of dear Father Crinnan."

"Saintly" was not a word that would have occurred to Penny to apply to Toby, but in the interests of investigation, she let it go. Instead she prompted the woman. "Father Crinnan?"

"Yes, he was one of the Redemptorist fathers who used to come here for three months at a time to say Mass for the nuns at the school. They were all nice, but he was far and away my favorite—so kind, so gentle, so trusting." A slight cloud passed over the once-beautiful face. "It's important when one is in one's teens to be believed. It's such a difficult time, particularly if one's parents don't understand one."

"It certainly is," Penny agreed heartily, having been momentarily bogged down among all the "ones." "I take it he helped you?"

"Always. Even when one doubted oneself."

"For instance?" Penny said, hoping to steer the conversation to a more personal level.

"Well, like the time I saw the plane and no one else did."

"Plane?" echoed Penny, beginning to feel like the village idiot.

"Yes, it was the strangest thing that ever happened to me,"

109

Mrs. Mitton said, gazing dreamily out at the bay. "And yet it is as clear in my mind as the day it happened. He—Father Crinnan, that is—had taken another girl and me on a walk up Soruba. It was a mild, misty day in October, so it was like walking in a cloud. I had kicked aside a piece of pine bark, and there, underneath it, was a primrose in bloom. Imagine that, a primrose in October. The two of them were a little way ahead of me, and I was just about to call out to come and look, when I saw the plane. A great big plane it was, come swooping out of the mist over Sheena. I was startled, because we were still thinking in terms of Germans and invasion back then, but then I saw the circles on the wings and knew it was one of ours. And as I looked, I realized it was making no noise. I called out, 'Look at that plane. I think it's crashing.' But by the time they had heard me and turned around, it was gone. It just disappeared into the mist, and then there was a kind of hissing sound, and that was all. When I told Father Crinnan, he got all excited and said I should run and tell my father, who was head of the local Home Guard here. So I ran all the way home." She stopped abruptly.

"And?" Penny prompted.

"My father didn't believe me. He had been outside but had seen nothing. He said I was making it up just to impress Father Crinnan."

"Oh, too bad." Penny feigned sympathy, impatient to get to the question she really wanted to ask.

"But Father Crinnan wouldn't let it rest there." Mrs. Mitton's face brightened. "He insisted that my father make inquiries, because he said I was a bright girl and that if I had said I'd seen it, then I had." She paused. "The authorities would not say anything, but there is one thing that has always made me wonder."

"What was that?"

"Well, my mother and I were walking along the beach by the jetty about a week later, and there was this lifejacket washed up. It wasn't like the ones the seamen wore. It was bright yellow, what they called a Mae West, and airmen used to wear them. So I've often wondered about that."

"Did you enjoy your school days at the convent?" Penny was determined to get down to cases.

"Oh, yes, very much. It's why I insisted on Deirdre going there. Not that Mitton was for it." It was somehow in keeping that she referred to her husband this way. "But I said to him, I said, 'We've just the one chick, and we've got to do right by her.' Even if it wasn't easy to manage and it meant her going away to Edinburgh."

"And did Deirdre enjoy it also?"

Mrs. Mitton's face clouded. "Not as much as I did, but she did very well there for all that. Got her Scottish A levels and could have gone on to college had she the mind to. And Mitton came to see the wisdom of it, too, once she got older. If she had stayed around, there'd have been no end of trouble with the riffraff, and most likely she'd have ended up marrying one of them. As it was, from ten to eighteen she was out of it and safe—at least while she was there—and then Hamish came along like a gift from God." Her face softened. "She got married, so all was well."

"At eighteen?" Penny could not hide the sharp edge in her voice.

"Yes." Mrs. Mitton looked a little disconcerted. "Mitton wanted her to go to college, but she was set on marrying, and I didn't see why not. Hamish is a good provider and a steady man."

"How old is Deirdre now? She looks so young still."

"She's twenty-six. They've been married eight years."

Just about the time Gareth McClintock took the plunge, Penny thought. "That must have been a year for weddings. Wasn't that when the McDougall married?"

Mrs. Mitton's face tightened. "Och, aye, but that was something else altogether. Not before time they wed. A fair scandal in the district it had become, and see where it has ended. And no proper marriage either, sneaking off to a registry office like they did. My Deirdre had a good kirk wedding, with the pipes and everything."

"Was Gareth the riffraff to whom you were referring?" Penny asked bluntly.

The housekeeper seemed flustered. "Och, there were worse than him around. Allen Gray for one." She almost spat the name. "Aye, it was a guid day for everyone when he cleared out. No, Gareth was more like a big brother to her. I mind when Mitton was teaching him his trade, Deirdre as a wee bairn used to tag around after him like a dog. A real pest to him she was, but to be fair, he was aye guid with her. Then, when she went away and he went off to the island, they didna see much of each other. But protective he has always been. After all, look what he did to Allen Gray because of her. No doubt you've heard Mrs. Gray's tale, but it's nae the truth.''

"Not the details, no,'' Penny said cautiously. "But I've gathered that she doesn't much care for the McClintocks.''

"Aye, you may say that, but Allen deserved everything that came to him. If Gareth hadn't done it, my man would have.''

"What did he do?''

"Made improper advances to Deirdre,'' the housekeeper said primly. "On a walk to the well she was, and up comes he all mean and heated after her. She's fleet of foot is Deirdre, so nothing happened, ye ken, but it gave her a nasty scare. Gareth put him in hospital, though.'' This was said with lively satisfaction.

"And after that Allen Gray went away?''

"Och, aye. The auld laird would have none of that, so he gave him his notice, and high time, too. He was nothing but a lazy layabout and no good to his mother at all.''

There was the sound of a car in the driveway, and Mrs. Mitton from her vantage point at the window exclaimed, "Losh, there's the Macdonell, and I haven't got lunch under way yet! You'll have to excuse me, Dr. Spring.''

There was more that Penny would have liked to ask, but she felt that she had made a good beginning and did not want to alienate the suddenly amiable Mrs. Mitton. "Of course. I'm sorry for having held you up.''

"Och, it's been nice talking with you,'' Mrs. Mitton said graciously, and turned to her work.

Heather and Alison came in giggling. "That woman,'' Heather exclaimed as she saw Penny. "She really is too much. She did everything but blindfold Dennis to keep him from looking at Alison.''

Alison, who was in very short shorts and a halter top, displaying glorious golden-brown legs and shoulders, grinned. "Well, there was quite a lot of me to see.''

"I'm afraid I've let us in for it," Heather said with a grimace. "They're dying to have us all for dinner tonight, and I couldn't think of a graceful way to say no. I hope you and Toby won't mind."

"I don't, and I don't think Toby is even going to be here. He said something about having dinner tonight at Craignish Castle."

"Oh, thank heaven. I was feeling so guilty about it. It's likely to be pretty painful, but at least the food will be enjoyable."

"Suits me," said Penny, always ready for a good meal. "Did you find out anything?"

"I don't know. I don't think I'm very good at this sort of thing," Heather confessed. "I couldn't think of what to ask."

"I got something that didn't quite jibe," Alison put in. "I asked him if he'd found the missing cow. He looked positively scared, and you should have seen the look she gave him. I don't think he had told her about it."

"Either that or it never happened and it was something he made up for our benefit on the spur of the moment," Penny said thoughtfully.

"But why?"

"To account for his presence in a hot and bothered condition in an unlikely spot. We may be on to something."

"But what on earth could Dennis Strachan have against Amy?" Heather cried.

"That's it again, the eternal why. Still, early days yet. We may come up with something. Anything else?"

"Just a little thing," Heather said. "Meg had a very nice sapphire ring. She told me that at one time it was her mother's, and she never takes it off. I've never seen her without it, but she wasn't wearing it today."

"How did they react to the murder?"

"Shocked, of course. Said all the right things, and she at any rate is prepared to believe Gareth did it. Called him a 'violent young man.' "

"Did you manage to work in anything about Deirdre?"

"The very name of a Mitton is like waving a red flag in front of Meg. She launched into her many complaints, most of them imaginary, I'm sure. He just sat there looking resigned.''

"Anything specific?"

"There was something about a couple of sheep having had their legs broken, as if they'd been hit by a car. She blamed that on Deirdre, who, according to her, drives like a madwoman over the estate roads.''

"Did she say when this happened?''

Heather looked at Alison, who shook her head.

"Well, at least it's a start. Maybe we'll find out something more tonight. Where are you two off to next?''

"The Macdonells' this afternoon for tea,'' Heather replied with a sly grin at Alison. "Ian is dying to see her again. No luck on Cranston. The boat is still out, so they must be on a long trip somewhere. What's on your agenda?''

"Mrs. Gray, if I can find her. I want to hear her version of the Gareth-Allen Gray fight.'' Penny then related what she had been told that morning.

An after-lunch check with Mrs. Mitton revealed that this was one of Mrs. Gray's nonworking days. Penny's visit to the lodge was forestalled, however, by the arrival of Toby.

He loped in, looked relieved at the sight of her, and said, "Ah, good. I have to get over to Corky's by five, so I came back a bit early, hoping to have a bit of a confab before I go.''

"Did you find anything?'' she asked eagerly.

"Not what you had hoped for, but a lot of ground clearing.'' He searched his pockets, coming up with several slips of paper. "In the first place, no dice on your Spanish galleon theory. My memory turned out to be correct. All elements of the Spanish fleet that were blown around to the west coast have either been accounted for elsewhere or are known to have fetched up off Ireland. There's no possibility a stray could have ended up here, so that's out. Also, no luck on the connection between the McDougalls and the Macdonells. Amy McDougall's great-grandfather made a bundle while a colonial official in west Africa, in the cocoa trade, I believe. No connection with the shipping Macdonell and no connection with the McDougall who drowned in the Corrievreckan. It's a completely different branch of the clan.''

"How about with Mrs. Mitton's parents?" she asked.

He looked a little pained. "Genealogy is very time-consuming, and I only had a few hours. I was trying to work on main themes, not remote possibilities."

"Oh, all right," she said hastily. "Go on."

"I had a quiet word with Jack Phipps, who, I must say, seems a lot more sensible than his aunt," Toby commented. "He'll make some discreet inquiries about Phillips and Rose, but if they have been smuggling or anything of that sort, it must be on a very small scale, because there have been no rumors of anything like that in Oban. However, he gave me two bits of information that were very interesting. Apparently, about three months ago there was an Irishman who wanted to hire a local boat to take a shipment over to Ireland. He was accompanied by a Scottish Presbyterian minister who is known to be a fanatic Orangeman. When the skipper of the boat asked what the shipment was, the Irishman blustered and said it was none of his business. When the skipper insisted, he said he was in the car business in Belfast, and it was a shipment of automotive parts. It sounded a bit fishy to the skipper—who is the brother of one of the Oban constables, by the way—because anything like that goes cheaper and faster out of Glasgow or Liverpool. When he said he wanted to inspect the shipment before loading, they thanked him and took off, and he never saw them again."

"Have they had anything of this sort before?"

"Not that the authorities know about, but the sentiments of this area on the whole are very pro-Orangemen and anti-Catholic, and it's pretty well known that both extremist wings in Northern Ireland are arming themselves, so gunrunning would not be too unlikely. I'll have a word with Corky and see if he has heard anything."

"What else did you find out?"

Sir Tobias looked positively smug. "I asked about Allen Gray. It seems that just a week ago, they had a routine enquiry from the Glasgow police about him. He was out on parole and had failed to report to his parole officer, so they wondered if he had turned up in his home district. Perhaps the prodigal son has put in an appearence, and this accounts for his mother's sudden turning off."

Penny frowned. "Did they say how long he'd been out of prison or what he'd been in for?"

"No, but Phipps is checking on that. He said that usually they don't go after a parolee quite as quickly as this unless his original crime was a violent one."

"Well, you have had a fruitful trip," Penny said. "I'm the only one who seems to have drawn a complete blank. Even Heather and Alison came up with a couple of interesting things." She then related the events of the day.

"Odd about that plane." Toby puffed on his pipe. "Can't see it's of any importance to the present situation, but it's odd all the same." He made a note in his little black notebook. "Probably not important, but I may as well mention it to Corky. He went straight from Winchester into the air ministry during the war—didn't finish up at Oxford until afterward, as I recall. He may be able to throw some light on it and get us further into Mrs. Mitton's good books. Oh, and why don't you postpone seeing Mrs. Gray until I can come with you? If her son, the ex-convict, is lurking around somewhere, it might not be too healthy to go alone. Any word from Alastair on Gareth the Silent?"

"Not a thing. Yes, I think I will leave Mrs. Gray until tomorrow. She's due here then, and maybe she'll be easier to tackle on home ground. Anyway, I have to get ready to go to dinner at the Strachans'. Heather and Alison should be back soon from their afternoon snoop at the Macdonnells'."

After Toby took his leave she went for a melancholy wander through the empty house. She studied the portraits in the dining room, peered into cupboards full of crystal and china, and finally ended up in the tower room of the south wing, gazing out over the empty bay. As she turned to descend, she noticed for the first time a framed map on the wall behind the door. It was of the Soruba estate and was dated 1865. She studied it with interest, noting the location of the Cameron farm and various other buildings. I wonder if any of those still exist, she asked herself. For if Allen Gray is around and is on the lam, chances are, he wouldn't stay at his mother's cottage. He may be holed up in one of those. I must ask Heather about them. With fresh purpose, she bustled downstairs as she heard the sound of the Mini turning into the drive. The query died on her lips as she saw their white, sick faces.

"What is it? What's happened?"

"Oh, Penny, it was just horrible," Alison managed to get out. "We were passing the chapel on our way back, and we saw the padlock was off, so I went to investigate." She gulped. "The inside was like a charnel house—blood all over. And then laid out on the couch—you know the one— there was a dead sheep. Its throat had been cut, and there was this wooden stake. Somebody had driven it right through its heart."

CHAPTER 13

As the long shadows of twilight gathered over the Craignish peninsula, two very disparate dinner parties were under way. In the gun room of Craignish Castle, a small and heavily laden gate-leg table was drawn up before a merry, crackling fire; a thick sea mist had turned the evening damp and chill. Here the two ennobled bachelors were browsing through an epicurean dinner, their contentment deepening as the choice bottles of wine Lord Corcoran had produced for each course were successively emptied. With the turtle soup came a choice Madiera; with the loch trout, a Yugoslav white; with the pheasant, a Mouton-Rothschild claret; with the raspberries and cream, a vintage sauterne; and with the savory, a Portuguese wine from an obscure vineyard that Lord Corcoran urged on his guest as his own discovery.

"What do you say to staying right here for our cognac and cigars?" he suggested. "Such a bother to move into the study, eh?"

"Excellent idea. I don't think I could move, anyway." His guest beamed back. "Lots to discuss, old chap, and we can do it just as well here. Now, if only I can remember what I'm supposed to talk about."

In the formal and evidently seldom used small dining room at the Strachan farmhouse, things were not progressing quite as smoothly. The hostess was overanxious, the host morose, and the guests more than a little distraught. It had been decided, after Penny had phoned the Lochgilphead police about the macabre discovery in the chapel, to say nothing to the Strachans about the incident until the police had had time to investigate. Alison and Heather were still very much shaken and squeamish. As they had piled into the Mini to drive the short distance to the farmhouse, Penny prayed silently that the main course would not be the inevitable mutton of the Western Highlands. She had a vision of her green-faced companions rushing from the dinner table in hopeless disarray.

Her prayer was answered, but as it turned out, the choice of the main course was almost as bad, for after an excellent cock-a-leekie soup, Meg Strachan had appeared with an entire beef tongue steaming gently in ungarnished glory on a large platter. Penny had become inured after her many years in England to English delicacies such as kidneys, tripe, and tongue but was well aware that her American compatriots regarded such things as unfit for human consumption. She watched in quiet agony as Alison and Heather pushed the tongue furtively around their plates and avoided their hostess's anxious eye, all the while keeping up a stream of desperately bright chatter. Things improved a little with the appearance of a black-currant summer pudding with thick fresh cream, but nothing appeared to cheer their silent host, whose main diet throughout the dinner had been increasingly strong whiskies and water.

Penny had abandoned all thoughts of judicious pumping and now was concerned only with keeping the conversation flowing until they could gracefully take their leave. "I was so impressed by your sheep dog," she said to Meg Strachan. "How clever they are, aren't they? They must take a tremendous amount of training."

"Aye, he's a good dog," Meg agreed. "My father raises them."

"Your father is a farmer, too?" Penny asked, hoping that this would be a fruitful topic.

"Aye, and a good one, too," Meg said, glaring at her unheeding husband. "Has a fine farm outside of Dumfries. Good land there, not like these Highland bogs." Her tone was bitter. "There's little profit to be made out of sour land."

"Do you lose many sheep in the bogs?" Heather asked

tentatively. "I found a dead one in the woods the other day, and I wondered if there was anything I could do to help, perhaps put up some fences."

"Och, there's nothing so daft as sheep. You could put up fences from here to Glasgow, and they'd find some way of doing themselves in, silly brutes! But it's a kind thought, for which I thank you." To their embarrassment, her large dark eyes suddenly filled with tears.

"I've noticed the sheep have red patches on their fleece," Heather said in haste. "Is that your mark?"

Meg cleared her throat. "Aye. With only the two farms active around here, we don't bother with earmarks any more. We daub ours with red, and Hamish does his with green, so there's nae mix-up between the flocks." Alison drew in her breath and gave Penny a wide-eyed stare as Meg went on. "Aye, Hamish has the right idea. Runs the farm as a sideline and does his main business elsewhere. And a mighty profitable business it is, too, so I've heard. Has he been after you yet for the things up at the house?" The question was abrupt. "He was aye pestering the auld laird about them."

"He has mentioned them," Heather said uncomfortably.

A grim smile was on Meg's pale face. "Then you'd best watch what you're about. Hamish is a very smart business-man and knows how to get what he wants." Her eyes slid to her husband, who suddenly snorted with laughter.

"Meg, you're havering," he said, reaching for another whiskey. "Hamish is not all that bright. He can't even see what's going on under his very own nose."

"Haven't you had enough of that?" she snapped.

"I'll have had enough when I say so," he said. They stared fiercely at each other, but her eyes dropped away first.

"You're neglecting your guests," she said feebly. "They may fancy another wee dram themselves."

The three women denied any such fancy, but their host seemed to have revived, and he continued, gazing with con-centration at Heather. "Meg's right about one thing, though. You'd best watch out. I like you, Miss Macdonell, I think you're a fine woman, but I must warn you that there are those here who do not feel the same way. Not at all.''

"Oh?'' Penny put in cautiously. "Do you have anyone specific in mind, Mr. Strachan?''

"Dennis to you, dear lady.'' He gave a little belch. "Och, it's not just one, ye ken. It's noses that are out of joint around here. I'll name no names, but there's a verra, verra disappointed man who lives nearby and who may speak you fair but has no guid thoughts for you. And there was one you thought of as a friend but was no friend. A schemer born she was. And there's them in your very house that'd be glad to see the back of you.''

"Dennis,'' Meg said on a rising note. "You've no call to say things like that, scaring poor Miss Macdonell here.''

"Och, the Macdonell knows I mean her well,'' he muttered, and lapsed back into dreamy contemplation of his glass.

After ten more minutes of stilted conversation, they took their leave, with their anxious hostess accompanying them to the gate.

"You'll have to excuse Dennis,'' she said defensively. "He has a lot on his mind now, and it takes him like that.''

They made their thanks and watched in silence as her ungainly figure loped back into the house. Alison let out an explosive sigh. "Phew. Thank God that's over. What a ghastly evening.''

"It got interesting toward the end, I thought,'' Penny murmured, peering into the mist. "Isn't that Hamish's car down by the jetty?''

"Yes.'' Heather was scrambling into the Mini as the gentle chugging of a powerful engine sounded from the bay. "And that sounds like Cranston's boat heading in. He must be a confident seaman. I surely wouldn't want to be out in this fog. He certainly must be in a hurry to get home.''

As they let themselves into the dark house, the phone was ringing. "It's for you,'' Heather called to Penny. "Sir Tobias.''

"Well, let's hope he got more out of his evening than we did from ours,'' Penny grumbled as she took the phone.

Toby spoke slowly and with great precision, as if speaking

to a very deaf idiot. "When did you say that plane went down in the bay?"

Penny's eyebrows lifted. "You're drunk!"

"I have drunk adequately, but I am not drunk," he informed her. "However, Corky and I are having such an interesting time, I have decided to accept his invitation to spend the night. I will rejoin you late tomorrow morning."

"After you have slept it off." She sniffed. "And to answer your question, I don't know other than that it was in October and that it was some time when the Germans were still threatening invasion. Why? Do you have something?"

"I will not know until I have a firm date," Toby said with ponderous patience. "Can you get it?"

"Yes, I suppose so. I can ask Mrs. Mitton tomorrow morning. Will that do?"

"It looks as if it will have to," he grunted. "Good night."

"Drunk as a lord. How appropriate," Penny said, grinning suddenly at Heather, who was hovering anxiously just out of earshot. "Oh, well, at least he's having a good time."

"I could use a drink myself," Heather said, heading for the lounge. "Honestly, it seems the ongoing problem around here. I hope I don't end up as a client for Alcoholics Anonymous. What was that ghastly thing we ate at dinner? Would anyone like a sandwich? I'm starved."

"Beef tongue is regarded as a great delicacy," Penny observed mildly, at which both Alison and Heather shuddered and headed for the kitchen. Penny trailed after them and supervised the making of three thick ham sandwiches.

"With all the brouhaha about the sheep," she said as they headed back with full plates to the lounge, "I never did hear if you got anything out of the Ian Macdonells."

Heather shook her head in discouragement, but Alison, her mouth full of sandwich, nodded and made incoherent noises. When she had swallowed and taken a swig of wine, she said, "I think I'm turning into a real snoop. I found two things. I went through the old boy's desk when they were showing Heather the garden."

"Alison, you *didn't*," her aunt exclaimed in horror.

"You have to do things like that if you're going to find out anything," Alison said in outraged innocence. "Anyway, besides a whole pile of unpaid bills, I found a very interesting letter from Amy McClintock; it was something about the repayment of the mortgage loan on the house. She was afraid she had to insist on him coughing up for it. It was a very mild 'or else,' but it definitely was an 'or else.' If he is strapped and can't pay, that could be a motive, couldn't it?" She looked at Penny as Heather continued to stare at her in shocked silence.

"Yes, very interesting. It could indeed. What else?"

"Well, it might not be anything, but Mrs. Macdonell kept talking about Ian's lodge nights. It's some association called the Sons of Orange. It might be worth looking into if they are all as nutty on the subject as he is."

"Yes, certainly," Penny said. "You've been doing fine."

"Oh, and there's another thing," Alison went on. "That sheep in the chapel—it was one of Hamish Cameron's. I remember the green patch on its fleece. Do you think it could be some kind of kooky warning for Deirdre?"

There came a sudden thumping on the front door, and they sat frozen for a second. "Who can that be at this time of night? It's ten-thirty," Heather declared.

"We'll all go," Penny said, and led the way. "Who is it?" she called through the locked and bolted door.

"Alastair McClintock," came the muffled reply.

"Oh, goodness. Hold it a moment." She wrestled back the bolts and peered anxiously out into the thick mist. "Has something happened?"

"Not that I know of," he said in some surprise as he angled his tall figure through the half-open door.

"Then why are you here?" she demanded.

He looked past her to where Alison leaned against the lounge door, still munching on her sandwich. "Er, I wondered if Alison would like to come for a ride on my motorbike. The moon is rising now," he said weakly.

"In this mist? You must be crazy." Heather then took in the situation and temporized. "Why don't you come in and keep Alison company in the lounge, play the stereo or something. Dr. Spring and I have some business to talk over in the study."

A look of relief came over his long, bony face. "That would be fine with me."

"Want a sandwich?" Alison said, waving the remains of hers at him.

"That would be very nice, too," he said, and followed Alison like a faithful shadow back into the kitchen.

"I guess we're stuck with the study," Heather said wryly. "As if we didn't have enough on our hands, we now have an amorous young man as well. I hope it doesn't get too serious. I can't see my sister being overjoyed by her daughter being courted by the brother of a suspected murderer."

"Well, look at it this way," said Penny, "if we do our thing right, he won't be a suspected murderer anymore." They settled themselves in the dimly lit, white-paneled room into which the mist seemed to have seeped.

Heather looked nervously at the light bulbs. "The lights seem awfully dim tonight, don't they? I hope the generator is not going on the blink again."

"Do you know how to fix it if it does?"

"Haven't a clue. I usually scream for Mitton, who knows its little ways." Heather sighed deeply. "I've said it before, and I'll say it again. You don't know how much it means to me having you, and now Sir Tobias as well, with me. When I came, I thought I soon had the measure of the people around here, but now with every day that passes, I see new angles, new depths, and I'm just not certain about anyone or anything anymore. Take Meg Strachan. I put her down as a horrible woman, and she *is* in a way, but tonight I found myself feeling positively sorry for her. It must be pure hell to be in love with a man who is such a loser as Dennis appears to be. Honestly, Penny, the more I see of marriage, the more thankful I am that I never took the plunge. Look at this lot around here. Besides Meg, there's Margaret Macdonell, who is such a blob. If she ever had a personality of her own—which I am beginning to doubt—it has long since vanished, and she is simply Mrs. Ian Macdonell. If anything happened to him, I have the feeling she'd disappear like a wisp of smoke. And then there's Deirdre—beautiful as all get out, married to a good provider, but obviously as miserable as sin."

"Frustrated women can be a lively source of trouble. Did Dennis upset you with what he said tonight? It struck me that he might be trying to make you panic for his own reasons."

"Not really. After all, I'm not exactly stupid. Though I talk a good fight and put up a front, it didn't take me long to realize it would take a while to be accepted here. But I did not understand his dig about Amy. Why would she scheme against me, and what about?"

"A good question, but one that may never be answered," Penny observed. "I think we're losing sight of the main issue. Amy certainly couldn't have taken a potshot at you in the woods; she was already dead."

"Oh, well, the hell with it, anyway," Heather said abruptly. "Let's talk about old times."

They chatted for a while, until Penny yawned and said, "I think we should fold our tents. I have to tackle Mrs. Gray tomorrow, and you're planning a descent on Cranston, so we both better be fresh for the fray."

Faint strains of music and gurgles of laughter came from the lounge as they made their way upstairs. "That's a good sound at any rate," Heather observed as she bade Penny good night.

Penny flopped into bed and was drifting off to sleep. She vaguely heard the grandfather clock strike the midnight hour, but shortly after that she was jerked into wakefulness by the sound of her door swinging open. She sat up, her heart thumping.

"Heather? Alison? Is that you?" she called.

There was no answer, and her ears strained for footsteps in the south wing, whose double doors she had carefully bolted in Toby's absence. She seized her flashlight from the nightstand and slipped out of bed. There was no light under Heather's door, no sound from the south wing as she pressed an ear to the double doors.

"Couldn't have latched it properly," she muttered crossly, returning to her room and shutting the door with a firm click.

She was just drifting off again, when it opened with a soft swish. This time she not only repeated the process but checked Alison's room. The bed was empty, with the party downstairs evidently still in progress. She shut the door again in exasperation, propped a straight chair under the knob, and retired to bed.

"To hell with it anyway," she said aloud. "And if the colonel is on the prowl, to hell with him, too. He's a bit late with his ghostly warnings. We've had our murder."

CHAPTER 14

"Alastair says that they've moved Gareth to Oban and that his lawyer is trying to get him out on bail, but he doesn't hold out too much hope," Alison reported over breakfast. "Alastair's afraid that the lawyer will get so pissed off at Gareth's silence that he'll quit on them."

"Alison! Do you have to use language like that?" Heather protested mechanically. "And what time did your little tête-à-tête break up last night, anyway?"

"Don't play mother hen, it doesn't suit you," Alison said with a grin. "There's no one here but us. Where's Penny?"

"She had to ask Mrs. Mitton something. And then I think she was going to phone Sir Tobias."

". . . It was some time early in October of 1941," Penny was saying. "And the airman's life jacket was spotted about a week later. Does that help?"

"It might. Last night it evidently rang a faint bell in Corky's head, but he didn't volunteer anything to me. Oh, and on no account go in search of Mrs. Gray if she doesn't show up at the house. I've had another chat with Jack Phipps, and his information was that Allen Gray had just done a seven-year stretch for manslaughter, so he's no one to mess with." Considering the amount he had drunk the night before, Toby was being remarkably brisk.

"Okay. Did you discover when he got out of prison?"

"About three weeks ago, so he could conceivably have been behind all the things that have happened at the house since you have been there."

"But not the things that happened before I arrived," she

pointed out. "Those have been going on for approximately two months now, which seems to rule him out, at least as the instigator." A dubious sound floated over the wire. "What is that supposed to mean?" she demanded.

"Just that you only have Heather's word for it that all those things did happen," he observed. "Including, for that matter, the supposed shooting. We never did find any trace of it, remember?"

"Well, her word is good enough for me," Penny said, bristling. "I'm surprised at you. Heather's not an imaginative sort; why should she make it up?"

"There you have me," he confessed. "But I still would like to see some sort of relationship between the murder and what has purportedly been going on at Soruba House. We have no linkage as yet."

But Penny was off on her own line of reasoning. "If we can prove Allen Gray is around," she muttered, "it might get the police to look in a new direction. Maybe Amy ran into him on her expedition to the Wishing Well, and he did her in because he didn't want his presence known, and then he tried to make it look like an accident."

"Yes, but look here, you can't have it both ways," Toby said. "You've just got through telling me about the slaughtered sheep and how you think it might be a warning from him to Deirdre to watch out. That's scarcely the action of a man who is keeping his presence quiet, and certainly not the action of a man who has just committed a murder that another man is under arrest for."

"I suppose not," she said, agreeing grudgingly. "Oh, and incidentally, I've found an old estate map here that shows quite a few places we should check to see whether he's been holing up in any of them. I think we should do it as soon as you get back, and I'll ask Heather what their present status is. When will you be here?"

"Oh, in about an hour or so. Did your dinner party bear any fruit?"

"Meager pickings," she said, and told him about the discussion.

She snatched a quick breakfast while Heather did some

phoning of her own, from which she returned looking somewhat downcast.

"No luck on Cranston. Bennett was positively snappish to
me. He said Cranston was off to Oban on business, and that
he had things to do at the house, so it wouldn't be convenient
for us to come today. The only thing I could think of was to
invite them here for dinner tomorrow. It may seem a bit soon
after Amy's death, but no one seems to be doing any particular mourning for the poor soul."

"Have you heard anything about the burial or whatever?"

"Yes, again something I did not expect. According to
Alastair, Amy left instructions with her solicitor that she was
to be cremated and no religious observances of any kind were
to be held. I believe they've already done it. I would have
expected something quite elaborate at the kirk with pipes and
plumes and family vaults. Her ashes are to be scattered at sea
by the next head of the clan, if and when he shows up."

"Sounds quite sensible to me," Penny remarked. "I'm not
a great one for death rites. If Cranston is a no-go, why don't
you and Alison zero in on Hamish and Deirdre? In fact, why
not ask them for tomorrow's dinner, too? It'll give Toby a
chance to look them over, and I don't imagine Hamish will
need much prompting if he has his eye on your antiques."

"That's another thing," Heather said thoughtfully. "Last
night Alastair got quite excited about those watercolors in
the lounge, so Alison tells me. Have you heard of Fergus
Macdonell?"

"Wasn't he your ancestor?"

"No, not that one—another Fergus. Seems he was a poet
in World War I and was killed in the general Macdonell
holocaust at Ypres. Well, it appears he has recently been
rediscovered by the Scottish younger generation, and there is
quite a cult grown up around him. Some of his poems have
been set to rock and roll music of all things."

"What's that got to do with the watercolors?"

"I'm coming to that. He was also an amateur artist. When
he was wounded early in World War I, he spent his recupera-
tion time here writing a cycle of poems called 'Across the
Western Waters' and painting scenes to go with them. Alastair
thinks those are the originals, and, if so, they may be quite

valuable as a cult item. He says that if you look carefully at the paintings, you can see Fergus's monogram interlaced in the scenery. It is the same one with which he signed all his poems. The funny thing is that somebody did make me a very generous offer for them just recently.''

''Hamish?''

Heather shook her head. ''No, Amy,'' she said in a low voice, and looked at Penny with troubled eyes.

''Dear lord. Yet another line to be followed up. And another possible reason why someone wants you out of here. I tell you, one thing I should do with all due speed is to have an appraiser look at all the paintings in the house. You told me it has never been done, and with everything else that has been going on, it might be as well to play it safe.''

''I suppose so. And yet for the moment everything seems so quiet.''

Penny briefly considered telling her about the door opening during the night, but she did not want to raise old fears. She said instead, ''Well, I'd better get after Mrs. Gray. Her son sounds like a very nasty bit of work, and you'd better warn Alison not to go for any solitary walks until we establish whether or not he is around here.''

''You think he might be?''

''It's a possibility. He may be behind the sheep incident, and, as he seems to be on the lam, he may have been the one who cleaned out the coins from the well. Could you fill me in on which of those buildings on the old estate map of Soruba still exist?''

They climbed up to the tower room, and Heather contemplated the map. ''The best person for this would be Jamey Mitton,'' she said after a minute. ''He took me all around when I first came, but I honestly can't remember where everything is. A lot of the old barns and sheep cotes have fallen into ruin; some of them are just piles of stones.''

Penny brightened. ''Good idea, and maybe I can get another slant on Deirdre and Gareth at the same time.''

As they descended, there was the sound of movement in Toby's room, and Penny popped her head around the door, hoping that he had returned, which would allow them to get right to their hunt. Instead she came upon her other quarry, Mrs. Gray, who was busy plying a dust mop.

The woman greeted her with a sly grin. "If it's the gentleman ye're after, he was noo here the nicht. His bed has not been slept in." The bruise on her face had faded to a pale yellow, and she appeared to be in good spirits.

"No, I was looking for you. I think it's high time we had a quiet talk about what has been going on. Just between us, you understand. I do not want to bring the Macdonell into it if it can be avoided." She gazed steadily at the old woman, whose dark eyes met her gaze with a wary glint.

"Och, and what could an auld besom like me have to tell a clever leddy like you?"

"Quite a lot. But first let me tell you some things." Penny perched on the edge of the bed and indicated the fading bruise on the old lady's face. "Your son did that, didn't he? He's hiding from the police somewhere around here, and he's been after you for help. In the meantime, he has been doing some mighty peculiar things, and I'd like to know why. The police are on his trail, you know, so the best thing for you to do, both for him and for yourself, is to make sure he gives himself up before he gets into worse trouble."

Mrs. Gray looked at her in silence as the tick of Toby's traveling clock sounded in the hushed room. Suddenly she spat out, "He's away again, and good riddance to the devil's whelp! I hope I never set eyes on him as long as I draw breath."

"But he was here."

"Och, aye, he was here. Not a sight nor sound of him for eight lang years, and then he has the gall to show up on my ain doorstep like a stray dog, whining for food, whining for money, and when I naysay him, he claps me a good one to mind my manners and close my mouth."

"And did you help him?"

"Och, I gave him what siller I had to get shut of him. It was little enough. And I gave him some food, but he didna bide with me."

"Was this before the McDougall's murder?"

"Aye, the day before it, he showed at the lodge, bold as brass, but the way he was acting, I ken he'd been around before that. Mean he was and excited, but not as excited as he was before he was away.''

"So you saw him twice?"

"Aye." A strange expression flitted across the old face. "Full of whisky he was that time. Came to boast and to rail at me. He said he'd show me what a clever lad he was, that he would be riding in style with siller in his pocket and with the gentry bowing and scraping to him before he was through, but I'd never see a penny of it because I'd been no proper mother to him. He said it was the last I'd ever see him but that I'd hear plenty and sorry I would be for all the harm I'd done him. So I cursed him, and he left." She stopped abruptly.

"And when was this?"

"The nicht before the nicht."

"You mean two evenings ago?"

"That's what I said," Mrs. Gray muttered testily.

"Do you know where he's been staying?"

"He didna say, but he knows every butt and ben around here, same as I. There are a thousand and one places he could have been where no one would find him."

"Then why do you think he's gone again?"

Mrs. Gray looked surprised. "Because he said he was away. Why would he lie?"

Penny let that go. "All right, now that we have the time framework, let's get down to cases. On the day we found the McDougall, was it he who shot at Miss Macdonell in the woods behind your place?"

"Losh, no. He hadna a gun or flourishing it he would have been to show what a fine braw man he is. Besides, Allen's a man that likes to use his hands; a great one with his fists is Allen."

"Did he use them on the McDougall?" Penny asked bluntly.

Mrs. Gray shook her eldritch locks vigorously. "Nae. If there's one person in the world he'd never have laid a finger on, it was puir Amy."

"But what if she had stumbled across him and threatened to turn him in to the police?"

"Nae, she'd never have done that, any more than he would have hurt her. They both had their reasons." The dark eyes were bleak.

"Did he say anything about the murder?"

"When I told him they had taken Gareth McClintock for it, he laughed and said that they had the right man for the wrong reason but that he could tell them a thing or two."

"Did he, now," Penny murmured uneasily. "And what about the sheep in the chapel and the money from the Wishing Well?"

The old woman looked startled. "I know nothing of the sheep, but what's this about the well?" There was a quaver of fear in her cracked voice.

"Somebody cleared every coin out of the well. And if he was as hard up as you say, he seems the most likely candidate."

Mrs. Gray was staring at her with wide, frightened eyes. "Och, the fool, the puir besotted fool. It's the doom he has brought upon himself for sure."

"Oh, come now, Mrs. Gray, there could not have been more than a pound or two in change. It's scarcely a capital crime."

"Ye're a Sassenach. It's not for you to understand."

Feeling that she was losing the old woman, Penny hastily changed direction. "What about this fight he had with Gareth McClintock? Why did he land in hospital if he is such a good man with his fists?"

"Because Gareth took him from behind. That's the McClintocks for you. Treacherous and devious they are. Ye'd be a fool to trust any of that ilk, for a stab in the back is all ye'd ever get for it."

The door opened suddenly, causing them both to jump. Toby's tall figure appeared on the threshold.

"Oh, there you are," he exclaimed peevishly. "I've been looking all over for you."

"I'll be about my business the noo," the old woman announced with relief. "Ye mind my words, Dr. Spring." She scuttled past Toby.

"What was that all about?" he asked, shutting the door behind her.

"I'm not entirely sure," Penny said, and repeated what Mrs. Gray had told her. "The worst of it is, I think she is telling the truth or what she thinks is the truth. One thing for sure, we'd better get right after him, because he obviously knows more about this business than we do.''

"Why don't we leave it to the police? Now that we know he is around, they can find him with their resources a lot quicker than we can.''

Penny frowned. "No. I want to get to him first. There are some things that just don't add up. He thinks Gareth is the murderer, and yet he has expectations of money from someone here, at least from what he said to his mother. That certainly can't be Gareth. So there's someone else involved. But who?''

"Deirdre?'' Toby suggested tentatively.

"Then why the business of the sheep? With the police swarming all about, why draw attention to the person you are in the act of blackmailing?''

"Maybe someone else did that to the sheep.''

Penny threw up her hands in despair. "But *why?* How many people can be involved in this thing? For God's sake, Toby, let's go find Jamey Mitton and start searching for Allen Gray. I have this awful gut feeling that we have no more time to waste.''

"All right. I've nothing better to do until Corky gets back from London.''

"He's gone to London? What for?''

"I haven't the faintest idea, but as soon as I relayed the information you gave me, he took off like a bat out of hell. I've never seen a man get so excited so fast.''

"Didn't he say anything?''

"Only one thing: to keep an eye on Mrs. Mitton and to see that nothing happened to her until he got back. He said that she might be more precious than rubies.''

CHAPTER 15

It was a measure of Penny's edginess that she had a spirited and totally illogical argument with Toby about which car to take. Since logic was entirely on his side, he won, and they took the Bentley. They located Jamey Mitton placidly fishing just off the jetty, and this exasperated her still further.

"We need you, Mr. Mitton, to guide us around the outbuildings on the estate," she said, fairly snapping at him. "We think Allen Gray has been hiding out somewhere, and we're desperately anxious to ask him some questions about the murder."

"Aye, I can do that. The fish are not biting, anyway," Jamey returned with no visible show of surprise, and proceeded to reel in his fishing line with maddening slowness. He cocked his head toward the bay. "There's some dirty weather coming. Listen to the Corrievreckan." They listened to the distant rumble, which did seem to be taking on a more menacing note. "There'll be a storm before this day is out," he opined as he rowed slowly back to the jetty. He tied up the boat and looked disapprovingly at the big car. "We'll not be getting very far in that."

"You see," Penny said triumphantly to Toby.

"In fact," Mitton continued, ignoring her, "where we are going, we'll not be needing a car at all, ye ken. It's walking we'll be doing, but if you'll just be dropping me at the house, I'll be getting my gun. Just a wee precaution, you understand. If Allen hasna changed his ways, he's nae a reasonable person and may need a mite persuading."

"Where to?" Toby asked as Jamey rejoined them, carrying a formidable shotgun.

"If ye'll drive to the auld gymnasium, we'll take a peek in there, and then there's a sheep path behind it that'll take us over the hills. There's but three or four places that he's likely to have used, but they're a guid step apart, so it'll take us the morning to cover them."

Penny's heart sank slightly, for this seemed to be at odds with Allen's mother's list of a thousand and one hiding spots, however exaggerated it may have been.

The gymnasium/badminton court yielded nothing but echoes and dust, and so they commenced the stiff climb up the hill behind it. Penny tried desperately to figure out how she could best introduce the delicate subject of Deirdre to Deirdre's father. Nothing brilliant occurred to her, and so finally she said, "What do you make of this business of the chapel?"

"The work of a madman," Mitton said calmly. "And Hamish Cameron is out a good ewe. Would ye be thinking Allen Gray is behind it, now?"

"That is so, and it also occurred to me that it might be some sort of warning to Deirdre."

He stiffened slightly. "And why would ye be thinking that?"

Oh, well, in for a penny, in for a pound, she thought. "Because I think Deirdre has been using the chapel to meet someone."

They had reached the top of the hill, and he stopped briefly to scan the unending vista of heather and bracken that lay on the tableland beneath them, on which some Highland cattle grazed.

"And ye have evidence for that?" he asked softly.

"No, but Miss Ingstrom and I did see something in the chapel that indicated that your daughter had been using it. We have said nothing of this to the police, but I wondered if you were aware she had been seeing someone and who that someone was. They may both be in some danger. If you know, it would be wise to tell us. We are not the police, and we are here only to help."

"My daughter is a woman grown," he said deliberately. "What she does is her business, and so I mind mine. If ye have questions to ask, ask her."

"I fully intend to," she said, realizing by the determined set of his mouth under the drooping moustache that so far as he was concerned, the subject was closed. She tried another tack. "Could you tell me something about Allen Gray? I've heard about his fight with Gareth and his attempt on Deirdre, but something his mother said seemed to indicate that he had strong ties with Amy McDougall. How was that?"

He did not answer immediately, for they had come to a semiruined stone building that crouched low in the heather; its slate roof had collapsed, exposing half the interior. "They used to use this at winter lambing," he explained briefly, and ducked his tall lean figure through the warped door.

Toby stooped behind him but reemerged in a minute or two, dusting his hands off and shaking his head. "Nothing. Where next?" he said to Mitton.

"About a mile and a half over yon, another like this for the Cameron farm. It's heavy walking," he added with a sly glance at Penny.

"No matter," she said resolutely.

"All right." He spoke with grudging admiration. "You were asking me of Allen? Ye ken his father died when he was but a bairn, and he never has got along with his mother. When he was fifteen, he ran away. It was when the auld McDougall was still alive, and it was Amy who found him on the streets of Oban and brought him back. She must have made some arrangement with Mrs. Gray, the auld besom, because he stayed over on Sheena after that as a sort of general handyman, even after the auld laird died. She was very guid to him, they say." His tone was carefully non-committal.

"When did he leave Sheena, then?"

"Just after Gareth went there as her gillie. The Macdonell of the time took Allen on here as a junior factor, but that didna last long."

"Mr. Mitton, I think there is a little more to it than that, so you might just as well tell me," Penny said firmly. "Was he romantically involved at all with Amy McDougall?"

"There was some talk," he admitted reluctantly.

"And Gareth cut him out?"

"Nae, there had been an unpleasantness before that. A falling-out, you might say. Allen never had guid sense. He started putting on airs, ye ken."

"I see," Penny said, thinking that she did. "And yet he bore no grudge against Amy McDougall?"

"Nae," he repeated. "For he didna leave empty-handed, and I never heard him, who spoke black of everyone, say a hard word against her."

"So you don't think there is a possibility he might have murdered her?"

He glanced sideways at her. "I have nae opinion. He's been long gone, and the years can change a man."

"Do you think Gareth did it, then?" she asked bluntly.

"Nae, I do not. He's nae more capable of murder than my Deirdre is." The dark eyes flashed a challenge at her, and he firmly clamped his mouth, closing the subject.

Toby suddenly broke in. "How easy is it to obtain a kilt of the Macdonell dress tartan?"

It was such an unexpected question that they both gaped at him.

"Well, I'm not a Macdonell," Mitton said, stuttering. "So I don't rightly know. They're a wee clan, ye ken, but the big kilt firms in Glasgow and Edinburgh would hae the bolts of it. It's not a popular tartan like the Black Watch or the Stuart or the MacNeill, which is mine, but they'd have the material."

"How about Oban?" Toby demanded.

"It's possible. They have a kilt shop there, right enough. Ye could ask."

Penny had finally guessed what Toby was after and looked at him with the pride of a doting mother for a precocious child, but she said nothing until Mitton was busy shooing some Highland cows out of their path.

"Why didn't I think of that?" she said *sotto voce* to Toby. "You figure we can get a line on who has been acting the part of the ghost from a kilt order?"

"It struck me as a possibility. I took a look at that tartan, and it is hideous, so only the devout or the devious are likely to want it. Of course, the most likely person to have one is Ian Macdonell."

"On whom we'll check," she said jubilantly.

They walked onward as the morning became increasingly sultry and dark thunderclouds gathered along the line of the outer islands. They reached the second lambing station, but it yielded nothing.

Jamey Mitton cast a knowledgeable eye at the clouds. "We have two hours at best before this breaks—time enough to get to the bothy, but we'll be veering back toward the Lochgilphead road, so it'll not be such a long step to the house."

By the time they reached the bothy, Penny was tired, sweaty, and extremely hungry. It too proved entirely empty, save for sheep droppings and the scuttling sound of creatures in the ruins. She sat down with a thump on one of the walls.

"Well, I've had it for today. I haven't walked as far as this since I crossed the Serengeti with the Masai, and I don't intend to walk much farther. You're right, Toby; we should let the police flush him out." Sir Tobias looked at her in some surprise but said nothing.

"It's but a short piece to the track to the house," Mitton said, coaxing them. "We'll come out by the memorial. You could rest there while I get the car, if Sir Tobias doesna mind me driving it."

Toby handed him the keys and watched him lope off with remarkable speed. "You didn't really mean that, did you?" he observed mildly.

Penny had taken off a shoe and was briskly rubbing her left foot. "No, but before we set out again, I'm having another word with Mrs. Gray, and we'll do better without Mitton. It couldn't have escaped you that he's more or less been walking us around in circles."

"Yes, I did notice that. It occurred to me that for some reason Mitton does not want us to find our quarry. Interesting, that. I am beginning to share your enthusiasm for a talk with the unpleasant Mr. Gray. What can he know that everyone is so afraid of?"

"I'm beginning to have the horrible feeling that when we do find out, it will be something we may wish we hadn't, for Alastair's sake, anyway. Mrs. Gray's remark about the right man for the wrong reason has shaken me." She shaded her eyes and looked at the bank of clouds boiling toward them. "I hope he hurries up with the car, or we are going to get soaked. It looks as if this lot will wash out any further outside activities today, so why don't we snug ourselves down in the study and draw up future battle plans?"

"And make some phone calls," Toby added with a yawn. "But frankly, my first order of business will be a nap. How about you?"

"Only after I've eaten. I'm famished. Ah, here he is." They stood up wearily, and as she climbed into the car, Penny went on. "Now that we know Allen Gray is equally at home on Sheena, I think we should suggest to the police that they also take a look around the island." She could not resist a sly glance at Mitton. "It would be easy enough for him to get to and fro with all the rowboats there are around the place."

"What was the point of that?" Toby asked after Mitton had left them.

"I thought we might give Mitton something to think about. It'll be interesting to see if he takes a little trip out there. There's no way he could warn him otherwise. They don't have a phone in the cottage. They always use the one up at Soruba, and he obviously can't do that."

"I can't see him going to any great lengths to protect Allen Gray."

"Neither can I, but in our present floundering situation, I figure that if we throw enough bait in enough directions, someone sooner or later is going to nibble. Oh, and when you've recovered from last night's orgy—" Toby looked suitably pained. "I wish you'd experiment with the floorboards in the south wing to see which of them triggers that damned door of mine. Well, I'm off to forage for food. See you later."

After a sandwich and a cup of coffee, she chatted again with Mrs. Gray, but the latter was now in a surly mood and provided little comfort.

"I told ye he was away," she snapped. "And it's wasting time ye are larruping around the estate with that auld fool Mitton. If Allen doesna want to be found, ye'd never find him in a thousand years."

Too tired to press the point, Penny collapsed into her bed and drifted into a long nap filled with disturbing dreams. She awoke finally to a dark greenish gloom, with rain lashing at the windows and the roll of thunder overhead. The storm, as predicted, was upon them, and it was impressive. She looked out the window at the bay that was covered in angry white-caps, and even through the closed windows, she could hear the angry roar of the giant whirlpool. I really would like to see that, she was thinking as a cautious tapping sounded at the door.

"Come in," she called, expecting Toby. But it was Heather's head that appeared.

"Oh, good, you're up," she exclaimed. "Isn't this storm something. I'm afraid we might be without lights tonight." She clicked the light switch up and down to prove her point. "Mitton's working on the generator now, but he says it looks as if something has mucked it up. We'll have to get someone out from Oban. I gather you didn't have any luck this morning."

"No, none. How did you get on with the Camerons?"

Heather joined her at the window. "Not too well. Hamish wasn't there—off on another trip and will be back tonight—but Deirdre was looking terrible. I feel so sorry for her. She looks so white and drawn, as if she hasn't slept in days. I suppose it could be the baby, but she seems awfully distraught. Alison tried to get her talking about the murder—I hadn't the heart—but she just would not be drawn."

"Are they coming tomorrow?"

"I hope so. She didn't seem very keen, but I said I wanted Hamish's opinion on some of the things here, and just to make sure, I'll phone him tonight—if the phone is still working, that is."

"Do you know if Toby got his calls through?"

"Yes, he did, and he sent a message with Alastair about something, too. He showed up to take Alison to the movies, of all things." Heather shook her head in disbelief. "Arrived like a drowned rat. What love will do! I made them take the Mini. They'd have been blown flat on his motorbike." She moved restlessly about the room, fiddling with her hair.

Penny watched her curiously for a few seconds and then asked, "What's worrying you, Heather?"

Her friend gave her a quick glance and looked away. "Two things. You haven't been into my medicine cabinet, have you?"

"No."

"Well, I can't be absolutely sure, but I think two whole bottles of the Valium are missing," Heather said in a worried voice. "I thought there were six, and now there are only four."

"There were six," Penny said flatly. "I remember counting them and being shocked. Have you any idea who might have taken them?"

Heather shook her head. "It could have been anyone in the house. Which, after what Dennis said, doesn't exactly cheer me up. And there's another odd thing. Margaret Macdonell called me up about an hour ago. She sounded very upset. Ian went out this morning and hasn't come back. She thought for some odd reason he might be here. I asked Mrs. Mitton, and she said she had seen his car going up toward the main gate about noon. He sometimes cuts through the estate to Ardnan— it's so much quicker, you see—but so far as she knew, he did not stop at the house."

"Mm, probably just waiting the storm out somewhere," Penny said reassuringly, trying to hide her own unease.

Someone knocked at the door, and Toby appeared, an odd expression on his face. "I put the enquiries in motion about the kilts," he said carefully. "And young McClintock has passed on the Gray information to the police. Not that there is anything they can do until this storm has spent itself." He lapsed into silence and looked expectantly at them.

"Well, I'd better go and see when and if we're likely to get dinner," Heather said hastily, and left them.

"What's up?" Penny demanded.

"Just that I've tried every inch of the south wing, and then I tried every inch of the north wing: floors, walls, windows, doors. And I found there is absolutely no way of opening this door from either of them. We'll have to think again."

They looked at each other. "Oh," said Penny in a small voice. "I see."

CHAPTER 16

"I have never met a case where so much time is spent around the dining table," Penny fretted. "If we are ever going to get to the bottom of this, it looks as if we'll have to eat ourselves to the solution." It was the following evening, and she and Toby, dressed for the upcoming dinner, were closeted in the study.

"Since we have no official capacity and cannot tackle these people directly, it's about the only way of doing it," Toby said mildly, fiddling with his Old Wykehamist tie. "Besides," he added with a touch of malice, "it should suit you down to the ground. You always complained on all our other cases that you never got fed enough."

Penny ran her hand through her already rumpled air so that it stood up in improbable spikes. It had been a frustrating and not very comfortable twenty-four hours, with no real developments. The few things that had happened had only served to increase the general feeling of unease that had settled over Soruba House like a sea fog.

The electrician from Oban had arrived that morning in the wake of the storm, inspected the generator, and announced gloomily that somebody had undoubtedly been monkeying about with it and that it looked to him like sabotage. This had upset Heather to no small degree.

It had also been a day for rows. Isobel Menzies and Mrs. Gray had had words, after which the former had appeared before them in tears, avowing that she was too upset to work any more that day. She had departed for Ardnan, leaving Mrs. Mitton, who was deeply embroiled in the preparations

147

for the dinner party, shorthanded. Alison and Alastair had had their first quarrel—subject unspecified—and so Alison had been moping around the house like a discontented Valkyrie.

A tearful Margaret Macdonell had phoned up to apologize to Heather for her ridiculous panic of the day before. "Ian is just furious with me for being so silly," she cried into the phone. "I can't think what came over me. I do hope I didn't upset your preparations for the dinner party tonight."

Heather, feeling boxed in, could think of nothing better than to invite them as well, thus adding to Mrs. Mitton's gloom.

Neither the Oban nor the Edinburgh kilt stores reported any sales of the Macdonell dress tartan, but their hopes were momentarily raised when a Glasgow firm called to say that a man's kilt in the dress tartan had been ordered and delivered seven weeks before. Unfortunately, the sale turned out to have been cash-and-carry, with no name or address given.

"Did the assistant remember anything about the person who had ordered it?" Toby had enquired, only to find that the shop assistant in question was on a two-week holiday to Spain and was unavailable.

"Well, it's a nice time fit," he observed to Penny philosophically. "So I suppose we'll have to wait until the assistant comes back and, if we're lucky, remembers something."

The police search of the Soruba estate had yielded no evidence of Allen Gray. In spite of the high seas that still roiled unappeased after the storm, they had seen the police launch docking on Sheena and were currently awaiting another call from the invaluable Constable Menzies. He apparently had taken an instant fancy to Toby and had therefore constituted himself as the latter's listening post. Another fruitless phone call had been made to Craignish Castle, where Toby had been informed that Lord Corcoran was still in London and that they had received no word about his return.

"Stymied," Penny had said, fuming. "Nothing to do but wait, wait, wait."

"Well, let's see if we can think of some new angles. I've an idea or two for which I need your help. One thought came to me," he said, drawing out his notebook. "Namely, that whoever staged that 'accident' with Amy McClintock's boat didn't know too much about sailing or sailboats. Would that help us narrow the field at all? Who are the good sailors here?"

"Heather could answer that better than I, but Ian Macdonell is a keen sailor, Mitton is good with any kind of boat, and since Gareth was his protégé, he is, too. And Cranston Phillips and Bennett Rose, I suppose."

"They operate a big powerboat," Toby pointed out. "They may not know much about sailing."

"No, I suppose not."

"So I'd better keep them on the possibles list," he said, busily scribbling in his notebook. "Along with the Strachans."

"Yes, he doesn't like the sea at all," Penny interjected.

"How about the Camerons?"

"I just don't know."

"And we don't know about Allen Gray either, so both of those are question marks. That doesn't get us a whole lot further. The only person it seems to take off the hook is Ian Macdonnell—the only one we've come up with who may have had a motive to wish Amy McClintock out of the way. Besides Gareth, that is," he added gloomily.

"What else did you have in mind?"

"To try to figure out where everyone was on the afternoon of the murder, between one in the afternoon when she set off from Sheena and about six o'clock, which is what the pathologist came up with as the *terminus ante quem* for her death."

"That's certainly easier," Penny said. "Because most of our characters were gathered together in one spot: Cranston's party. We got there a little after six, and they were all there ahead of us."

"Who wasn't there, then?"

"The Strachans. I'm not sure whether they just did not come or weren't invited. The Mittons, who don't move in this set at all, and, of course, the McClintocks."

"And Allen Gray, who we now know was around there then," he added, busily writing. "That certainly narrows things down a bit, although if she was killed shortly after setting out, it would still have given the murderer time to get back to the party. Did anyone seem at all odd in his behavior?"

"Hamish was semi-polluted by the time we got there, and

neither of the Macdonells was feeling any pain. The mixed drinks were very strong. Oh, I've just remembered, Cranston wasn't there when we arrived. He came in a bit later with a fresh supply of booze.''

''So we can't rule him out entirely, either.''

''It seems to me we can't rule anyone out entirely,'' she said with some asperity. ''As you say, if the murder was committed earlier, anyone there could theoretically have had time. I don't think this is really getting us anywhere.''

''But if the murderer had to be at the party, it might account for the fact that he sabotaged the boat but didn't have time to stay around to see whether it actually sank,'' Toby insisted.

''That's possible. But it could just as easily have been a lack of knowledge about sailboats. Which would seem to me, putting everything together, to put Dennis Strachan squarely back on the hook.''

''How do you make that out?''

''Because he was snooping about near the scene of the crime the day after the murder, remember? What if he had committed the murder the day before and gone back to see if all was okay. He spotted the sailboat, which he thought had been sunk, and in a panic was on his way back for a rowboat or something to tow it out to deeper water and sink it, when he had the misfortune to run into us. So he made up this cock-and-bull story about his cows getting out and rushed on with his errand. But then, before he could get back, we had discovered the boat and the body, and that was that.''

''It is possible. But that brings us back to the question of motive. Why would he want Amy McClintock out of the picture?''

''Well, we do know from Alison's snooping that Amy had been lending money to Ian Macdonell. We also know that the Strachans are struggling financially. Maybe she lent him money and was making 'or else' noises at him as well.'' Penny was warming to her subject. ''In fact, it would also make a certain amount of sense if he were behind the happenings at Soruba, the motive being the same. If Heather weren't on the spot and they could not pay their farm rent, they would have a hell of a lot more breathing space to come up with the money than if she were camped on their doorstep, saying, 'Hey, where's this quarter's rent?' Also, he is a piper, he does know the grounds and house inside and out, and he would be active enough to climb the ivy. Yes, the more I think of it, the more the cap fits.''

"Except for one little anomaly," Toby said dryly.

"What's that?"

"Allen Gray." She looked at him in surprise, and so he elaborated. "You said Allen Gray talked big to his mother about getting money. Our presumption, therefore, is that he had something on someone about the murder. If Strachan is the guilty party and is as financially strapped as you say, what money would Allen Gray be likely to collect from him? Certainly not enough to ride around in cars and have the gentry bowing and scraping, as he is reported to have said."

"That could have been just a drunken boast," she said doubtfully. "But, yes, you do have a point there."

They were interrupted by Alison, who announced abruptly, "Phone call for Sir Tobias. Constable Menzies," and slammed out again.

Toby was gone for some time. When he returned, he had a look of deep concentration on his face.

"News of Allen Gray?" Penny demanded.

He shook his head and slumped back into his chair. "Not exactly, but something that indeed gives one food for thought." He proceeded to fill his pipe at a snail's pace.

"Well, what is it?" She was almost dancing with impatience.

"The police made a very thorough search of Sheena. There's a small building at the southern end of the island, a sort of combination boathouse and fishing shack. Somebody has been using it as an observation post," Toby said with great deliberation. "They found a chair pulled up at the window, a traveling rug, a thermos, and a pair of very powerful binoculars."

"Allen?"

He shook his head. "They showed the things to the servants at the castle. The rug, the thermos, and the binoculars all belonged to Amy McClintock. There were fingerprints on the glasses which they are now matching against hers." He paused. "I asked Constable Menzies what could be seen from the shack. Apart from the bay itself, he listed the track from the Lochgilphead road to the house, the farm cottages, Soruba House, and the chapel."

"So Amy might have known what was going on in the chapel and who was going there," Penny said. "She might also have seen someone climbing the ivy at the house. It's all beginning to make a little more sense, at least as to motive. I'm really starting to look forward to tonight's dinner party. I think we may be able to stir up some fireworks."

"I know you did not take to her, but what kind of woman was Amy McClintock? In the light of this, I think it is very important to know."

Penny reflected. "Putting aside my own feelings and adding together the bits and pieces I have got from the people around here, I would say that she was not overly intelligent and had, because of the isolation of this place, been very deprived all her life in the social sense. Her father was a bigoted old man who kept her on a very short rein right up until his death. And yet . . ." She paused. "One gets the feeling that she was determined and indeed reached out for what she wanted, and one of the things she wanted was a man, preferably young. Allen Gray was her protégé, and so was Gareth, and she went ahead with both of them in the teeth of the social disapproval she knew must come from it. I also get the impression that although she was not very likable, she did have a tremendous curiosity and a tremendous need for people, and this observation post business seems to bears that out. I'm not talking about blackmail, just that she liked having a little edge of knowledge that she could show on occasion, perhaps a little moral blackmail at most. Also, good Scot that she was, she was interested in money and pretty sharp about getting her money's worth out of anything. I must confess I cannot see her as a schemer. Dennis Strachan may just have thrown that out as a smoke screen for reasons of his own. She didn't strike me as bright enough for that."

"What if, in her snooping, she came across the unpleasant fact that her husband was cheating on her? What do you think her reaction would have been to that?"

"Obviously she'd have been upset," Penny said slowly. "Even if only half the testimony of the servants at the castle is true, it is evident that she did light into Gareth, but I think she would have been realistic enough not to let it break up the marriage. Letting him go would have been the last thing she'd have done.''

''In that case, not letting him go may very well have been the last thing she did,'' Toby said. ''I must say that after all our digging, our silent friend is still far and away the most likely candidate.''

''Or Allen Gray. I still feel, in spite of all that has been said, that a man with a record of violence like his would be quite capable of biting the hand that had fed him in the distant past. Suppose, for example, he had been hiding out around here and needed a stake to get away. His mother has no money, and anyway, they are on bad terms. Who else would he turn to? I'd say the woman who in the past had helped him. He contacts her, puts on the squeeze, and she says, 'Sorry but.' He gets mad and throttles her and then makes a clumsy attempt to hide the crime with the sailboat accident.''

''Somehow that just does not satisfy me. I mean, what about those dark hints of money and power he made to his mother after he knew Amy was dead? He could not have meant Gareth was to be the source of it, because he has none he can readily lay his hands on. We've pretty well ruled out Strachan for the same reasons. If the sheep is Gray's handiwork, we are almost in the same position with Deirdre, who, in any case, would not have the kind of money he was talking about. No, I still have the feeling we are missing a gigantic piece of this jigsaw puzzle, and until we get it, we are not going to arrive at the truth.''

''For that matter, no one around here has that kind of money,'' Penny stated. ''With the possible exception of Phillips and Rose, who seem comfortable but not affluent, I'd say Heather was the best fixed of the lot, and yet she does not have what anyone would call a fortune. Unless someone has expectations we don't know about.''

The door opened again, but this time it was Heather. ''Cranston and Bennett are just pulling up, and the Macdonells are right behind them,'' she announced.

''Right, we'll be with you in a second,'' Penny said. ''Well, the curtain's going up. We're on.''

They started toward the formal drawing room where the pre-dinner drinks were laid out but were intercepted by Mrs. Mitton, who beckoned to them frantically from the kitchen corridor. "I don't want to upset the Macdonell," she whispered urgently. "But I thought you ought to know. Mitton has just come up from the cottages. He says there's an ambulance at the Strachans', and they are taking her away to Oban."

"Meg Strachan?" Penny exclaimed. "What's the trouble?"

"Suicide, drug overdose," Mrs. Mitton hissed. "I knew he'd drive her to it one of these days; a thorough bad lot is Dennis Strachan!"

CHAPTER 17

It was a difficult evening, as if the sense of unease in the house had intensified everyone's personal quirks. Margaret Macdonell was timorous and silent, regarding the company out of rapidly blinking, fearful red-rimmed eyes. Her husband, as if to compensate for her silence, was loud and blustery, but his usual heavy-handed gallantries to Alison had a hollow ring, indicating that his mind was firmly fixed elsewhere. Penny was shocked by both the Camerons. Deirdre looked so strained and taut that she had the impression that only an effort of will was keeping the pregnant woman from fainting. Her husband appeared totally heedless of her wretched state and was almost sickening in his attentiveness to his hostess, while his handsome eyes roved hungrily over the antique items. Penny would not have been a bit surprised to see little white price tags sprouting from them.

Not that she had a lot of opportunity to observe, because while Hamish was monopolizing Heather, Cranston Phillips had made a beeline for her. As expertly as a sheep dog, he had cut her out from the crowd and literally cornered her, his great bulk looming intimidatingly over her. She let it happen, for if he was set on pumping her, she had similar designs on him and hoped that Toby was doing the same with Bennett Rose. She was keeping an eye on them as best she could, but they didn't appear to have much to say to each other. Bennett was hovering solicitously around the pale-faced Deirdre, who, unlike everyone else, was sitting down.

She turned her attention back to Cranston, who was saying, "I was counting on you to fill me in on all that's been going on. Too bad Bennett and I were off on that trip. We missed all the excitement, and God knows, there's little enough of that around here. I hear that you and Sir Tobias have been helping the police. Had no idea you were an amateur detective as well as all your other fields of expertise.'' His muddy brown eyes challenged her mild hazel ones.

"Oh, no," she lied resolutely. "We're spectators just the same as you are. Pure accident that we happened to be here."

He let out a guffaw of disbelief. "Oh come now. I've done a bit of checking up. The two of you have quite a reputation as a mystery-solving team. You don't expect me to believe you are both here just by accident."

"If you recall, I was here quite some time before Amy's murder," Penny said severely. "And Sir Tobias had been invited up to look at the long barrow on the estate. In fact," she could not help adding slyly, "if Alison and I had not been checking the barrow out for him, I doubt whether Amy's body would have been found or the murder ever discovered."

"Well, it's not much of a mystery, anyway," he muttered. "Seeing they've already got the murderer."

"Have they? You think it's as simple as that?"

"Stands to reason, doesn't it?" His voice was sharp. "He'd been playing around, and Amy had got fed up with it and was preparing to throw him out, so he did her in."

"Who was he playing around with?" she demanded, watching him closely.

His eyes slid away from hers. "I've no idea; probably one of the household help. That'd be about his style. Let's face it, he's a peasant through and through. Act first and think afterwards, and now that they've nabbed him—brutish silence. Silence gives consent, you know."

"There are some things that don't quite jibe, though," she said. "Gareth is an expert sailor. I doubt whether he'd have made such a stupid mistake about the sailboat, and according to his brother, who is a policeman, he has an alibi but does not choose to reveal it at this time."

"An alibi. I can't believe it," he said, stuttering. "Then why hasn't he told the police?"

"The obvious thing that springs to mind is that he is protecting someone. Why? I have no idea. Have you?"

"What do the police think? What else has been happening?"

"I should think the murder was quite enough to have happened in a quiet place like this," she answered tentatively. "What else could have happened?"

"I heard that there had been some odd business at the chapel, something to do with Hamish."

"Oh, that. Just a rather nasty piece of vandalism," she said offhandedly. "The police seem to know all about it."

"Oh. And there's been nothing else?"

"Nothing of any importance," she assured him blandly. "How was your trip? We heard you heading home in the fog the other day. You must know these waters like the back of your hand to have attempted it in that weather."

He preened slightly. ":Yes, these waters don't hold any secrets from me. No, it wasn't an exciting trip, just picking up supplies for Bennett and odds and ends like that. It was mainly tiring."

He did look tired; the wrinkles around his eyes were sharply etched, and there was a certain tautness about his face that made him look a lot older than she had first thought him to be. She could not help wondering what supplies Rose could possibly need that could not be found in Oban and that warranted a sea trip of several days, but to press the point would seem overly curious, and he volunteered nothing further.

"Just as well you made it in before the storm," she observed. "That really was something."

"A damn nuisance," he said morosely. "It'll be several days probably before the sea calms down enough for Bennett to get on with his work. You'd be surprised how a storm like that stirs up the bottom. This year, it seems it has been one bloody thing after another." His tone was savage.

"So that Bennett has not be able to do his underwater photography or whatever it is he does?"

She said it idly, but he gave her a sharp, suspicious glance. "He has several contracts, and this weather means he's falling behind on his deadlines."

"Does it interfere with your painting?" she asked innocently.

"I'm having a bit of a dry spell." His voice was offhanded. "Like a writer's block, you know? It will pass, but in the meantime I'm glad to give him a helping hand."

"Mrs. Macdonell was saying what a help you have been to everyone around here," Penny said. "So nice to be looked up to by your neighbors."

"Well, one does what one can," he mumbled. "Is Sir Tobias going to excavate that barrow for Heather? What does he expect to find, buried treasure?" His laughter had a forced ring to it.

It was such an abrupt change of subject that she was caught off guard. "There are no immediate plans. He may try to establish a date for it before he goes. It's so large that he thinks it may even be a Viking longboat burial."

"You mean like that one they found at what's-its-name, Sutton Hoo?" He sounded more astonished than interested.

"That was Anglo-Saxon, but there are Viking legends about the barrow, and it is remarkable how often these old tales hold a kernel of truth."

"Like the Macdonell curse?" he said with a little laugh. "I hope you haven't been scaring poor Heather with this truth-in-legend idea."

It was her turn to give him a sharp glance. "No, I haven't, though as it happens, I do know about the curse. I am quite anxious to see this fabled whirlpool. It certainly sounded impressive the other evening."

"Oh, you must. It's quite a sight. Get Heather to run you out in the powerboat. Sailing around it is a bit dicey, but you are safe enough on a good day at low tide in a powerboat."

"Do you do much sailing around here?" She tried to make the question casual.

"No, too slow for me. Never could see the sense in depending on wind and tide when you can get an engine to do your bidding. Bennett is the sailor."

Their tête-à-tête was ended by the announcement of dinner, but when they all gathered in the large formal dining room, Penny found that she was sitting between Phillips and Hamish and that Cranston was at Heather's left at the top of the table, with Ian Macdonell on her right. Toby had been accorded the master's position at the other end of the table and was flanked by Mrs. Macdonell and Deirdre, with Rose facing Hamish and Alison across from Penny.

The first thing Cranston said to Heather when they were all

seated and the soup was being served was, "You've got to run Penny out to the Corrievreckan; she's just dying to see it. You've been out there, haven't you?"

Heather glanced at Penny and said something to him in a low voice, but Penny's attention had been captured by Hamish, who was enthusing about the dining table, and so she missed what followed. His enthusiasm shifted from the table to the sideboard and then to the portraits. Penny tried to keep track of his raptures as she took in the rest of what was happening.

A glum-faced Isobel Menzies, she noted, had rejoined the staff, and there was a younger edition of Isobel helping in the butler's pantry that served as a hatch between the kitchen and dining room. Constable Menzies had evidently put his foot down and sent his daughters back to work. Alison was listening, with a slightly disgusted look on her face, to Ian Macdonell expounding on deer stalking. Bennett Rose was being very attentive to the white-faced Deirdre and had even managed to bring a faint smile to her pale lips. When she looked over at Toby, Penny's heart sank, for there was an expression on his face that she knew only too well. The attack of melancholy she had been anticipating since he had arrived at Soruba had evidently struck in full force. He was immersed in deep gloom at the head of the table, where Mrs. Mitton hovered at his elbow, darting little anxious glances at his lugubrious face. His silence was matched by that of his right-hand partner, Margaret Macdonell, who, so far as Penny could see, had not opened her mouth once.

Tiring of Hamish's raptures, she tried to divert him to a more fruitful field. "I suppose every old house has its quota of treasures," she observed. "Is Sheena Castle as well endowed as Soruba?"

"Well, if your taste runs to Victoriana, it has some interesting pieces, but nothing to compare with Soruba. Amy was always talking about doing parts of it over. She even consulted me, but it never came to anything. Didn't want to put out the money it would have taken to do a good job." He gave a little embarrassed laugh. "*De mortuis* etcetera, but Amy didn't like to part with ready cash too easily, although she liked to rake it in well enough. She sold me a few things from the castle, but at a stiff price."

"Was she interested in art?" Penny asked, thinking of the watercolors in the lounge.

"No, not in the slightest. No talent or taste along those lines at all. So far as I know, poor Amy only had two talents. She was a very good sailor."

"And the other?"

"Rather an unusual one. She could lip-read." Again he gave an embarrassed laugh. "Damned uncomfortable on occasion, that. You had to be very careful what you said to someone else when she was around. I remember once I muttered to my dinner companion at her table that the soup was stone cold, and she boomed right down the table at me, 'It's supposed to be; it's vichyssoise.' I was very embarrassed."

Penny was highly intrigued. "How on earth did she come by it?"

"She told Deirdre once; something to do with a bad mastoid attack when she was a child. It left her deaf for the best part of a year, and she learned to lip-read then. She covered it up well, but actually she was still quite deaf."

Which probably accounted for the queer seesawing pitch of her voice, Penny thought. Another idea suddenly occurred to her. "At what distance could she do this?"

"I've no idea."

"Did everyone know she was deaf?"

"Again, I've no idea. We knew. Presumably Gareth must have known, but as I said, it was something she covered up extremely well."

"Speaking of Deirdre, she is not looking too well. Is the baby causing her problems?" Penny enquired.

He glanced up the table to where his wife was pushing the food around her plate, with a sick expression on her face. His gaze shifted to his mother-in-law, and he frowned. "Och, no. Her mother has been clucking over her like a mother hen, filling her with auld wives' tales and putting all sorts of silly ideas into her head. I've no patience for it. She's been on at her to move back home, of all things. Says it's not good for her to be by herself so much." He snorted. "As if I can help it if my business takes me on the road a lot. And who's to look after things at the farm if she moves back, I'd like to know. I had to put my foot down, and now they are both of them sulking. She'll get over it.''

Penny marveled again at his complete lack of sensitivity and wondered how much of Mrs. Mitton's motherly concern had to do with the knowledge that Allen Gray was once more in the area. She became aware that Alison was staring meaningfully at her, and she turned her attention to the conversation across the table. Alison had contrived to get everyone talking energetically about tartans.

"As a Sassenach, I don't find tartans a very enthralling subject," Cranston murmured into Penny's ear. "Most of them offend my color sensibilities as an artist, and the kilt as an article of masculine attire I always find faintly ludicrous. I say, your friend at the end of the table doesn't look as if he is having a very good time. Deirdre is not looking her best, I admit, but I have never seen anyone quite so unaware of her many charms."

"Er, Sir Tobias tends to get preoccupied like that when he has a lot on his mind," Penny said hastily, but was saved the need for further explanation when Heather suddenly rose after a whispered consultation with Mrs. Mitton.

"Shall we leave the men to their port and cigars?" she said a little self-consciously. "They can join us later for coffee."

It took them all by surprise, but the women obediently rose with her. Alison, whose good temper seemed to have been restored, gave Penny a wink as they filed out. "My, aren't we the proper ones," she whispered as Heather led the way to the drawing room, looking very distracted.

No sooner had the coffee been handed around than she came over to Penny and whispered urgently, "Follow me out."

With a falsely bright smile for the rest of the women, she led Penny away to the lounge. Two figures rose to meet her, and Penny let out a gasp of surprise. One of them was a broadly grinning Alastair, but the other was a rather dazed-looking Gareth.

"I didn't mean to break in on your dinner party," Alastair said, almost chortling. "But I wanted you to be the first to hear the good news and to ask a favor if I may. They've let Gareth out on bail, and I was wondering if he could stay the night in the room above the garage, Miss Macdonell. He'll not be troubling you for food or anything, but I've only got a room in a boardinghouse at Lochgilphead myself, and it's a bit awkward with my landlady. So if you could give him shelter . . ."

"Does this mean they've got a line on Allen Gray?" Penny broke in eagerly.

Alastair shook his head, and his smile faded. "No. We don't quite understand it ourselves, but it is something to do with a phone call from London, at least so the lawyer says. He was so eager to get Gareth out, he didn't ask too many questions. It's a fair puzzle, isn't it, Gareth?"

"Aye, it is that," his brother agreed gloomily, and then stiffened, his eyes wide with disbelief.

From behind Penny came a little choked cry, and she turned to see Deirdre poised in the doorway, her hands clasped to her throat. She had an anguished, pleading look on her face.

"I knew . . . I know," she stammered, and then fainted dead away at Gareth's feet.

CHAPTER 18

If Penny had had any doubts remaining about the relationship between Gareth and Deirdre, they were quickly banished by the scene that followed. With an inarticulate cry, he gathered her up in his arms as tenderly as a baby. Penny got the impression that had his brother not restrained him, he would have rushed out into the night with her, never to be seen again. As it was, he was persuaded to put her down on the couch, where he remained at her side, clutching her limp hand until the heavily fringed eyelashes flickered open upon violet eyes.

"It's all right, my Deirdre," he whispered. "It's going to be all right noo. Dinna fash yourself for me."

Heather cast an agonized glance at Alastair. "It's quite all right about the garage room," she said. "But I really think you'd both better go now. It will be very awkward if the rest of them see you."

He nodded and took Gareth by the arm. "She's fine now," he said warningly. "It was just the shock. Let's get out of here. We've caused Miss Macdonell enough trouble. There'll be plenty of time for this later." He steered the unwilling Gareth out of the front door.

Heather and Penny gazed dazedly at one each other over the prone girl. "What'll we do now?" Heather asked.

"I'll stay with her, and you go back and send Alison in. You'd best stay with your guests. I can hear the men getting up from the table. Then I'll corner Hamish on the quiet and get him to take her home."

"Why on earth did they let Gareth go?" Heather said as she went out, shaking her head in disbelief.

Alison quickly appeared in her stead, her blue eyes round as saucers. "This is one for the books," she whispered. "What am I supposed to do with her?"

"Nothing. Just try to see that she doesn't go into hysterics," Penny whispered back. "I'm going to tackle Hamish now and get him to take her home. Tell her mum's the word on Gareth, but I don't think it'll be necessary."

Before she could leave, Alison laid a restraining hand on her arm. "Oh, by the way, unless Ian Macdonell is lying in his teeth, he doesn't have a dress tartan kilt; he can't stand it either. And what's the matter with Sir Tobias?"

"I've no idea."

When she returned with the reluctant Hamish, who had still been busily taking inventory of the antiques, she was relieved to see that Mrs. Mitton had joined Alison in guarding Deirdre. Feeling that Hamish could safely be left in the hands of his redoubtable mother-in-law, she went back to the party. She went over to Toby, who was standing in a corner with a demitasse in hand, looking like a discontented stork.

"Gareth's out," she hissed in his ear. "Something to do with a phone call from London. You didn't cook this up with your Craignish Castle friend, did you?"

His round blue eyes widened slightly, but his gloom remained undiminished. "No," he growled.

"What's the matter with you?" she demanded. "You've been doing fine so far; now is not the time to get in one of your moods. Obviously something big must have happened."

"I'm trying to remember something," he snapped at her. "And I can't do it with people chattering at me. Leave me alone."

"Well, really!" She flounced off in a huff.

Alison came in and gave her a little all clear sign before Penny was approached by Bennett Rose. "Has something happened to Deirdre?" he asked. A worried frown was on his face.

"Just a fainting spell," she explained. "Hamish has taken her home."

"I thought she was feeling poorly. This murder and then

the nasty business with the sheep has really got her down." It was more of a question than a statement.

"The early months of a first pregnancy are often difficult," Penny said.

He flushed. "I suppose so. I hear you're off to see the Corrievreckan."

"Oh, yes, some time before I go."

"You're leaving?" He sounded almost eager.

"No, not for a while." She looked blandly at him.

"Well, the sea should have calmed down by tomorrow. I'm hoping to get in some underwater time myself. Now that the excitement around here is over, let's hope we can all get back to normal. I saw the police launch over at Sheena today. Any idea what they were after? More evidence to put poor old Gareth on the griddle, I suppose."

"No, I understand it had nothing to do with the murder. Something about an ex-convict who is supposed to be in the area," she said, and watched his reaction; there was none.

They were joined by Margaret Macdonell, who was clasping a large snifter of brandy and who seemed a lot more animated than she had been all evening. "After the ladies again, I see, Bennett," she said archly. "Is this a private conversation, or can anyone join in?"

After a few desultory remarks about the storm, Bennett left them and joined Cranston, who was talking to Alison. Damn, Penny thought, I was only just getting going with him. She dutifully turned her attention to the bleary-eyed Margaret.

"You and Sir Tobias simply must come for tea," she was saying. "I'm afraid our home is a humble one compared to this, but our garden is at its peak right now, and if I do say so myself, it is worth seeing. I do so love to garden. Do you care for water lilies?" The odd question made Penny blink, but it had evidently been a rhetorical one, for Margaret kept right on. "Ian dammed a wee burn, you know, and we have a pond with really the most colorful water lilies. So pretty with the Japanese goldfish; they're another wee hobby of mine," she confided with another little coy smile.

"How nice. Yes, I'd love to see them. But I'm afraid Sir Tobias is going to be very busy for a while." As she watched, he put down his coffee cup and stalked out of the room in the direction of the study.

"My son will be home on leave in the next day or two," Margaret went on. "I'd like you to meet him, too. It will be so good to have him home for a while to take his father's mind off things."

With an effort, Penny brought her mind back from the wandering Toby to her companion. "He's concerned about the murder, is he?"

Mrs. Macdonell looked a little taken aback. "That too, of course, but mostly about this awful violence in Northern Ireland. You know it's a terrible thing, Dr. Spring, when a man in the prime of life has to retire. Ian has so much energy and nothing to spend it on, and he was such a good organizer. He gets very preoccupied with things." A worried frown creased her plump face. "I don't hold with violence myself. There's altogether too much of it in the modern world, and violence begets violence, I always say." She produced this cliché as if it were an original pearl of wisdom.

"Quite," Penny murmured. "Both on a national and a personal level, as witness this murder. What does he think about it?"

"Well, we were both extremely shocked, of course. But I cannot say we were too surprised. That's what you get when you try to mix classes, particularly in marriage. It never does, never! Of course, we put up with Gareth for poor Amy's sake, but he was really very trying and sometimes downright embarrassing. He was so uncouth."

"Then you think the police have the right man?"

Her pale blue eyes widened in astonishment. "Don't you?"

"I understand the police are not entirely satisfied," Penny said, equivocating. "And that they are looking for an ex-convict who is thought to be in the area."

Margaret Macdonell gasped. "An ex-convict? Good Heavens, I must tell Ian, and we must be very careful to lock up very carefully from now on. We have quite a lot of family silver, you know. Poor Heather must be absolutely terrified in this big house and with all these lovely things." Her voice was wistful as her eyes ranged around the room.

"I think he was originally from this estate," Penny said, watching her carefully. "Allen Gray?"

Her companion looked faintly puzzled. "I don't recall anyone of that name. It must have been before we moved here, but I'll ask Ian. He'll know. He knows everything there is to be known about Soruba. He has shot over every inch of it."

"He's a keen hunter, is he?" Penny asked, thinking of the deer's head.

"Oh, yes. Guns, guns, guns." The pale eyes rolled expressively. "He and Bennett are always at it. Any new gun that comes on the market, they simply have to have. You'd think they were about to start a private war. Men are such children, aren't they?"

"Chattering too much as usual, I see." Her husband had broken in. "I hope you haven't been boring Dr. Spring." He favored Penny with a hard look. "I think it's time we said our good nights, old girl. Our hostess is looking tired. Mustn't outstay our welcome. We may not be asked back."

The party began to break up. Cranston leaned over, his arm firmly encompassing Heather's thin shoulders. "Well, your trip to the Corrievreckan is all arranged," he informed Penny. "Heather is all set to lay the Macdonell curse once and for all. We'd offer to take you out ourselves, only with Bennett being so far behind, we're going to be hellishly busy. Great party, Heather. We'll all be after you now to do it again."

When the door had closed on the last of them, Heather sank into a chair. "Well, that was certainly exhausting, but they seemed to have had a good time. Was the dinner all right?"

"Oh, fine, just fine," Penny said quickly, and realized that she had been so preoccupied that she could not recollect a single thing they had eaten.

"Thank God for Constable Menzies," Heather said piously. "He marched Isobel and her sister back in very short order. I don't know what we'd have done otherwise, because Mrs. Gray had a 'fey' fit and departed for home, muttering darkly about trouble brewing."

"Did she indeed? I wonder if she picked up on Gareth getting out."

"Wasn't that a stunner? Looks as if you were right about him and Deirdre. I felt I was on the set of *Wuthering Heights*."

"And if I'm not mistaken, he's not the only one that cherishes a tender passion for our local belle. Bennett Rose's concern for her seemed way above and beyond the call of friendship."

"Which is a lot more than you can say for Hamish," Alison chimed in. "What a creep he is. I expected him to present you with a price list somewhere along the line. If Deirdre has been cheating on him, I don't blame her one bit. Still, if Bennett is dippy about her, it probably explains why I had less than my usual success with him. I sort of angled to get invited to go diving with them and got royally snubbed."

"Sir Tobias seems upset about something," Heather observed. "I hope it's nothing I did. What's become of him, by the way?"

"Oh, Toby is just suffering from an overdose of amiability. You've only seen his sweet side so far. Now we're in for a little of the sour. Nothing to worry about. I can handle him. It's best to leave him alone at the outset to come to terms with his own grumps."

"You know, for a horrible moment there, when Deirdre keeled over, I wondered if that's where my Valium had gone to," Heather said worriedly.

Penny gave a guilty start. "That reminds me. I've got to make a phone call."

"At this time of night? It's after midnight," Heather protested.

"Yes, well, there was a bit of drama earlier that in the interests of your peace of mind we kept from you. Mrs. Mitton told us just before dinner that Meg Strachan was taken off to Oban in an ambulance—a drug overdose."

"Good God, do you think . . ."

"That's what I want to find out." Penny was gone for quite a while, during which time aunt and niece went around collecting glasses, emptying ashtrays, and plumping cushions in worried silence. When she got back, her face was grim. "It was a very near thing," she announced. "But she is going to be all right. And it was Valium. Have you any idea when either of them could have gotten hold of it?"

"Both of them were at the house at separate times on the day I missed it. But to think they'd come into my room—it's almost unbelievable. What does Dennis have to say?"

"That is just what the hospital has been asking me. There is no sign of him, and she can't—or won't—say anything. They have no idea whether she took it or was given it."

"Oh, no. Then however was she found?"

"Mitton apparently. He heard their sheep dog howling up a storm and went to investigate. He let the dog into the house, and it went rushing upstairs. So he followed it, and there she was, flaked out on the bed with the bottle beside her. No sign of Dennis, then or since. I must say this has cemented a growing suspicion I've had about him."

"You mean you think he might have murdered Amy?"

"I feel that it is a very good possibility and that something has panicked him and he's on the run."

"But what?"

"Possibly the elusive Allen Gray."

"But why on earth should Dennis have wanted to murder Amy?"

Penny shrugged. "That we still have to find out. I think I'll go and find Toby. This really alters everything."

"Well, I'm all in. I'll lock up and say good night," Heather said wearily.

Toby was run to earth in the study, hunched over a book. "New developments," she announced tersely. "So if you will emerge from your melancholy fog for a minute, I'll fill you in." She told him the story quickly. "Well?" she challenged at the end.

"Well what?"

"What do you think of that? Sort of bears out what I was saying earlier, doesn't it?"

He roused himself slightly. "Could be, or from what you have told me about them, he may have just walked out on her, and she decided to end it all. She sounds the absurd sort of female who would do something ridiculous like that."

Penny restrained herself with an effort. "But you obviously have other ideas," she said sarcastically. "Would it be too much to ask that you share your great thoughts?"

"I have indeed been given much food for thought tonight."

Toby was at his most forbidding. "And I think this may be a whole lot deeper and darker than we supposed, but I am too tired to discuss it now."

"Just so long as you don't dry up on me tomorrow," she said warningly. "But I'm all in, too, so let's go to bed."

"We'd better check the doors and windows first," Toby said to her surprise.

"Heather has already locked up."

"Then we'd best recheck them just to be sure," he insisted.

"For any particular reason?"

"Yes, for a very good reason," he said calmly. "Somebody has been standing in the rhododendron bushes at the head of the drive for the past two hours. I could see the glow of the cigarettes he or she has been smoking. Somebody is watching the house."

CHAPTER 19

Penny overslept and awoke to a brilliantly sunny day and a cloudless azure sky. She went down to breakfast to find Toby presiding in solitary glory and contemplating the honey pot with deep gloom.

"I hate liars," he announced by way of greeting.

"Oh?" she said, and waited for more.

"And Bennett Rose is the most barefaced liar I have encountered in a long time. And I don't see the sense of it."

"Oh?" she repeated.

"I must get to a decent library, but my memory is usually trustworthy, so I am certain I am right."

"Quite. May I ask about what?"

"The moment I laid eyes on him, his face rang a bell," he continued, ignoring her question. "It took a lot of digging for, but finally I came up with it and tackled him. Strangely enough, it was about a Spanish treasure ship."

"Not that again. I thought you said you'd eliminated that as a possibility."

"I did. Would you kindly let me finish?"

"By all means." She buttered a Scotch pancake and poured herself some coffee.

"Do you remember the finding of the Spanish treasure ship *Concepción* in the Caribbean during the 1970s? Well, this whetted the appetite of treasure seekers, who then went after others of the Spanish fleet scattered in the same storm. There was one treasure galleon located just off of Key West; a Miami salvage outfit got the rights to it. But somebody else had gone in ahead of them and cleaned out the wreck. Suspicion fell on a smaller salvage operation that was in the vicinity. They were suspected of some long-distance underwater looting. There was even a court case about it, but nothing was ever proved. Now, I am certain Bennett Rose was the principal diver for the smaller outfit, but Rose was not the name he used then."

"Well?"

"He claims never to have been in the Caribbean; never was connected with a treasure operation. Yet I know I'm right," Toby boomed.

The door opened, and Alison's head popped in. "Ah, Sir Tobias. Lord Corcoran from Craignish Castle on the phone for you. Urgent!"

"At last," he exclaimed, springing after her and leaving Penny to glare gloomily at the honey pot.

She could not make any sense of this news. She was not left alone for long before Heather came in, looking very upset. She slumped into a chair and poured herself a cup of coffee with a shaky hand.

"What a lousy start to a beautiful day," she groaned. "I've just had to throw out our overnight guest."

"Gareth. But why?" Penny exclaimed.

"I haven't the faintest idea. Constable Menzies was here when I got up this morning, all secretive and urgent. Would I please ask Gareth to leave. Of course I said no. Why should I? Still all secretive and urgent, he said that the police were very anxious for Gareth to return to Sheena Castle and that he wasn't likely to if I let him stay on here. I protested how awful that would be for him, what with all the servants there being so ghastly about him, but Menzies said that was all taken care of, because the servants had all been taken off yesterday by the police launch. The only one left is an old gardener as a sort of caretaker. I asked him what the police were after, and he said that he didn't know himself but that it was very urgent and would I cooperate."

"Did you?"

Heather nodded miserably. "I made him come with me, and luckily Alastair was already there, so that helped. They were very nice about it, said they understood my position, but I feel just awful. Alison is simply furious with me and is off to the island with them. I don't know if she intends to come back or not."

"They are going there, then?"

"Oh, yes. Constable Menzies managed that very smoothly. He offered to take them across, even had some supplies for them. Isn't it all odd?"

"Yes, very strange. I was going to ask you if you would run us over there yourself this morning, not to the castle but to that little shack I was telling you about yesterday. I found out something about Amy last night that might alter things considerably, but I want to test it out right there on the spot."

"What about Amy?"

"She could lip-read. Did you know she was deaf?" Penny asked.

Heather shook her head in astonishment. "I had no idea, none at all."

"Let's get Toby, then. We'll need his binoculars," Penny said, rising. "I'd like to leave right now."

They had to settle for the binoculars without their owner. They were informed by Mrs. Mitton, who seemed to be gripped by some intense inner excitement, that after his phone conversation Sir Tobias had departed immediately for Craignish Castle.

"In the mood he's in, probably just as well," Penny said, and went to hunt for the glasses.

Their arrival at the jetty coincided with the return of Constable Menzies in the Soruba launch. "If ye're going out, Miss Macdonell, have a care," he counseled. "There's still an awful great swell out there from the tempest; it's not a sea to take chances with."

"We're only going to take a look at Sheena," Penny informed him. "And would you do something for me? Do you have any transport here?"

"Aye, I have my bike up at the house," he said cautiously.

"Then would you cycle down to the chapel, and when you get there, talk to yourself?" He looked startled, and so she explained further. "I want to see how much we can make out on the mainland from that little shack."

"And what would you be wanting me to say?" he asked.

"Anything you like. Just move your lips. We'll wave a handkerchief at you when we're ready."

"Oh, all right."

As they moved out into the heavy swell, they saw Cranston's big white powerboat approaching slowly. He leaned over the rail of the wheelhouse and shouted down in a worried voice, "You're not going to try for the whirlpool today, are you, Heather? This sea is far too high."

"Not to worry," she called back. "I'm just taking Penny for a spin around Sheena. If the sea goes down, maybe we'll take a crack tomorrow."

"Oh, fine. Have you heard the big news? The police have let Gareth McClintock go."

"Really? How amazing," she called back innocently as they passed. "Where did you hear that?"

"Ian told me. It's all over Ardnan. The constable . . ." his voice floated faintly back to them.

"Well, that blows another theory," Penny said when they were out of earshot. "I thought they wanted Gareth over on the island to keep his presence under cover, but evidently the police want it known that he's out. I wonder why."

"Could it be that they want to lure Allen Gray out of hiding?" Heather suggested nervously.

"That's an uncomfortable thought: Gareth as a possible target."

"I do hope Alison doesn't stay over there," Heather said, fretting. "Oh dear, what will her mother say?"

"Could you land us out of sight somewhere?" Penny asked. "I don't particularly want Cranston to see what we're up to."

"Yes, there's a little cove just around the end of the island. We can put in there, but you'll have to wade in. There's no jetty, but the water's quite warm."

"I don't mind getting wet in the interests of science," Penny said. When they had anchored, she rolled up her slacks and slid into two feet of water with surprising agility. "Ugh," she exclaimed. "This bottom is all muddy and slimy."

"Yes, there's a terrific silt problem all around here. Something to do with water drainage from all these streams; we even have to have our little jetty dredged from time to time."

They made their way cautiously to the little weather-beaten shack at the southern tip of the island, where the big double doors stood ajar. It was musty inside, trapped flies buzzed futilely around the window, curiously trying to escape. Only the chair remained as mute testimony of its former occupant.

Penny sat down and focused Toby's powerful binoculars. "Ah, there's Menzies on his bike. He's almost at the chapel. Go out behind the shack and give him a wave, will you, Heather?"

It was evident from his actions as he reached the chapel that he had spotted their signal, but fiddle with the binoculars as she might, she could not make out his face in enough detail to spot lip movements.

"All right, you can give him the all clear signal, Heather," she called out resignedly. "This one's a no-go and yet another theory down the drain. Amy could have seen who went there, but she never could have made out what they said."

After a minute or so, the constable remounted his bike and pedaled slowly back towards Soruba. She swept the seemingly deserted mansion, saw that the ivy-clad south tower was clearly visible, and then looked over at the farm cottages, which appeared startlingly close but equally devoid of life.

Heather rejoined her. "Anything?"

"Not yet. Wait a minute—well, I'm damned," Penny exclaimed. "Will you look at that, down on the south side of the jetty." She handed the glasses to Heather.

"Why, it's Mrs. Mitton with Sir Tobias. And is that Hamish, too?"

"No, I thought so at first, but it's someone tall and dark like him, but older."

"Could it be Lord Corcoran?"

"I don't think so. He's older than Toby, and this man looks to be in his mid-thirties." Penny took the glasses back and watched as the two tall figures fell in on either side of Mrs. Mitton and moved slowly off in the direction of the Laird's Walk. "I've no idea who it could be. However, you can distinctly see their lip movements from here; I wish now that I could lip-read."

She continued her survey, and Cranston's boat suddenly sprang into sharp focus. They had just dropped anchor, and

Cranston could be seen leaning upon a large packing case on the deck and talking gravely to Bennett, who was in his wet suit and buckling on his aqualung. She studied them intently for a time.

"Well, if that's their usual parking spot, it would not have given Amy any problem at all," she said at length. "Even I could make out some of the things Cranston said, to wit, 'bloody nuisance' and 'fix it.' "

She watched Constable Menzies pedal back down the track toward the Lochgilphead road. "Menzies is certainly hanging around," she observed. "I wonder if he's keeping his eye on someone."

Heather was getting a little restless. "I think it's because he finds all this a lot more exciting than sitting around Ardnan waiting for some tourist to drop litter in a public place, which is about the gamut of his usual activities. Have you seen enough?"

"Yes, I suppose so." Penny reluctantly put down the glasses. "Maybe we should get back and see if we can nab Toby and the tall stranger."

They chugged out on the bay again, and Heather set the boat into a wide sweep, bringing them in underneath the small headland on which the chapel was perched. Then they followed the shoreline back toward the jetty. It was scattered with huge mounds of leathery sea kelp that had been torn from the sea bed by the storm and was now rotting under the warm sun, to the delight of a buzzing horde of insects.

"Faugh," Heather exclaimed as they passed one particularly noisome area. "It's like living next to a sewage plant. I really must get to Mitton and see if there's anything to be done with it. I'm sure it can't be healthy."

"Short of carting the whole lot inland and burning it, I can't think what," Penny said mildly. "And it would be a regular Augean stable enterprise, never-ending and expensive."

"I must do something," Heather said stubbornly. When they had docked, she marched firmly up to the Mitton cottage and banged on the door. Mitton emerged in his shirt-sleeves, looking surprised.

"She's up at the house," he announced.

"I was looking for you, not Mrs. Mitton," Heather said.

"We simply must do something about all this rotting sea-weed. There's an area quite close to here which is simply atrocious, and for your own health's sake, I think you should clear it out. Would you come, and I'll show you where?"

He hesitated. "I'll just get my jacket." As he stepped back inside, they could hear a low murmur of voices from within, one of them female. He reappeared, shrugging into his coat.

"Deirdre with you?" Penny hazarded.

"Aye," he said shortly. "After last night's upset and with Hamish off again, her mother thought it best."

Heather led the way back along the shore. "It's just around this bend," she said. "One of the deep rock pools, I suppose." They passed several smaller ones where the seaweed had rotted into a fetid pink froth that emitted a cloying stench. "The one I'm talking about is much worse than this," Heather muttered grimly as she mounted a small rise. Here the stench was overwhelmingly noxious. "Down there." She pointed and then froze. "Oh my *God*." Her hand trembled and dropped.

Penny, coming up behind her, looked over her shoulder and at first could see nothing in the big rock pool that was piled high with the detritus of the storm. Then she saw it: first a boot, then the unmistakable outline of a human leg. Heather turned and clutched at her blindly.

"Dennis?" she choked out.

"Ye'll stay here," Mitton ordered in a thick voice. "I'll go and see."

He waded down into the rock pool and bent over the body beneath the seaweed; his broad back blocked their view. After a few seconds, he straightened up and came back to them, his dark face now a grayish white. "It's not Strachan," he announced.

"Then who is it?" Penny asked, her arms around her shivering friend.

His eyes met hers with an unfathomable look. "It's Allen Gray," he muttered. "And by the looks of him, he's been dead for some time. You ladies best get back to Soruba. I'll go for the police."

But the police had come to them. A voice hailed them from above, and they looked up at the red face of Constable

Menzies grinning down at them from the road above. He was accompanied by another policeman.

"Could I trouble you to come up, Miss Macdonell, and have a word with the inspector here?" he called.

Penny was the first to get her voice back. "You'd better come down here," she shouted. "We've just found Allen Gray—dead." She pointed downward.

The inspector let out an exclamation and came plunging down the slope toward them, with an angry expression on his face. As she watched him, the thought uppermost in her mind was that their main hope for a fast solution to the case had just vanished, that the secret only Allen Gray had known now lay buried forever under a pile of rotting seaweed.

CHAPTER 20

"He is without doubt one of the most aggravating men alive, and one of these days I'm sure I'm going to do him in out of sheer exasperation," Penny said, glaring at a note written in Toby's small, neat hand. "To go off now of all times, when things are breaking so fast."

"What exactly does he say?" Heather was still looking sick and wretched from their harrowing experience at the beach. Penny handed her the note.

A matter of some importance has come up, requiring my presence at Craignish Castle for a few days. Please make my excuses and apologies for this sudden departure to Miss Macdonell (Heather). As Corky and I will be out a great deal of the time, you may not be able to reach me directly; however, messages may be safely left with the butler. I shall be in touch with you as soon as it is feasible.

Toby.

They had returned to find him gone, bag and baggage. Mrs. Mitton was gripped by the same inner excitement Penny had noticed in the police inspector and was stubbornly mute about what had transpired at Soruba that morning.

"I have been asked by the authorities not to say anything, so kindly do not ask me," she had said definitively, and there had been no budging her.

"Messages may be safely left with the butler, indeed," Penny snorted. "I've just talked to him on the phone, and he sounds as if he swallowed a poker. A butler, in this day and age. Honestly, this area is so out of this world that I wouldn't be a bit surprised to see a dinosaur wandering down the drive. But two can play at that game. I told him that Allen Gray had been found dead, period. If Toby wants details, he can damn well phone me for them.''

"What could it all be about?" Heather asked.

"Well, I don't need a crystal ball to know that this Craignish Castle business has something to do with that plane Mrs. Mitton saw go down in the bay. But what the hell can be so important about a World War II crash that no one did anything about at the time?"

"What plane?" Heather said blankly, and Penny had to repeat the meager recollections of the young Moira McDougall.

"Do you suppose that is what Cranston and Bennett are after out there?" Heather suggested.

"Certainly in the light of all this other interest, their presence out there is beginning to look fishy, but then, what doesn't?" Penny sighed. "Did you hear the inspector down at the beach? An immediate autopsy ordered and no press release allowed on the body. I thought for a while he was going to take us all into protective custody to keep our mouths shut. And all this because of what, in other circumstances, we'd have taken for a simple drowning in the storm."

"It was odd about those coins, though," Heather murmured.

"Yes, at least it seems to have cleared up one of our minor mysteries, even if it has augmented the major ones."

The body had been clothed only in a shirt and trousers, but in the pocket of the trousers had been three coins: two American quarters and a queer bronze coin with a hole in the middle, which Penny had identified as of west African origin. It seemed in all likelihood that this was what remained from Allen Gray's looting of the Wishing Well.

"I hope Constable Menzies doesn't dry up on us now that Toby has taken off," Penny went on gloomily. "I took him aside at the beach and asked, as a great favor to Toby and me, that he let us know the results of the autopsy as soon as it came in. He promised he would but said that they wouldn't have the preliminary results before this evening and that it may be several days before they have a full report. More bloody waiting. It's enough to drive one frantic. Did you ever find out what the inspector wanted a word with you about?''

Heather frowned. "Yes, again extremely odd. It was to ask me to tell Mitton not to do any shooting on the estate in the next few days, and if he saw any strangers around not to chase them off or even draw attention to them in any way. He also wanted to ask if they could station a policeman up in the tower room of the south wing.''

"And he still wants to do this, even though they've found Allen Gray?'' Penny asked.

"Yes. I'm so confused and worried, I'd give anything to get out of here for a while.''

"Then why don't we take a run into Oban?'' Penny said briskly. "I'd like to see at first hand how Meg Strachan is doing, and maybe she'll talk to us. I'd certainly like to know where Dennis has gone and what the hell that was all about.''

"All right. I'd better let Mrs. Mitton know we won't be here for lunch and to leave a cold dinner for us tonight,'' Heather said, and went off to put her house in order.

Just after they turned on to the Lochgilphead road, they met Hamish's car coming from the direction of Oban. He gave no sign of having seen them, and Penny, watching out of the back window, saw him opening the gate into the estate road. "Looks as if he's going to collect Deirdre,'' she observed. "I wonder if he knows about Gareth and if the balloon has gone up there yet.''

"I feel so bad about Mrs. Gray,'' said Heather. "Thank heavens, she didn't come in today. I don't think I could have faced her, knowing about her son and not being able to tell, I mean. What is happening around here? It seems as if the whole place has gone mad since Amy's death.''

They had a slight hassle at the hospital about getting in to see Meg Strachan. Penny was again impressed by the acute class consciousness of the area, when the deciding factor in their favor was Heather's revelation that she was "the Macdonell.'' At once doors opened, and they were directed to the small private room in which Meg lay.

A nurse escorted them in and said briskly, "You have visitors, Mrs. Strachan. Not more than fifteen minutes, mind.''

A small, sandy-haired man who had been sitting by the bed

in the room's sole chair stood up protectively in front of the bed, looking at them under beetling brows. "She no' wants to be bothered by any visitors," he announced in a creaking voice.

"It's all right, Father," a faint voice said from the bed. "It's the laird herself. I don't mind talking to her."

Heather approached the bed, awkwardly clutching the flowers and fruit she had picked up in town. She smiled nervously at the gaunt-faced woman in the bed. Meg's eyes were not on her but on Penny.

"If you don't mind," the faint voice said pointedly, "I'd like to talk to Miss Macdonell alone."

Penny had no choice but to leave.

"Did she say anything?" the nurse hovering at the door asked eagerly.

"About what?" Penny snapped, feeling more than a little put out.

"About the overdose. Nobody has been able to get a word out of her, not even the doctor. The police have asked us to keep a close eye on her."

"How is she? Is she going to be all right?"

"Och, she's out of danger, but she'll not be feeling any too frisky for a spell." The nurse looked at her expectantly, but seeing that Penny was not about to be chatty, she moved away reluctantly.

Left to her own devices, Penny paced up and down the sterile corridor, until the door finally opened and Heather emerged, looking even more shaken. "Well? Any luck?"

Heather made a little shushing motion as the nurse reappeared. "I'll tell you outside," she muttered, and scurried out.

In the hospital's parking lot, she leaned against the Mini. "Well, it looks as if I've got the home farm back on my hands. Dennis has taken off; he's cleared out, left her. And they are flat broke. That's what she wanted to talk to me about. I was right about the ring; she gave it to him to sell to cover this quarter's rent, and instead he has apparently taken the money and skipped."

"Has she any idea where?"

"No, not an inkling. He must have planned his getaway

carefully. She went into Kilmelfort to do some shopping in their pickup, and when she got back, he was gone and so were all his belongings. No note, no explanation, nothing.''

"How did he get away, then, if she had the car?"

Heather shrugged. "I've no idea, unless someone picked him up."

"So it was attempted suicide?"

"She wouldn't say, and I didn't have the heart to press the point. She was so upset not being able to pay me. She kept going on about taking the cattle for the payment, as if I cared about that!"

"But she's going to have to say something sooner or later to the police. Suicide is a crime, you know. They won't let her go until it's cleared up."

"Her father strikes me as a shrewd old bird. He kept talking firmly about 'the accident,' and I think that is the story she is going to stick to. As soon as she's well enough, he told me he is going to take her back home to the Lowlands. Her mother's dead, so I imagine he'll be glad enough to get her back. All he said about Dennis was that he'll get what's coming to him."

"Did she say anything about the Valium?"

"No, and it would be impossible to prove. She was on it herself, 'for her nerves,' she said, and the only bottle they found by the bedside was her prescription."

"So we're not one bloody bit further along," Penny said disconsolately. "Honestly, I'm beginning to feel I'm losing my grip. There is no way I can see to track Dennis down."

"I suppose the police could look for him?"

"On what grounds? It's no crime to skip out on your wife. And all the rest of our suspicions about him are just that, suspicions. We haven't an atom of proof that the police would even look at for a second. Look, let's go and have something to eat; maybe that'll cheer me up. God knows, when my own partner walks out without even a fare-thee-well or an explanation, it's no wonder I'm not making any progress."

At that moment, in the magnificent setting of the hall of Craignish Castle, Toby's deep voice was sending thunderous echoes off its stone walls. "I really must insist that my colleague be informed of this. I have laid out the case for you as I see it, but most of the actual findings are to her credit. She has a right to know."

The suave young man who stood before him was in no way perturbed by his thunderous plea. "I'm sorry, Sir Tobias, but it is out of the question. In a situation like this, which is as sensitive to her own nation as it is to ours and is also in the interests of national security, I'm afraid I cannot allow any information to go beyond these four walls. We are hoping for a speedy resolution, but this may take days or even weeks. Since you know all there is to know now, I'm afraid I shall have to insist that you stay here, incommunicado. It is not as if she were in the least danger, and in any case, the police will be right there. And if you are thinking of appealing to Lord Corcoran, you may as well save your breath. He is bound to tell you the same thing."

Toby, stalking out in a fine Celtic fury, did precisely that and was told the same thing by the discomfited peer. "Then I insist on taking part in the watch," he growled menacingly.

"That I am sure can be arranged," his intimidated friend said soothingly, and with that Toby had to be content.

After a meal that calmed Penny somewhat, she and Heather went off to the movies to distract themselves. It was fairly late by the time they headed home along the coast road, where the twilight was fast gathering. To Penny's stretched-out nerves there seemed to be an air of brooding menace over the desolate landscape as they turned into the estate gate and bumped up the now-familiar track. She felt as if unseen eyes were upon her, although she could see no sign of the silent watchers. It was with a sense of relief that she spotted the round yellow light of the constable's bicycle wobbling toward them down the hill from the main gate as they drew up before the house.

"Here's Menzies," she exclaimed. "Let's hope he has something good for us."

They waited outside the house in silence, with only the tinkle of the burn below intruding upon their temporary peace. Menzies's bicycle swung into the drive as he peddled toward them; suppressed excitement was writ large on his round red face.

He swung in beside them and dismounted. "Och, it's guid

to find you ladies outside. I dinna want to say what I have to say inside the house, ye ken. Forby I shouldn't be telling you at all."

"You have the results of the autopsy?" Penny asked breathlessly. "What were they?"

"Allen Gray was drowned and so full of whisky he was well nigh pickled," he said, his little eyes dancing with excitement.

"Oh." Her voice went flat with disappointment. "Then it was just an accident of the storm, after all."

"Wait up." He was too excited to be polite. "I didna say he was drowned in the sea now, did I? The autopsy was verra, verra interesting. Drowned he was, but in *fresh* water, and in verra, verra special fresh water at that. In his lungs were found ant eggs, the kind they feed to goldfish, ye ken? And in his lungs also were found fragments of water lily weeds. And there's but one place around here you find yon."

Penny looked at him. "You mean . . ."

"Aye, I do that. It seems Mr. Ian Macdonell is going to have a lot of explaining to do, a lot. And they canna pin this on Gareth, neither. Allen Gray had been dead, the doctor says, before that storm ever struck. Dead he was when he went into the bay, but then the storm gave him back. Even the heavens and the sea are against this murderer, so we'll get him for sure."

CHAPTER 21

"Naturally I'm glad it gets Gareth out of immediate jeopardy, but I'm not very satisfied in my own mind that Ian Macdonell is the right man, either," Penny stated. "Granted his fish-pond was used to murder Allen Gray, it's still a long way from proving that Ian killed him or that he was involved in the other murder. There are too many factors pointing away from that."

It was the next morning. Her audience in the lounge of Soruba consisted of Heather; Alison, who, much to her aunt's relief, had returned the night before; and Alastair McClintock, who had unexpectedly been recalled to duty, thereby indicating that the police had definitely changed their minds about Gareth.

The young couple were sitting hand in hand and were evidently far more interested in each other than in her theorizing. Alastair roused himself sufficiently to say, "Well, the police do seem to be on the track of a gunrunning operation Ian was involved in. That would have made a good blackmail motive for Gray, because even if Macdonell didn't have any money, presumably the men behind him did. Also, he's by far the most likely person to have wanted Heather out of here and so would have mounted the war of nerves that has been going on."

"Then why kill Amy?" Penny demanded. "And in such a curiously unskillful manner?"

"Perhaps she tumbled to him, saw something from that observation post of hers," Alastair suggested.

"I must say I agree with Penny, just on general grounds.

Ian strikes me as mostly hot air and bluster. I don't think he'd have either the guts or the brains to plan all this," Alison insisted.

"What does Sir Tobias think?" Heather asked hastily, hoping to avert another spat.

Penny looked vexed. "I have no idea. I talked with an unidentified someone at the castle again last night, but I could not contact Toby or Lord Corcoran. I'm fed up to the teeth with him!"

"Well, not to worry, Dr. Spring," Alastair said, "I have to go to work now, but perhaps I can be the bearer of glad tidings when I drop in tonight on the way back to the island. In the meantime, why don't you all relax and take it easy until I see what has developed."

But Penny was in no mood to relax. Impatience boiled within her, and she fumed and fretted around the house to such degree that Heather finally said, "Why don't we all take a run out to the Corrievreckan? It'll use up the morning, and then if you still have had no message from Sir Tobias, maybe we can drive over to Craignish and see what is going on."

"Count me out," Alison said promptly. "I simply must write home, and I've got all sorts of forms to fill out for Edinburgh University."

Her aunt looked pleased. "You've decided to transfer, then?"

Alison went a little pink. "Yes, I have."

"Oh, I'm so glad, particularly if it means you'll be spending your vacations here."

"You can count on it," Alison said with a twinkle.

Penny was peering with deep suspicion out of the window. "What about the weather?" The skies had had another change of mood and were pearly gray, while a light mist lay on the calm waters.

"Oh, I think it will be fine." Heather joined her at the window. "There's no storm forecast, and if we go now, the tide will be all right. It's low at the moment, and it won't turn until after midday. It's very calm. Listen!"

It was true; the sound of the great whirlpool was only a sullen murmur.

"Okay, then," Penny said as she went off in search of jacket, binoculars, and camera.

On the way down to the jetty, they passed the Cameron car with Hamish at the wheel, driving at a furious pace, an expression of thunderous anger on his face.

"I wonder if we shouldn't pop in and see Deirdre," Penny said, her interest reviving. "It looks as if the balloon may have gone up there."

"Let's not," Heather said quickly. "I feel I've had all the complications I can stand for the moment. We'll do it on the way back if you still want to. I just feel like putting all this behind me for a while."

They cast off and chugged out onto the oily swell of the bay. Their momentum created a slight breeze that set the light mist swirling and tugged at their hair with gentle fingers.

Looking landward, Penny saw that Jamey Mitton had emerged from his cottage and was on his way to the jetty; he was staring fixedly after them. On the Lochgilphead side of the bay, she saw Cranston's boat just pulling away from its mooring. She trained her glasses on Sheena, but there was no sign of movement either at the castle or down at the jetty, where the castle's powerboat was secured. Whatever went on at the Mittons didn't involve Gareth, she thought with a small twinge of satisfaction. I hope he stays put on the island and out of trouble.

As they chugged past the point on which the boathouse sat, she again sensed the unseen eyes and wondered whether the police had taken over Sheena to the same extent they had Soruba. Why? she asked herself as the islands of Jura and Scarba became more sharply defined and they headed toward the narrow strait that separated them. Who were they watching?

Emerging from her reverie, she sniffed the air and said, "There's an awfully strong smell of gas, Heather. Is that normal?"

"Yes, I noticed that, too." Heather's concentration was fixed firmly on the compass. "I think this mist must be keeping the exhaust fumes around us. There's usually more of a wind. Here, would you take the wheel for a minute and keep on that heading while I make sure that the exhaust isn't fouled in any way." She slipped out of the seat and headed for the stern of the boat as Penny gingerly took the wheel. Heather shrieked and then laughed shakily. "Penny, look off to your left. It gave me quite a shock."

Sticking out of the water were the bristling moustache and grave, innocent eyes of a harbor seal, who was inspecting them solemnly. Suddenly the water around him was dotted with other sleek heads.

"Why, it's a whole school, or whatever it's called, of seals," Heather exclaimed delightedly. "Let's circle about and see what they do. I'll take some pictures."

Penny took the boat around in a circle, and the seals, entering into the spirit, followed them; some of them dove under and popped up ahead of the boat, and then dove back to rejoin their companions. After about ten minutes, they tired of the game and then, as if on a signal, disappeared at once with graceful flicks of their flippers.

"I got some good pictures. That was fun, but we better get back on course now, I suppose," Heather said, putting down the camera.

"Was there anything in the exhaust? The smell is still strong."

"No, it seems to be okay," Heather said a shade uneasily as she took back command. "We should be coming into the tidal pattern of the whirlpool soon. If you look dead ahead, you'll see a kind of swirl on the surface, and there's a funny optical effect that goes with it. I'm going to bear off toward Jura in a minute. The center of the Corrievreckan lies directly ahead, and we'll skirt around it—I don't dare go too near— and then we'll come around the other side of it and come back in by Scarba."

Penny gazed obediently ahead. After a circular current had become visible on the surface, the whole ocean seemed to dip slightly, sliding away to an unseen vortex; it was a curiously vertiginous sensation. "Yes, that's really something," she began, when suddenly the engine coughed a warning, spluttered, and died.

Heather let out an exclamation and started to fiddle feverishly with the starter and choke, but nothing happened.

"Any idea what it can be?" Penny asked nervously.

"Not a one."

"Could we be out of gas?"

"No, I checked before we left; the gauge read full." Heather's voice was sharp with anxiety.

"How do you check it?"

Heather pointed to a metal cap in the side toward the stern. "There's the tank." She produced a long steel rod. "And here's the gauge."

Penny unscrewed the cap and plunged the measure down until it scraped metal. She withdrew it and examined it closely. "It appears to be empty," she said in a carefully controlled voice.

"What? Impossible." Heather repeated the process. "You're right," she said in a shaky voice. "I don't understand it. Maybe we've sprung a leak in the gas tank. No matter, I always carry a spare can. We'll use that and head for home pronto."

She reached into the storage compartment in the bow, where a red can was visible. "Ah, here we are," she said in relief, and removed it. "Oh, God, it's empty," she whispered.

"So we're without power," Penny said grimly. "Well, thank heavens the tide hasn't turned yet. You carry a rescue kit, don't you? We'd better send up a distress flare, fast!"

"Of course!" Heather groped in the storage compartment and pulled out an oilskin packet. "Here they are." But as she opened it, she fell silent. The flares sat in a neat row, but every single one of them had been emptied; all that remained was the hollow tube. "Oh, my God, it's happening again—the curse."

"Curse, nothing," Penny snapped. "It's sabotage as clear as daylight. We've been set up. This is one trip we weren't meant to come back from. This is no time to make like the Lady of Shallot. I need a screwdriver and a can of oil or grease, anything flammable."

"Screwdriver?" Heather echoed feebly, and then dazedly pulled herself together. "Yes, right here."

"Well, at least the murderous Mr. X left us something," Penny said, getting to work. "This wooden grille we're standing on comes off, by the looks of it. We'll stay with the boat as long as it's feasible, but if necessary, we can bale out with the grille and take our chances in the water. We've got flotation jackets, and with the grille we'd have a fighting chance of swimming for it.''

"But the whirlpool!"

"Remember the survivor from the wreck? If he could make it to Jura in a storm, we have an even better chance in flat calm. But in the meantime, while I work on this grille, you get together every rag you can find. We'll contribute our clothes, too, if necessary,and douse them in any oil that's around. We can't signal, but we can light a fire. Someone should see that on the islands and investigate.''

"But we'll set the boat on fire," Heather protested.

"What odds? If we stay with it, we'll just go faster. It's the principle of the bottle and the cork. The boat is the bottle that will be swept more quickly into the centrifugal force of the whirlpool, and we are the corks that can keep out of it longer.''

They worked in desperate silence, and Penny, glancing over the side, saw that they were being swept in a circular clockwise pattern and that their speed was beginning to increase.

"I've found all there is, including a bottle of lighter fluid and a can of oil, but I don't know what good it's going to do us. Look ahead." There was a note of helplessness in Heather's voice.

A bank of fog was curling toward them through the strait. "Holy hell," Penny swore. "We could have done without that, but let's get the fire lighted anyway." There was another delay while they searched frantically for something to light it with. "I knew I should never have given up smoking," Penny said bitterly as she delved feverishly through her tote bag. "But I usually carry some for Toby."

At the very bottom, she found a crumpled matchbook with six or seven paper matches remaining, and she sacrificed a notebook and her address book to add some paper to the small pile of greasy rags and bits of rope Heather had assembled. Even so, it took five of the precious matches to coax the paper into a blaze. By that time the sea fog was upon them and had swallowed them in its gray maw. After the brief blaze produced by the paper, the rags caught but then settled into a sullen smoky smolder, which sent a column of darker gray into the fog.

"A fat lot of good that'll do," Heather said bitterly. "God, why did I ever leave New York?"

"We can still see Jura," Penny said, trying to be encouraging. "As soon as we're swept a bit closer, I think we should abandon ship and make a try for it."

"Okay, but in case we don't make it—well, I'm very sorry to have gotten you into this," Heather said bleakly.

Silence fell, and to their straining ears the sinister murmur of the whirlpool seemed appreciably louder.

Then Penny exclaimed, "Listen, I think I hear an engine." In counterpoint to the whirlpool's growing voice came a deeper, duller note. "Yes," she commanded. "Yell as loud as you can."

They shouted themselves hoarse for a few minutes, until a deep-voiced shout answered them, and the dim shape of another small powerboat appeared out of the mist. It slid quietly alongside them, and the figure at the wheel took on definition. It was Gareth McClintock.

He grappled the boats expertly together and cut his own engine. "Lively noo, ladies, we've no time to waste. They're right behind me," he said as he helped Penny on board and held out his hand to Heather.

She shrank away from him. "What is he doing here? How did he find us?" Her voice held a note of hysteria. "How do we know he isn't the one?"

"Och, woman, there's no time for craziness. I'm not a murderer. Them that fixed your boat are right behind me. Get aboard, I tell ye!"

"Come on, Heather, he's right, I can hear another boat," Penny shouted. "Get aboard like he says."

He grabbed at Heather's slight figure, dumped her unceremoniously into the cockpit, and with desperate speed unhitched the grapple and restarted the engine. But even as he did so, a powerful yellow beam shot through the mist, swept over and past them, and then quickly settled back upon them.

"Cut your engine, you young fool." A muffled voice came out of the fog. "There's a gun aimed at your back, and in the next five seconds you could be dead."

Gareth shrugged helplessly and cut the motor. "Keep your

wits aboot ye,'' he whispered. "We may still get out of this."

A large white prow loomed out of the fog. "Cranston, is that you?" Heather called hopefully. "Oh, thank God you've found us in time."

A grim laugh answered her, and the outline of his burly figure could be seen at the rail. Out of the corner of her eye Penny saw Gareth quietly pick up a large wrench.

"Now that young idiot has poked his nose in, we'll have to take care of him, too. No matter, the whirlpool can accommodate three just as well as two. Maybe it'll clear it all up. You should have heeded our warnings, because now I'm afraid we'll have to give the curse of the Macdonells a helping hand again."

"Shall I shoot them or put one in his gas tank?" Bennett asked.

"Neither. With the luck we've been having, we don't want any bodies washed up with bullet holes in them. You can see by the current that they're almost at the point of no return now. We'll ram the boat, cut it in half, and let nature take its course. Then we'll get out of here fast." Cranston laughed again grimly. "Just as well we checked. I've no idea why they're not in the middle of it already."

Penny saw Gareth's hand tighten around the wrench. "When I let go," he whispered, "ye're to hit the deck fast and pull the Macdonell doon with ye. Right?"

She nodded imperceptibly. With a sudden wild cry, he hurled the wrench. There was a crash of glass, and the light went out. Penny hit the deck and pulled Heather down with her as Gareth tripped the engine back to life. There was a startled oath from the figure above them, who disappeared from the rail, and then a cry of "Shoot, damn you, shoot the engine, while I ram them," from Cranston.

As Gareth revved the engine and started to cut across the bow of the larger boat, Penny could hear the splat and hiss of bullets hitting the water. Chips flew through the fog as the bullets ricocheted off the hull.

Suddenly another voice boomed out over a loudspeaker: "Phillips, Rose. This is the police. Cease fire and kill your engines. We are armed, and you cannot get away. A navy cutter is coming up on your stern and will put a shot into you if you do not comply with this order.''

The chatter of the gun died as two powerful searchlights outlined the white boat. After a coughing roar of defiance, its engines fell silent.

Penny crept over to Gareth, who was slumped against the wheel, blood streaming down his left arm. "Help," she cried. "Help us down here. Someone's been shot."

A gray shape slid out of the mist, and she looked up to see a familiar head peering over the side. "Hallo, down there. Are you all right?" Toby called.

"Oh, it's you, and about time, too! Of course I'm all right. So's Heather," she snapped. "But Gareth isn't. He's shot and bleeding all over the place."

"A police paramedic will be right with you," he boomed. "Congratulations on solving the case, but do you always have to be so dramatic about it? What pickles you do get yourself into, to be sure. It's getting so I can't leave you alone for a moment."

"You—you—oh, I give up," she spluttered, and started to laugh helplessly.

CHAPTER 22

"One moment Heather and I are alone on a wide, wide sea and tottering on the verge of the maelstrom, and the next this place is as busy as Times Square: naval pinnaces and police boats, not to mention one boatload of murderers and a local hero. What the devil was it all about?" Penny was leaning over the railing of Cranston's boat, watching with intense satisfaction as the handcuffed duo were led on to the naval pinnace under heavy police guard. The police launch bearing the injured Gareth had already sped off into the mist toward the jetty on the main road, where an ambulance had been summoned by radio.

"It's a very long story, but I can give you the crux of it in one word: plutonium," Toby said.

"Really, Sir Tobias, I must protest. You cannot breach security in this manner." The young man who was hovering at his elbow like an agitated harbinger of doom was no longer urbane.

Toby wheeled on him. "Sir," he roared. "This country is still a democracy—though, by God, sometimes I have my doubts on that score—and I will not be muzzled. These ladies, at risk of their very lives, have cleared up the case in a manner which will allow you to cover up the real truth of the matter and maintain your damned security. They have a right to know. In the long run, as laird of Soruba, Miss Macdonell will have to know, anyway, if the plans Lord Corcoran has related to me are to be implemented. And since it was Dr. Spring who dug out the facts in the first place, she has an equal right. So be quiet!" Having vented his spleen to good effect, he turned back with a seraphic smile to Penny. "As I was saying, plutonium, five pounds of pure plutonium. Worth several million dollars on today's market, particularly to several minor powers who are desperately eager to develop their nuclear potential."

"So that was what the plane was carrying. But why did it take so long before anyone did anything about it?"

"Please." Toby held up a magisterial hand. "Let me explain the sequence of events, and spare me the questions until I've finished. I point out the date of the crash: October of 1941, just before Pearl Harbor, when the Americans were still officially neutral. It was a grim time of the war for us, and a bunch of our back-room boys at Cambridge were feverishly working on the development of a superbomb to give us an edge. After long negotiations, the Americans had agreed to supply the raw material, but because they were supersensitive about the security aspects of this, the plutonium was secretly shipped across the border to Canada and flown from there in a British bomber. We still don't know what actually happened aboard that bomber, whether, in spite of all the security, it was sabotaged or whether it was just damned bad luck. The weather was good enough, although the visibility was terrible, and their destination was to be Prestwick, outside of Glasgow. It had been a routine flight pattern over Labrador and Iceland, and they were over Mull on the final leg when something went wrong. Their radio didn't go out entirely, but it was terribly garbled. Anyway, the last message received was, 'Ditching over S. . . . island,' and that was all. Mrs. Mitton's report, relayed through her Home Guard father, seemed to confirm this, but it was assumed that the plane had gone down near *Scarba* and had been swallowed up by the Corrievreckan. Unfortunately, what was not reported was her finding of the Mae West jacket, indicating that at least something from the plane had floated ashore. This would not have happened if it had all been sucked down into the whirlpool but had, in fact, crashed quite close to shore between Sheena and Soruba." Toby paused for a moment.

"However, to get back to 1941—before negotiations could get under way for a new supply of plutonium, Pearl Harbor was attacked, the Americans were drawn into the war, and, of course, they went ahead with the development of their own nuclear bomb. The whole thing was just written off as an accident of war.''

"But how on earth did Cranston and Bennett ever get on to it?'' Penny couldn't help breaking into his recitation.

"We still don't have all the facts. We must hope that one of those two thugs will break and give us the details, but again you have provided us with a probable answer. You mentioned that Rose's father had been in the Royal Canadian Air Force and stationed near Oban. Corky did some checking and found that he was a radio man there at that time. Anyone at that station must have known there was something special on or about that plane by the amount of security that surrounded it. He may even have received those last messages. Like his son, he was a very shady character. He was dishonorably discharged from the RCAF later on for a host of shady deals and a strong suspcion—never proved—of selling information to unfriendly powers. And we must surmise that in later years he probably mulled over the incident in talking about his war experiences. And when his son developed his own taste for treasure trove—I was right about his involvement in the Key West incident, by the way—he remembered this odd tale, and so the search began. It is just a guess, but he may initially have been under the delusion that the plane was carrying gold bullion.''

A frown creased Penny's brow. "Five pounds of plutonium. That would have to be a very small package,'' she said. "So why all this elaborate effort to get rid of Heather and polish off Amy? They could have gotten the package from the sunken plane, and no one would have ever been any the wiser. I mean, they weren't doing anything illegal. Salvage from sunken vessels is a legitimate enterprise.''

"Not quite. I must confess their motives in intimidating Heather had me baffled until I learned two things: the nature of this bay and what was in this packing case.'' He patted it fondly. "It's a Cousteau airlift.''

"A what?'' Heather, who had been listening to all this with growing amazement, could not contain herself any longer.

"A Cousteau airlift,'' said Toby in his best lecturing manner. "A compressed-air suction pump, which is a very valuable instrument in underwater archaeology. To put it simply, it sucks up mud and debris, allowing an excavator to get free access to what he is investigating. This whole bay happens to be beset by a silt problem. It is in all probability why they took so long to find the plane and why, when they did find it, it was not only buried in the silt but also full of it. And to find a small package in tons of mud without the aid of this little gadget''—again he patted it fondly—''would be well-nigh impossible.''

''But how can you possibly know all that?'' Heather exclaimed.

''Think about it,'' he insisted, as if encouraging a not-too-bright student. ''We know that the plane made a soft landing from Mrs. Mitton's testimony. 'A sort of hiss' was the way she described it. It did not break up or burn but shot straight to the bottom and buried itself in the mud. But something did break open—a door or a porthole, perhaps—as witness the Mae West jacket that floated free and was washed ashore. Ergo, over a period of forty years the currents would not only have buried it more deeply in the silt but would have filled it up, too.''

''But I still don't see . . .'' she began.

''Please, let me continue,'' he said with a ponderous patience that increased Penny's urge to kick him in the shins. ''An airlift was necessary, as I've said, but for an illegal operation it also had its drawbacks. For one thing, it is bulky, and for another, when it is in use, it creates a visible disturbance in shallow water, such as this is. When they located the plane and discovered their problem, they found that they had an added one in that their operations would be in full view of Soruba House. They were screened from the other houses of the area by the bulk of Sheena itself, and the farm cottages on your estate are too low-lying for anyone to see what is going on out in the water. But Soruba stands on a shelf of land and looks down on the bay. With it untenanted, they could operate, for even if the servants did notice and get curious, they could probably have fobbed them off with some technical gobbledegook about underwater photography. But they could not bank on that with you sitting in the house. So, when you announced at that dinner party that you intended to be a permanent resident of the area, they had to make plans to get rid of you. At that juncture, I may point out, there was no thought of murder, hence the rather bizarre method they chose. They were primarily thieves, not murderers.''

"But they weren't even thieves," Penny broke in. "This is what baffles me. Salvage is a legitimate operation."

"In this case, no," Toby said portentously. "I'm not sure about how the law operates in the States, but over here two factors made their search illegal. One, they were after government property, and two, the law of treasure trove, which, under English law, entitles the owner of the property on which it is found to collect the lion's share of the value.''

"But nobody owns the bay."

"Wrong," he boomed. "You should have studied that estate map more carefully. The waters between Sheena and Soruba are owned by the lairds of the two estates. Had their operation been an overt one, all they would have been left with at the end would have been a small percentage of the total worth of the plutonium, a few thousand pounds at most—a vast difference, I think you'll agree, from the several million dollars they would get if they took the lot covertly. As I see it, the murder of Amy was almost as unfortunate for them as it was for her. I doubt that murder was ever part of their original plans.''

"I'm not so sure about that," Penny murmured. "But go on.''

He shot her a questioning look but continued. "Anyway, her death pressured them into abandoning caution and going full steam ahead, as witness the fact that the day after the murder was discovered, they took off on the trip to pick up this vital bit of equipment. My belief is that if their little scheme to get rid of you two had succeeded, they would have gone right to work on the plane, grabbed the loot, and fled before Gareth could be brought to trial. They had no idea, of course, that anyone besides themselves was aware of the treasure sitting at the bottom of the bay. The news that Gareth had been let out must have sent them into a quiet panic, for it seemed to indicate that the police were not satisfied with their original assessment of the case and would be looking elsewhere.''

"Is that why the police released him and set up all those watchers?" Heather said. "You wanted to smoke them out and catch them diving for the plane?"

He looked a little uncomfortable, "Er, not quite. You have to remember that this all happened rather rapidly, and we still did not have some vital bits of information, like the airlift here. Naturally they were under a certain amount of suspicion, since they were the only ones around who had been consistently active in the area where the plane went down. But suspicion isn't proof."

Heather shook her head in bewilderment. "I must say I'm totally confused. How does Allen Gray fit into all this? Did they kill him, or was Ian somehow mixed up in this, too?"

"Allen Gray has indeed been the joker in the pack, and unless one of them talks, we may never know what he knew or what role he played in the whole thing. One might make an educated guess. I think the sequence of events went something like this: Allen Gray, from everything we've heard about him, was an unbalanced, vengeful sort of character. I feel he broke his parole and returned primarily to get back at the people around here who had harmed him and because he knew, in spite of all their differences, that his mother would help him and would not turn him in. But after he arrived on the estate, he stumbled on something that gave him bigger ideas. I don't know what that was. Maybe he saw who took the potshot at you in the woods, or maybe he had seen them up to their monkeyshines about the house, or maybe he had even witnessed Amy's murder. Anyway, he did get some hold on them which they initially went along with, hence all his boasts to his mother about coming into a lot of money. But he was a constant danger to them, particularly after he had pulled that stupid act of terror on Deirdre with the sheep in the chapel, which again brought the police to the estate."

Toby paused briefly. "I have a feeling that he may have been holed up in their house while they were away on that trip and that when they got back, they decided he was too dangerous to keep around. So they drowned him in the most handy place—the fishpond of their next-door neighbor—and then dumped him in the bay. It was just too bad for them that the storm came up and dumped him back again. Otherwise, they would have got clean away with that one and probably even Amy's as well, since the police, if they were satisfied with Gareth's alibi, would probably have settled on the absent Allen Gray as the culprit. Yes, as murderers they really were extremely unlucky.'' He lapsed into a temporary silence as if overwhelmed by the fickleness of fate.

Penny laughed briefly. ''Yes, they certainly were unlucky. I've just thought of something. Heather and I owe our lives to a bunch of harbor seals. They must have jiggered that gas supply on the boat so that it would conk out just when we were closest to the whirlpool and so would have gone under quickly, but we wasted about ten minutes of our gas circling around the seals and taking photos of them, so actually the boat conked out a lot sooner and gave us a chance to do something about our predicament.''

Heather chimed in. ''Yes, when you think of the panic I was in—but we weren't in any danger at all, really. They were following us out to see if their plan had worked, and the police were following them, so we'd have been saved, anyway.''

Toby was looking very uncomfortable. ''Well, not quite. You see, we weren't following them. We were following Gareth.''

They looked at him in blank astonishment. ''What,'' Penny exclaimed. ''You mean you still suspected him?''

''You must realize we didn't have much to go on,'' he said hurriedly. ''And when Corky found out about the plane, and that, in conjunction with Gray's statement to his mother about 'the right man for the wrong reason,' well, it looked as if he had been acting in conspiracy with someone else. We wanted to find out who that someone else was. So, we thought if he was let go and then watched carefully, he would eventually lead us to his associates, and we would have the evidence we needed. There was a very powerful electronic bug placed aboard his powerboat so that we could hear and record any conversations that took place. When he came flying down to the jetty this morning like a bat out of hell, we thought we were on to something, and so we followed him. Then, of course, when we heard what went on, we closed in.''

Heather was looking at him aghast. ''But he saved our

lives," she cried. "He rescued us, and he nearly got killed doing it."

Penny was watching Toby closely. "You're still not satisfied he's not a part of it, are you?" she said softly.

"No, I'm afraid I'm not. For if ever a man had a powerful motive to want his wife out of the way, Gareth did."

CHAPTER 23

Toby's hypothetical reconstruction concerning the plane was rapidly confirmed by a team of navy frogmen. So secure had they been in their conviction that their operation was totally secret that Cranston and Bennett had conveniently marked the location of the plane on a contoured map of the bay, thereby saving Her Majesty's Navy a lot of time and effort. Diving into the marked location, the frogmen found the plane completely buried in the deep mud, but for a small section of the tail fuselage, which stuck out among the fronds of waving kelp like the fin of a basking shark. They also came quickly to appreciate the need for the compressed-air pump, for the mud was of such a nature and consistency that no sooner was one small section cleared, than the section behind it was once more buried in the dark-brown clinging silt. It took them the best part of two days to work their way down to the back hatch of the plane, which had apparently blown out on impact and which revealed that the interior was indeed entirely filled with the same gluey substance. At this point the frogmen called it a day, and operations were discontinued until heavier equipment could be flown up from Portsmouth to take care of the problem.

An expectant hush had fallen over Soruba. Although the feeling of lurking menace had lifted, there was still no sense of relief, since so much remained obscure and so many questions were as yet unanswered.

If it had not been for the invaluable Constable Menzies, Penny would have gone frantic with frustration, for Toby had been ejected from the councils of the mighty because of his determined breach of security. Alastair McClintock, for some unaccountable reason, had been sent on an assignment to Edinburgh, and the police watch had been promptly withdrawn from the estate. Their one tenuous link with what was occurring was the red-faced constable, who gallantly pedaled up once a day with his slim packet of news.

It didn't amount to much. So far, the only charges brought against Cranston and Bennett had been for the attempted murder of Heather, Penny, and Gareth, who had been more seriously injured than had first been supposed. He still lay in critical condition in Oban Hospital from a bullet that was lodged perilously close to his spine. Heavy security had been clamped on the case, and so they were spared the ordeal of reporters; but by the same token they were equally deprived of information. Menzies had discovered that Cranston and Bennett were being held in separate jails, location unspecified, and were being questioned in the hope that one of them would break. So far they had remained silent.

On the home front there had been some minor developments: some predictable, others very much unexpected. The first of these happened the day after their near escape from the whirlpool. Heather, still a little wan from the delayed shock of it all, was summoned by a grim-faced Mrs. Mitton to a conference.

"A Mr. Urquhart from Kilmelfort wishes words with the Macdonell," she announced tersely. "I have put him in the study. He seems very upset about something."

"Oh, what now?" Heather groaned. "Come with me, Penny, I feel in need of moral support."

They went in to find a big, thickset man glaring out the window at the naval pinnace that was still parked over the sunken plane. He wheeled around as they came in. "Which of ye is the Macdonell?" he demanded in a husky voice.

"I am," Heather said a little nervously. "What can I do for you?"

"It's aboot one of your tenant farmers," he thundered. "Dennis Strachan. It's his whereaboots I'm after. I've been doon to the farm, but there's not a sign of him nor anyone. The man's a thief, and it's my rights I want of him."

"What did he steal?" she asked in surprise.

He swelled with inner rage. "My prize bull and my daughter," he roared. "Both of them gone without a sign. And me thinking the bull was at the Ardrishaig fair with her and she safe at her auntie's. A thousand pounds that bull cost me."

He went on at some length to describe the fascinating features of the bull before he moved on to a less flattering description of his daughter. Penny had to turn away to hide an involuntary grin, for the thought of Dennis Strachan wandering somewhere in the world saddled with one large bull and a farmer's comely daughter was almost too much for her.

"Have you been to the police?" Heather said weakly.

He looked faintly shocked. "Nay." His voice sank to a confidential whisper. "I didna want to bring scandal doon upon the estate, ye ken. Go to the laird, says I to myself. She'll fix it in the auld manner."

"But I'm afraid I have no idea where Dennis Strachan is," she spluttered. "Neither does his wife, who lies sick in Oban hospital. I can't help you. If he has taken something of yours, you should go to the police. They may be able to track him down and find your daughter."

He brushed her answer aside impatiently. "But in the matter of the bull, ye can do something," he persisted. "I'm not saying he has anything the worth of it, mind ye, but his own bull and a couple or three of his cows should square the deal. I'd be satisfied with that."

"But I couldn't do that," Heather said in horror. "Those belong to him and his wife."

"Och, but ye've every right," he insisted. "If he's skipped out on ye, ye've a right to what's left."

"But that would not find your daughter," Penny couldn't resist interjecting.

"She's no longer any daughter of mine. Silly bitch, to let her head be turned by a flighty, no-good skellion like him, who is married to boot. Besides," he added sadly, "she's over twenty-one."

Penny's interruption had given Heather time to pull herself together. "As to the matter of scandal, Mr. Urquhart, that is of little importance to me," she said firmly. "I shall certainly inform the police of this and will consult with Mrs. Strachan on how the matter can best be settled. That is all I can do, and I will let you know in due course what has been decided. Leave your name and address with my housekeeper.''

He looked rather taken aback by her sudden grand manner. ''Weel then, I'll be thanking ye kindly and taking my leave. It is just my rights I'm wanting, ye ken,'' he mumbled, and shuffled out.

Penny began to chuckle. ''So that was it. Dennis and the farmer's daughter, not to mention the bull. All my dark suspicions for nothing.''

Heather joined in after a few seconds with a weak laugh. ''Yes, I suppose it is rather funny when you think of it. Poor Meg. But I'll have to do something about it.'' She sighed. ''This feudal business is getting a bit wearing. At the moment, my yearning for Manhattan is getting to be obsessive. I'd even consider taking my chances in the south Bronx.''

When the matter was duly placed before Constable Menzies, he too chuckled. ''Aye, I'm not surprised. So it was Maureen Urquhart, was it? Aye, I can see that. Daft but bonny, and a pleasant way with her. Weel, I'll look into it, but nae doubt the bull is long gone, sold, and them off to the colonies with the proceeds, I'll be bound. If I were ye, Miss Macdonell, I'd leave the bargaining to Mrs. Strachan's father. Leave two farmers at it, and they'll have a right good haggle and come to some satisfaction, I warrant.''

Farmer Urquhart's parental feelings were eventually assuaged by the Strachan bull, one cow, and a choice ewe.

''The ewe, I take it,'' Penny couldn't resist commenting, ''being in full compensation for Maureen.''

Heather's next feudal duty was of a more somber note. Mrs. Gray came seeking audience, dressed in her best Sunday black and radiating a strange dignity.

''It's aboot my son,'' she said. ''Would the Macdonell aid me?''

''Yes, I am very sorry about Allen, very,'' Heather said. ''What can I do?''

''It's to get his body for proper burying from the police. If ye would ask for me?'' The old woman paused. ''He brought his doom upon himself, and he was not a guid man nor a guid son, but he was all I had. I'd like to lay him in the kirkyard beside his father.''

And so with considerably more pomp than had ever been accorded to him in life, to the skirl of the bagpipe's lament, which sent shivers up the laird's spine, Allen Gray was duly laid to rest in Ardnan churchyard.

It was not the end of domestic pain. Mrs. Mitton appeared at the dinner table, red-eyed and with her normal dignity thrown to the winds. Only Penny and Heather were present, for Toby had gone into Oban to take Jack Phipps out to lunch and find out what was going on, and Alison had departed for Edinburgh, ostensibly to look over the university. When Mrs. Mitton had begged for a private word with the Macdonell, Penny had gotten up to go, but she was waved back by the distraught women.

"No, Dr. Spring, you may as well hear it, too, since you know all about it, anyway." She caught back a sob.

"Sit down, Mrs. Mitton, and tell us about it, then," Heather said resignedly. "Would you care for some coffee?"

This lèse majesté brought a momentary return of outraged dignity. "No, I could not do that, but thank you kindly." She sat down, though, primly at first, but then her shoulders slumped and she let out a sob. "She's away to him. There was no stopping her, no reasoning. Away to Oban to be near him, she is. There's no hiding the scandal of it now."

Since there seemed to be no suitable reply to this, they waited in silence for her to go on.

"And it's me she's blaming for it all," Mrs. Mitton said in a trembling voice, wiping at her eyes. "And her father takes her part. But what I did, I did for her own guid. I mean, all the village was saying that Gareth had stepped into Allen Gray's shoes over at the island, and there was Hamish, such a fine-looking, well-spoken man and with such good prospects. What was a mother to do? Poisoned her mind, I did, Mitton says, leading to misery for both of them. But I thought her feeling for him was just what any young girl would feel for a bonny lad, and it would pass when she was married herself and settled down."

Penny felt that it was time to interrupt. "Mrs. Mitton," she said quietly. "The child Deirdre is carrying, is it Gareth's?"

The housekeeper pressed her handkerchief to her lips and nodded. "Och, the scandal of it. There'll be no hiding it now. She says Hamish can do as he pleases, but she'll never go back to him, that she'll be staying with Gareth no matter what happens."

"It might help in the long run if you would tell us what actually did go on during the period between the dinner party we attended at the castle and the murder. We surmised they had been meeting at the chapel. Did they meet other places, too?" Penny asked.

"Aye, sometimes at the farm when Hamish was away, sometimes at the castle garage on the main road, but it was at yon dinner party that Deirdre slipped Gareth the word that she thought she might be pregnant. They were very careful, I'll say that for them."

"How was she so sure it was his?" Penny asked bluntly.

"Och, Hamish looks the part, but he's not much of man," Mrs. Mitton said with devastating frankness. "He'd have been pleased to think it was his, but it wasn't likely. Anyway, the day before the murder, they went into Oban to a doctor's, and he confirmed it. So Gareth said as soon as he got his hands on some money, they'd go away together."

Heather shot a quick horrified glance at Penny, but Mrs. Mitton was too engrossed in her narrative to notice. "Ye see, the McDougall brought him or bought him everything he wanted, but he never had any cash for himself. She was funny that way. But when he got back that night, the fat was already in the fire. Careful they had been, but not careful enough. Somebody had tipped off Amy McDougall they'd been seeing each other."

"And my bet is on Bennett for that little good deed," Penny murmured under her breath.

"There was a terrible row. Amy went on like a madwoman about how she'd never let him go, that he'd never get a penny of hers, that she'd drive Deirdre out of the district. Oh, just terrible it was. The next day he slipped off to see Deirdre and said they'd have to go without the money and take their chances, that he wasn't going to stay around and let Amy have her way. Deirdre was frightened, but he was busy getting in touch with his brothers and sisters to see what money they could let him have and finding out about passports and things like that.''

Heather let out a little exclamation before the woman went on. ''And when it got time for that party, he sent Deirdre off home and said he'd be along later. Of course he never showed up, and the day after, he called her to say that Amy had taken off and that maybe they had better sit tight for a wee while. He might be able to raise some money from things that would never be missed around the castle, and whatever happened, she was to keep silence until he could get to her. When he was arrested, she did not know what to do, but now that he is free—'' She stopped and shook her head hopelessly. ''To think it has come to this. That's why I need your help, Miss Macdorell.''

''Naturally I'd be glad to do anything I can, but what do you want me to do?'' Heather said.

''If you'd talk with her, reason with her before the scandal breaks,'' Mrs. Mitton said eagerly. ''Hamish is in a rage now, but I'm sure he would take her back, and for all we know Gareth may be a dead man.''

Heather was firm. ''I'm sorry, but I would not even consider it. For one thing, Deirdre and Gareth are obviously very much in love; for another, he is the father of her child. For a third, I think it is high time everyone stopped interfering in their lives; and for a fourth, I called the hospital this morning, and Gareth is out of danger. The operation to remove the bullet near his spine was a complete success, and he's reported as strong as a bull.'' She softened her tone a little. ''Mrs. Mitton, divorce is very easy these days, and there is absolutely no disgrace to it. Let them work out their own destinies.''

''That's what Mitton says,'' Mrs. Mitton mumbled.

''And, believe me, he is absolutely right,'' Heather said. ''So be comforted. It'll all come out all right. You'll see.''

When the door had closed on her housekeeper, she turned to Penny. ''I wish I could believe that myself.''

''Yes,'' Penny mused. ''We are faced with a paradox. An overwhelming motive, plenty of means, but, if that alibi is true, no opportunity whatsoever. He could not have done it. And I, for one, do not believe he did.''

"And you are quite right, I'm glad to say." Toby, beaming like a Cheshire cat, came into the room in time to hear her last statement. "He didn't do it. I may not have made much of a contribution to this case, but at least I am a good herald. I bring good tidings from Oban. The case is closed, the murderer identified, and all is very well with the world."

CHAPTER 24

"Fortunately, the old saying about there being no honor among thieves seems to be a true one. In this instance, the police ploy of separating our two conspirators worked. Bennett Rose, to use one of your colorful American phrases, decided to spill his guts to save his skin." Toby was settling down to enjoy his role of narrator. "Mind you, it will probably mean that he won't get his just deserts. He bargained with them, but I'm happy to say, he won't get off scot free, either."

"I should damn well hope not," Penny exclaimed heatedly. "He was all set to shoot us, and he did shoot Gareth. Get on with it. Who did he implicate?"

"Oh, it was Cranston, all right. But without Rose's testimony, I doubt the police would ever get a conviction," Toby said with maddening vagueness. "There's not enough factual evidence, and a good defense counsel could make mincemeat of the circumstantial case. What pleases me most is that our theoretical reconstruction comes so close to what happened."

"Will you get on with it?" Penny demanded.

"I shall relate it from the beginning; then things will be clearer," he rumbled. "First, Cranston Phillips: a not-very-successful artist who had got in with a smuggling ring in London and made a fair income from bringing in illicit booze, pot, and perfume by boat from the Continent. About three years ago he fell in with Rose, who, after his illegal successes in the Caribbean, had been sniffing around over here for something similar. They got together, and somewhere along the line Rose told him about the treasure-carrying plane. The

213

south coast was becoming increasingly risky for the smuggling operations, so Phillips persuaded his bosses to let him run a similar operation up here, and in their spare time the two of them started the search for the plane. They didn't actually find it until September of last year, and preliminary work showed that they would have to do something a lot more elaborate than just a simple skin-diving operation. But then the winter came on, and the weather closed down operations until this May. No sooner had they started up again than you, Heather, showed up as the new laird and shortly thereafter announced your intention of staying. They'd been having difficulty laying their hands on the equipment they needed, but they knew that once they had it in operation, you would have to be got rid of. So they started on their campaign of intimidation, hoping to drive you out. When Penny showed up unexpectedly, this threw a temporary spanner into their works, but worse was to come."

He turned an accusing blue eye on Penny. "You put ideas into Amy McClintock's head at that dinner party with your talk of Spanish galleons and treasure. Not being very swift, she had not thought much about them up to that point, but then she zeroed in on their boat from her observation post and lip-read enough to know that they were up to something. According to Bennett, she called Cranston, all coy and secretive at first, indicating that she knew they were after something other than underwater photographs and pointing out the law of treasure trove, meaning that she wanted her cut of what they did find. This was disaster, but Cranston temporized, said it was all hush-hush but they'd meet and he'd tell her all about it.

"In the meantime, she had had this blowup with Gareth, so when he did call her for a meeting, she was in a mean mood and said she was going to consult with you, as laird of Soruba, about the whole matter. This, of course, would have scuppered everything, so Cranston went after her. She played into his hands by making that unexpected and pathetic excursion to the Wishing Well. He followed her, tried to reason with her about the need for secrecy, and failed because she was so upset and unreasonable; and so he strangled her. He then tried to arrange the accident, but he was pressed for time. The party had been set up, and if he wasn't there, he knew that once Amy was eventually missed, his guests would certainly remember an absent host and would wonder about it. So he left before he was certain the boat had sunk, grabbed some bottles from their secret store, and arrived late but with a plausible excuse. He thought that was the end of it. Then, to their great consternation, you found the body, but Gareth was quickly nabbed for it, and they thought they were safe, until Allen Gray showed up and they found that they were back in the soup."

He paused to light his pipe and then went on. "What Allen Gray's motives for coming up here originally were we'll never know—perhaps revenge on Deirdre, perhaps just to steal from Soruba House. But his motives were quickly altered. He had spotted one of them on a surreptitious excursion to the house and had started to keep an eye on them. He showed up at their house one night full of whisky and bluster, saying he wanted in on their operation. Cranston decided to play along with him. He agreed to Allen's demands but laid down a set of ground rules: Allen was to contact no one, was to wait in the house while they fetched the equipment, was to help them when it came. To ensure this they kept him drunk most of the time but, unfortunately for them, not drunk enough, because he paid that one last visit to his mother to boast of his success."

"But what about this business with Gareth?" Penny broke in.

"I was coming to that. When the murder occurred, Allen was upset and accused them of having a hand in it. They denied it but said that Gareth was a silent partner in their enterprise and had killed his wife because she was getting too nosy. This, because he hated Gareth, satisfied him, and he repeated the information to his mother, which led us all so merrily down the wrong path. In the meantime, they had got the airlift and even had him help get some underwater acetylene torch equipment aboard, which they thought they might need to cut into the hull of the plane. After that his usefulness was at an end, and so was he.

"According to Bennett, he had no hand in the killing. He had gone into Oban, and when he returned, Allen was gone.

Cranston eventually told him that Allen had turned on him in a drunken fury and demanded a half share of the future profits, that they had a fight and he'd knocked him out, disposed of him in the Macdonell's fishpond and then had flung the body into the bay from the boat. Not only did that solve their immediate problem, it also provided another possible scapegoat if the police weren't satisfied with their case against Gareth. They already knew from local gossip about Allen's insane killing of the ewe in chapel and about his fortuitous cleaning out of the Wishing Well.''

After pausing for breath, he continued. ''Incidentally, Gareth has identified that third coin that was found in Allen's pocket as Amy's lucky piece, which she always carried, so her presence at the well is established even without Rose's testimony.

''They were by now determined to get rid of you both, this time permanently. Penny was beginning to be altogether too successful in her nosing around. So they arranged another accident. Cranston, who is an expert mechanic, jiggered your fuel line so that it would give out at the edge of the whirlpool, and there, but for the grace of the harbor seals, you would have been. However, they were pretty shaken by this time, for the waters of the bay had not only rendered up Amy's body but Allen's as well; so, just to make sure this time, they followed you.''

''But why did Gareth follow us?'' Heather interrupted. ''I must say I don't understand that at all. When he showed up out of the mist like that, I was convinced he'd come to finish us off.''

''Ah, yes, but very lucky for you he did,'' Toby said benignly. ''Illustrating yet another old saw that to be uneducated never means that one is unintelligent. And part of the thanks for your rescue has to go to Alison. When she was over on the island, she mentioned your proposed trip to the Corrievreckan. In the meantime Gareth had been doing some quiet thinking himself about the murders and had come to the right conclusion: that Cranston was the most likely person. He had been keeping an eye on their activities from the island and had seen Cranston fiddling about down at your jetty. He saw you set out for your trip, but when he didn't see you come back, the alarm bell sounded in his mind, so he came out to find you. And that was that," he finished triumphantly.

"That was very nearly that for him," Penny said. "Glad as I am that this is over and done with, I wish things could have turned out a bit better for our young lovers. They seem a bit star-crossed, don't they? I hope Hamish isn't going to make trouble for them now."

Heather sat up straight and said briskly, "Baloney! If my estimate of Hamish is right, he's not going to make trouble. You are forgetting one important fact. Now that Gareth is in the clear, he stands to inherit Amy's money, and that, as I understand it, is quite a pile. My guess is that Hamish will want to be bought off, and Gareth will be only too happy to do it. In fact, I'm going after a piece of the pie myself, I've just had a inspiration, and I think I'll get right on with it. See you." She hurried out, leaving Toby and Penny rather taken aback by her sudden departure.

"Well, that was a quick change," Penny remarked. "Wonderful what a therapeutic effect we have on people, isn't it? So, the job's done," she went on. "What do you say to us getting out of here? I've had just about enough of the raw and rugged passions of the Western Highlands."

He roused himself. "There is still the question of the long barrow," he said mildly. "While I'm here, I suppose I might as well take a good look at it. We could go there tomorrow morning."

In the interests of science, they delayed their departure for three more days, while Toby measured and probed and pondered, and Penny lay back on the springy heather, basking in the cooperative sunshine and snoozing to her heart's content.

On the third day she roused herself to enough interest to ask, "What's the verdict?"

He joined her in the little nook she had made for herself in the heather and lit up his pipe. "Oh, very interesting," he said between puffs. "A nice chambered long barrow with possible solar alignments. It has an east-west axis. And if those stones on the outside are to be believed, early Neolithic, as you surmised."

"Are you going to excavate it?"

"Goodness, no. I'll turn this report in to the Office of

Works and the Scottish Department of Antiquities, where doubtless it will molder until Kingdom come, judging by the present state of things. There's no money around to dig something like this, and anyway, it is quite safe. It has sat here quietly for the last four thousand or so years. It can wait awhile longer. I'm not one for digging something just because it is there; I'm all for waiting until it can be done properly and completely. With the vast technological strides archaeology is making, the longer we wait, the better it will be."

"Oh. Then we can go home?"

"Any time you like," he returned amiably.

They had seen little of their hostess during this time, and when they announced their intention of leaving on the morrow, she made only a token attempt to dissuade them. "I've been very busy," she announced with satisfaction. "But all my wheeling and dealing has paid off, and I'll be off to the States—probably in late September. I'll need a Manhattan rest cure by that time."

"Is it all hush-hush, or can you tell us about it?" Penny asked in surprise.

"Oh, I'm so proud of myself, I had every intention of telling you. I've got the home farm tenanted again." Heather beamed. "Gareth is going to have to leave Sheena, so I suggested to him that the farm might be a profitable investment. He jumped at the idea. To preserve the local decencies, Deirdre is going to stay at home with the Mittons until the divorce is through and then move in officially. The farm cottages will be a regular enclave of McDougalls: three generations living side by side. I rather like that."

"But with Hamish on the other farm, won't that be very awkward?" Penny spluttered.

"My masterstroke number two," Heather replied complacently. "Hamish isn't going to keep it. With the money he is gouging out of Gareth, he is planning to open up a larger antique store in Edinburgh. To sweeten the pot, I offered him the commission on selling the Fergus Macdonell watercolors. Of course, he couldn't resist. I figured since they are a current cult item, they probably won't hold their present worth for long, and I'm not all that fond of them, so I'll use the money to restore the Italian garden and the chapel."

"But that'll leave your other farm untenanted," Penny pointed out.

"No, it won't," Heather said triumphantly. "Because Ian Macdonell is taking it over. I did a really good sales talk there and was greatly aided by the son, who seems a lot more sensible than either of his parents. Ian's a very shaken man. The police have been after him, but I don't think they'll prosecute, and I think he had a pretty good notion of what Cranston and Bennett were up to, so he's feeling guilty as well. Anyway, I pointed out to him how much sense this would make, since no one knows this estate better than he. He is an active man with not enough to do, and this would give him plenty. Eventually, of course, it will come to him or his son, so it's in his own best interests. They'd sell their house, which is too big and expensive for them in any case, and move in to the bigger farm when Hamish moves out."

"When you wheel and deal, you really do, don't you?" Penny was a little dumbfounded by all of this.

Heather grinned at her. "Yes, and it has brought me back to my senses, too. Now that the euphoria of being a lady laird has worn off a bit, I realize how right you were. I couldn't take this on a year-round basis. I'm off to set up a tax consultant business in New York. I don't care if I make any real money at it or not, but I'll spend the winters there and the summers here. The way things are looking on the Alison-Alastair front, Soruba will not be untenanted for long. I think they'll make a match of it before she's through at the university. Alastair's going there, incidentally, to read law, again courtesy of Gareth. By the way they fight, you'd think they were married already, but they both seem to enjoy it."

"So all must change that all may stay the same," Penny quoted absently. "I'm very happy for you, Heather."

"And it is all thanks to you both," Heather said tactfully. "We will all be indebted to you to the end of our days. You'll have to come back again soon to see how it has all worked out."

The next morning, after fervent farewells from their hostess and most of the remaining local inhabitants, the little green Triumph and the large black Bentley set off in stately procession. When they reached the Lochgilphead road, Penny signaled for a stop and got out of her car, where Toby joined her; an enquiring look was on his face. She looked up at Cranston's untenanted cottage and then back across the calm waters of the bay to Soruba.

"There is one final irony in all this," she murmured. "From that one little sentence Cranston let drop out at the whirlpool, I think the old laird of Soruba was the first of their victims. It makes sense, because he was drowned just after they had discovered the location of the plane. They thought that Ian would come into the place, and they had enough on him to keep his mouth shut. So Heather really owes her inheritance to them. What is more, if they had left well enough alone and allowed the old laird to die peacefully in his bed, chances are, they would have gotten away with their own scheme."

"Perhaps," Toby said. "What are your plans now? Since I'm already in Scotland, I thought I'd spend a day or two in Edinburgh, and then I'm off to the Lipari islands. An interesting new site has turned up there. Care to join me for either or both?"

"What's the date? I've completely lost track of time back there in never-never land."

"It's the middle of August."

"Umm, nearly two months before Michaelmas term begins." She debated silently with herself. "No, but thanks for asking. I think I need more of a rest than that. Chances are, if we go somewhere together, we'll trip over another body, and I've had my quota for this year. I think I'll make for somewhere nice and quiet, like among the Oros of Fiji."

"Fiji," he echoed. "Hardly a rest cure, I'd say."

"Compared to all this, they lead such nice uncomplicated lives out there," she said dreamily. "And I'm not sure that baked lizard won't seem a real treat after all the Scotch broth and porridge I've consumed."

"Well, to each his own, and *chacun à son goût*. Shall we have lunch together and part company afterward?"

"Right. I know a very good place at Dalmally: the Crown and Thistle."

"That doesn't surprise me in the least," he said, getting back behind the wheel of the Bentley.

Penny made for her own car and then paused, her hand on the door handle. "There's one mystery we never cleared up," she called back to him. "We never did figure out the opening door."

"Oh, that's simple enough," he said, starting his engine. "When you have eliminated all but the improbable, then the improbable is the answer. Obviously it was the colonel's ghost warning you of dirty work afoot." He passed her with an airy wave of his hand. "See you in Dalmally."

She stood looking after him with a faint grin on her small pixie face. Then she shrugged. "Well, that makes sense," she muttered as she started her own engine and waved her hand at her surroundings. "Thanks a lot, Colonel. See you around."

She sped gaily down the road after her partner in crime.